The Season of
Lillian Dawes

ALSO BY KATHERINE MOSBY

Private Altars

The Book of Uncommon Prayer (poetry)

The Season of
Lillian Dawes

Katherine Mosby

HarperCollins*Publishers*

HarperCollins books may be purchased for educational, business, or sales promotional use. For information, please write: Special Markets Department, Harper-Collins Publishers Inc., 10 East 53rd Street, New York, NY 10022.

FIRST EDITION

Designed by Jill Bauer

Printed on acid-free paper

Library of Congress Cataloging-in-Publication Data

Mosby, Katherine
    The season of Lillian Dawes / by Katherine Mosby. — 1st ed.
      p. cm.
    ISBN 0-06-621272-3 — ISBN 0-06-093695-9 (pbk.)
    I. Title.

PS3563.O88384 S4 2002
813'.54—dc21   2001042408

02 03 04 05 06 RRD❖ 10 9 8 7 6 5 4 3 2 1

For my mother

Human speech is like a cracked kettle on which we beat melodies fit to make bears dance when we long to make the stars weep.

—Flaubert

The Season of
Lillian Dawes

There is in most lives, a defining moment, a point dividing time into before and after—an accident or love affair, a journey or perhaps a death. For Spencer, all four, like the points on a compass, combined in the shape of Lillian Dawes. And because it is not possible to witness a tragedy without carrying away some of its stain, she became my watershed as well.

I was seventeen when the Renwick School for boys decided, despite my family's long affiliation with the school, to discharge me midterm. My father had died the year before, and out of deference to his name, and perhaps also his bequest, they had kept me on through a number of earlier infractions. However, when I was caught smoking a cigar in the chapel after curfew, it was plain I had exhausted the sympathy due my orphaned state. The masters were so eager to return me to what remained of my family that rather than wait for my aunt Grace to retrieve me at the end of the weekend, they sent me to New York, to my brother Spencer, which amounted to divine intervention in my opinion.

Spencer was ten years older than I, at boarding school by the time I was able to say his name. Our relationship therefore had been forged on holidays, in equal measures of jealous admiration on my part and amused affection on his. Spencer had assumed, at the time of our mother's illness, the role of family diplomat, a position for which he was singularly suited: his wit and lean good looks made him a favorite among even the most petulant of relatives, and his indifference to his status only furthered it. That is, until he declined to pursue his role professionally: after a brief stint with the State Department, he renounced his interest in foreign affairs. Then, much to everyone's surprise, Scribner published a slim collection of essays Spencer had written his final year at Yale, entitled *Apropos of Nothing*. Our father particularly, and the family generally, understood these two events as a repudiation of the tradition that had put Gibbses in the Senate, the Supreme Court, and two European embassies in the last century. It was also noted, a bit hysterically, that Spencer omitted from his wardrobe the hat and sock garters that were the mark of a gentleman.

Spencer's decision to go to law school had mollified my father initially; it was still possible for Spencer to "come around." But after graduating with honors, Spencer went to Italy, where he spent the next several years translating the obscure Renaissance poet Lapadini into English for an academic publisher.

It was at that point that Spencer's past underwent review, and then revision: childhood activities, earlier thought to indicate promise, were now taken as signs of oddity. For example, the Christmas pageants he had written for Hadley (our only cousin, five years my senior and five years Spencer's junior) and me to perform, featuring spectacular death scenes involving pomegranate explosions, were now seen to be morbid, though at the time he had been praised for the ingenuity of his plots and the historical accuracy. It should also be said that at the time, the relatives were so grateful to Spencer for having found a way of keeping Hadley and me occupied that they would have applauded a reenactment of atrocities far more tasteless than those Spencer actually chose.

Spencer's fall from grace, such as it was, did not, as I had initially feared, put greater pressure on me to succeed. It had, in fact, the opposite effect. I think it was felt that if Spencer, with all his gifts, could become a disappointment, then it was better not to hold out any major expectations for an ordinary fellow like myself. Indeed, it seemed to excuse my own lackluster efforts in the classroom and on the playing field because a precedent had been set—if I was not achieving my potential, it was because Spencer had squandered his. I might have felt guilty about letting my own failures fall on Spencer's shoulders, but I didn't. At the time, I felt relief.

Spencer met me at the station and took me to the Oak Room for dinner. Not only did he let me order a drink, but after the meal had been cleared, he offered me a cigar.

"I hear you've developed a taste for these."

"Actually, it was Bixby's idea," I explained, taking the cigar. "He was outside taking a leak when Mr. Thrush came in, which is why I was caught and he got off."

"Gabriel," Spencer said quietly, holding out a match for me to light the cigar, "I don't give a damn if you smoke cigars and I don't think your expulsion is a world-class tragedy. And I am

3

happy to take you in for the remainder of the term, only don't try to bullshit me."

He blew the match out just before it singed his fingers and dropped it disdainfully in the ashtray.

"I chose your name, you know. Mom wanted to call you Alfred, after her uncle, but Father thought the name was too plebeian because he had had a chauffeur by that name, who was apparently a coarse fellow who had to be let go. I was the one who suggested Gabriel. Gabriel is an archangel in three of the four world religions. And in all of them, Christian, Jewish, and Muslim, all of them, Gabriel is a messenger of truth."

I blew a series of near-perfect smoke rings in the air, aiming them up over my head. "And you knew all that at ten," I said, smiling at Spencer. He grinned and, hooking his finger through the elongating center of each wafting ring, said, "As a matter of fact, I did."

Lavinia Gibbs, in her silk knit suit, a herringbone of dour browns and black, with her sharp nose and high forehead, looked more like a bird of prey than a woman with a daring past. There was something severe about her posture, and the thin line of her mouth suggested rectitude. Only the theatrical, plumed millinery and the jangling bracelets riding up and down her wrist with the random insistence of a wind chime departed from the staid, austere appearance.

She had lived in Paris for almost two decades, with a married man whom our family referred to in hushed tones as "the Jew." Aunt Lavinia had made a few visits to the family before I was born, but they were awkward occasions which merely reinforced the discord that existed between her and her siblings. Neither her younger brother, Gordon, our father, nor her older brother, our uncle Ambrose, the judge, and least of all her sister, Grace, Hadley's mother, had made any further attempt at reconciliation.

Spencer remembered only one visit, during the Thanksgiving holidays—he must have been eight or nine—when Aunt

Lavinia had appeared in a fur coat with a fox's head at the collar. The fox had glass eyes that stared in perpetual surprise at its paws, which were crossed daintily under Lavinia's chin. It had somehow been arranged that she would take Spencer with her to the city for the day. Like many adults without children of their own, she had no understanding of what was involved in entertaining an eight-year-old—but that didn't seem to trouble her in the slightest. Lavinia took him to Rumplemeyer's for an ice cream sundae, but only after he had endured the boredom of watching her choose a pair of ostrich shoes at Bonwit Teller, an event no amount of sourballs, dug from the deep of her handbag, could make interesting.

While she had discussed the lasts of various shoemakers with the salesman, Spencer had tried to amuse himself by rummaging through her handbag, a privilege our mother had never allowed him. He was, he recalled, briefly intrigued by a gold cigarette case, with swirling initials on the cover, which clicked open to display a row of cigarettes, lined up like a cartridge of bullets, an accessory he thought about pinching for the games he played under the piano, where, behind the paisley shawl that draped over the sounding board, he fought wolves and bandits.

There was a dark red lipstick, which he swiveled up and down a few times before he surrendered to the urge to smear it on something, which turned out to be the lid of a shoe box, where he made a large glaring X, but otherwise, the secret realm of a woman's handbag was a disappointment. The other women in the store made silly expressions at themselves in the long reflecting glass at the end of a carpeted runway, posing for no one in particular, which made Spencer feel as if he was watching something private and perhaps forbidden. He contrasted this with Mrs. Belmont, who had briefly lived across the street from us and who used to sit at a vanity in her bedroom wearing only underclothes. Spencer had watched her apply her makeup and brush out her hair without the slightest notion that there was anything untoward in either his or her behavior until the morning Father inquired about Mr. Belmont and Spencer volunteered that Mrs. Belmont was a widow. Father put down his paper and asked Spencer what made him think that, and he replied, with great pride in his deductive ability, "Because she wears black underwear," for which he received his first and only spanking.

As was so often the case with stories that Spencer told, it was hard for me to know how much his version had been shaped by the subtle demands of narrative, to which Spencer readily conceded the authority of fact. In any case, his account of the visit concluded with Aunt Lavinia holding his hand very firmly as they walked along the park, through the slick of fallen leaves, to Rumplemeyer's. They sat at the counter, where Aunt Lavinia smoked Egyptian cigarettes through a holder, rotating the gray head of her cigarette in the ashtray as if she were sharpening it. The harsh smell of the smoke, the tiny pyramid imprinted on the cigarette paper, and the way in which she exhaled through her nose all impressed Spencer; she seemed as deeply exotic as the women occasionally featured in *National Geographic*, who wore veils, or who tattooed their hands. Spencer had a sundae with both butterscotch and chocolate sauce, hazelnuts, and extra whipped cream. Either the ice cream sundae or Lavinia's less than ladylike driving on the way home made him ill. He had vomited copiously in the guest bathroom off the foyer, making the family's good-byes to Lavinia even more perfunctory than usual. That was the last time he had seen Aunt Lavinia before our father's death.

Over the years, there was gossip of course, and if Uncle Ambrose was present, Lavinia's sanity would inevitably be questioned, in long, perplexed hypotheses, as if dementia could be the only explanation for such inappropriate behavior in a Gibbs. Often Ambrose would return to the time Lavinia had rolled off the changing table as a baby, or the fever she had had the winter before her ninth birthday. Our mother would purse her lips, making them tight with disapproval she could not express. We heard from our cousin Hadley, who was not necessarily a reliable source, that Aunt Lavinia had permanently offended our mother by sending her, as a wedding present, a douche bag.

While Aunt Lavinia never sent me anything but her best wishes at Christmas, she had sent Spencer a few presents, mostly books, an odd selection of volumes ranging from a monograph on cannibalism to a manual on training Indian elephants, never however commemorating a birthday or Christmas. As he grew older, she had written to him in a desultory fashion, abrupt and animated letters, inspired monologues that required no reply. Despite, or perhaps because of, the family line on Lavinia, Spencer had developed a smoldering fondness for her that had expressed itself during his adolescence in irregular postcards to her Paris address, full of odd intimacies: snatches of dreams, quotations from favorite authors, confessions of despair, and aspirations that he shared with no one else.

It was Hadley who told us Aunt Lavinia was back in town. Hadley had not seen either of us in almost six months, not since the painfully long afternoon when the family had gathered to bicker over Father's personal effects. The house, unburdened of Father's imposing presence, had lost much of the academic *gravitas* associated with family gatherings, the ostensibly festive occasions such as Christmas lunch during which we had to raise our hands before being allowed to speak.

But it seemed to me as though Father was there nonetheless, oppressing the parlor in the blinding brightness of an unshuttered noon, beating in like a searchlight, exposing his family's greed as they argued beneath the chandelier, flecked with shards of light from the Viennese glass, illuminating their blunt and rapacious purpose as it dispersed with evenhanded indifference its harsh beauty. Hadley's father had tried clumsily to mediate, but he was extraneous in his gray wool suit, nervous and placating as a salesman. Spencer, only recently returned from Italy, lay on the chaise longue, a room away, not bothering about his wing tip shoes on the silk brocade, drinking port from a cut-glass decanter and chain-smoking, a small ashtray balanced on his chest.

I wandered through various rooms, feeling sorry for myself. At one point, I went into Father's study and sat in his leather chair. I could smell the faint scent of cherry pipe tobacco and the citrus wax used to polish the desk, but I couldn't summon any tears, a fact that made me sad in an aching, hollow way, and I wondered when we would go out to eat.

I was sitting by Spencer's feet, studying the laces he had double-knotted, like a child, when Hadley came over. She leaned over him, replacing his overflowing ashtray with a clean one, and he said, "Hello Kitten," in a voice that had the gravelly thickness of sleep, "peculiar, isn't it, how this family cares more for its goods than its members?" Hadley just stood there, searching for something to say, while a queer smile swelled Spencer's mouth and his eyes blinked furiously against the smoke that rose between them, separating them like a partition.

It was, in fact, for Spencer and his double-knotted laces that I finally cried, and having at last produced my tears, I hurried into the living room to find an audience for my grief. Hadley annoyed me at once by remarking, "I see he has traded sullen for sad." The word *sullen* I found a particularly wounding interpretation of my attempt to display a somber dignity. Uncle Ambrose took me aside and handed me his monogrammed handkerchief, gesturing for me to wipe my nose. Without thinking, I blew my nose vigorously, eliminating the possibility of being able to return the handkerchief. I realized with a frisson of panic that I had no idea what the etiquette was concerning soiled linen: Do you put the befouled thing in your own pocket and just keep it? Does it get returned later, after a wash? Or did he expect it back now? While I was bunching the handkerchief awkwardly, stalling for time, Uncle Ambrose gave me Father's gold pocket watch, which I think he had intended to keep for himself.

In any event, I lost the watch at poker within the month and added it to the list of things which occasioned remorse when I was trying to fall asleep. It was a surprisingly short list, by the way.

I was returning from the corner market where I had gone to pick up a newspaper and a quart of milk for Spencer when I saw Hadley going up the steps of our building. As I mentioned, we hadn't seen her in a long while, but I was still not entirely ready to forgive her, so I slowed down rather than try to overtake her. She paused for a moment on the stoop of the redbrick building, checking the address. I imagine our row of brick buildings on West Ninth Street, huddled in the shadow of the Women's House of Detention, didn't seem grand enough to her. Withered veins of ivy crazed the facade, like a cracked eggshell, giving it a scruffy, disheveled verdancy. But knowing Spencer, it should not have surprised her: it was just the kind of place he would find charming; Spencer had the maddening ability to see beauty in the worn or broken, in detritus that she found only depressing.

As she rang the bell, I came up the stoop behind her. Hadley had plucked her eyebrows and was wearing a gingham sundress that ill suited her, making her seem innocent and naive, attributes that clashed with her husky voice and vixen temper. I suppose she had a kind of blonde allure if you liked that sort of thing, which I didn't, unless it was Veronica Lake.

Hadley straightened the seam of her stocking as a way of ignoring me a moment longer. Then, she made a dismissive comment for my benefit about the building looking like the master's house at a second-rate boarding school. Hadley was familiar with the subject, having attended one, so I said, "I guess you should know."

Hadley snorted contemptuously and pressed heavily on the buzzer.

"Oh, Hadley, how astonishing," Spencer said, opening the door. He hadn't shaved and his hair still held the distraught posture of sleep. The clothes he wore under an old silk dressing gown had clearly been slept in, and the gown itself dusted the floor with several inches of hem, dragging its belt from a back loop like a limp tail terminating in a frayed tassel, too weary to wag on the cool marble floor of the vestibule.

He held the heavy wooden door ajar for her as she entered and leaned her cheek toward him for a kiss. But she kept moving forward and his kiss grazed the air she had just vacated and languished in that hollow pocket of space, becoming notional, an insignificant flutter in the high-ceilinged hall.

"Were you up late?" she asked.

"No, I'm just naturally indolent," he answered, closing the door and winking at me.

"I hope," she said, "I'm not disturbing you. You're not busy or anything, are you?" The question sounded vaguely like an accusation, but she was clearly not prepared to be put off by a threadbare dressing gown.

"As a matter of fact, Hadley, I was in the middle of a very delicate business and won't be able to entertain you right now."

She had already started for the front parlor. "Don't be ridiculous. I have an important piece of news and, besides," she added with a smile, "I know better than to expect you to be entertaining."

She settled down in the center of the sofa and kicked off her high heels immediately, tucking her legs up under her on the seat cushion. Then, with more concentration than the task required, she pulled her gloves off slowly, with exaggerated drama, draping them neatly over the saddle of her handbag, while Spencer shuffled into the living room, skidding slightly in his socks on the parquet floors. I lingered in the hall, pretending to sort through the mail, most of which had sat unopened on the sideboard for nearly a week.

"Your impudence, my dear, is staggering," Spencer said, shaking his head, imitating Uncle Ambrose's crackly baritone, "but I'll let it pass because you're my only cousin and not without decorative value."

Hadley smiled; she was a pushover for a compliment, and she could wring enough pleasure from an adjective or two to make herself blush.

"So, what is it?" she asked, swiveling her feet down to the floor and crossing her legs, running a stocking in the process. I slouched over to the piano wedged in the corner of the parlor, where I could view the visit without being compelled to participate, but Hadley was making a point of ignoring me anyway.

"What is what?" Spencer returned, dropping his thin frame into a large armchair near her and tossing his head back against a sagging cushion.

"What you're doing right now that is so very important."

"Oh that." Spencer reached for the silver cigarette box on the end table and after peering into it for a moment selected an Old Gold and tapped it vigorously against the lid.

After he had lit the cigarette and exhaled a prodigious amount of smoke, he scratched his head and smoothed down his hair in a single nervous gesture, and replied, "As a matter of fact, I'm composing a very beautiful love letter. The lyric poignance is stunning."

Hadley reached over for a cigarette, making a showy display of effort because Spencer hadn't bothered to offer her one.

"That will make the family very happy. You must know everyone abhorred your last girlfriend—that Rita creature."

Spencer laughed and slid a heavy glass ashtray across the coffee table in her direction. Then he leaned back again and swung his feet up to fill the edge of table that the ashtray had formerly occupied, crossing his legs loosely at the ankle.

"That was by far the most delightful thing about Rita," he answered, still smiling as he puffed his cigarette and blew the smoke up toward the chandelier. The smoke rose in a loose blue spiral, disintegrating into the recesses of plaster rosette that crowned the ceiling. I had never met Rita, but Aunt Grace had excoriated her with the single word "Rockette."

Hadley pulled at a snag in the upholstery fabric, unraveling a thread in the damask weave. "Spencer, you *must* get some sun. Your legs are positively fluorescent," she said, dismissing Rita with an ellipsis. I turned to look at the band of skin exposed by the gap between Spencer's sock and the cuff of his trousers. His ankles looked bony and fragile, and Hadley's expression registered a brief conflict, as if she felt both protective and slightly squeamish. Perhaps she was remembering the time at the Waldorf cotillion, when she had overheard a girl in the ladies' room dismiss Spencer as "one of those tall, charming men you know would be absolutely useless in an emergency." He had always been bookish, it was true, apt to leave the tennis court in pursuit of a lost ball only to be found ten minutes later with a volume of poems someone had left on the lawn, or staring at the carp feeding at the edge of the lily pond. One of his professors in college had told Father that Spencer was brilliant, which had only made Father suspicious of the quality of education being offered there.

Spencer pulled up his socks and rearranged himself against the faded upholstery of the chair.

"You're not supposed to say that sort of thing to a man unless you've married him. I hope you don't make those kinds of careless comments with your beaux."

I struck a couple of chords on the Bechstein and laughed heartily at this, sounding, even I could hear it, a little forced at the end. But Hadley laughed too and glanced around the room; it had the same boyish whimsy Spencer's rooms had always had. His model schooner was prominently displayed on top of the bookcase and the brown cowboy hat he had worn as a child perched on a bronze bust of Lincoln, throwing the scale off, making Lincoln's brow seem huge and encephalitic. A striped tie drooped from the wall sconce, waiting to be pressed into service or just waiting to be pressed, and the wadded contour of a black sock was partially consumed by shadow under a reading chair that had been savaged by the Siamese cats he had kept in his dormitory room at Yale.

I assumed Spencer could have afforded a swankier apartment, but chose the parlor floor of a wide old brownstone for those architectural details suggesting an earlier grandeur without actually providing it. I would later learn that Spencer's irreverent attitude toward the comforts of wealth and convention was more than the quirky inflection of personality. The dilapidation of his surroundings calibrated a complicated equation: pride multiplied by privilege, divided by guilt.

Years later, when I read about the sham Potemkin villages in

Russia, I would remember the elegant transience that permeated Spencer's decor. His apartment had a restless charm, suggesting, like a stage set, a plywood world that could be dismantled overnight. It was this indifference to material stability that our relatives felt to be a dangerous flaw, which, unchecked, might bring about some greater dishonor.

Aunt Grace was fond of attributing this to our upbringing: "It's because he lost his mother. *She* understood: too much is a sign of vulgarity but not enough is the mark of failure. Minginess and ostentation are equally distasteful. Constance understood all this, and, above all, she was clean. It was one of her great qualities, but obviously she didn't pass it along. If you don't take pride in appearances, everything unravels eventually. It's a slippery slope, you know."

Hadley's eye rested briefly on a blue china vase in which a few lily stems wilted, giving off a vague sour odor, a peevish smell hinting at neglect. But the quirky appointments (the Bechstein piano, where I now slumped and chewed my thumbnail, wore a black sock garter around one of its stocky legs, and the toenails on the claw-foot bathtub had been painted with red nail polish, probably by Rita) seemed unaccountably cozy. I had the feeling, as the sounds from the street sifted by, like a tide pulling the traffic out to one of the avenues, of floating, drowsy and safe, like the child to whom Spencer had read aloud Hardy boys stories, when reading was still a kingdom I could not enter by myself.

"Who is she?" Hadley asked, lazily stubbing out her cigarette; it continued to smolder but she made no further effort to extinguish it.

Spencer looked absently around the room, then rose and

stood before the mirror that overhung the mantle; mottled like the pewter scales of a fish, murky and silver at once, its reflection was as watery and dark as the surface of a pond.

"Tell me who she is," Hadley repeated. "Do I know her?"

Spencer addressed her distorted profile in the mirror. "Who is who?"

"Your new gal. I promise I won't breathe a word," Hadley said, making a quick but fumbled combination of cross and salute that was meant to reassure him of her integrity.

"What new gal?" Spencer asked again, a confusion spreading across his features.

"The one you're writing to. The love letter. The epic poignance and all that." She picked up her gloves and tugged on the fingertips, a nervous gesture that Spencer had once described to me as "milking the dugs of old kid gloves."

If Spencer noticed, he refrained from teasing.

"There is no new inamorata," he said. "I just thought I ought to keep my hand in. I never have the time or inclination when I am actually seeing anyone. Besides, I think having a particular person in mind rather limits the creative flow."

"Oh, Spencer," Hadley said, coming quickly to the mantel where he slouched and tenderly adjusting the satin lapel of his robe, on which there was a small, dark stain, "you're hopeless. Let's go eat. That's what I've come about anyway. Aunt Lavinia is in town and we're all invited to lunch. It's kind of a command performance, so don't say no."

Spencer cracked a knuckle. "Lavinia's in town? How extraordinary. Why such short notice? Is she only here for a quick tour of duty?"

Hadley leaned up against the mirror, reapplying lipstick, her lips pooched out, making it hard for her to answer: "Nooo, she's here for good. The Jew died. She called a week ago. Your phone's out, which annoyed her. I think that's the only reason she invited me." Hadley paused to press her lips together before puckering up and planting an imprint of her lips on the mirror. "You really should pay the bills, Spencer. It's just squalid not to."

Lavinia was enthroned on the red plush banquette, with her bulldog, Mr. Phipps, seated beside her, when we arrived. She had already had the table service changed; apparently Aunt Lavinia always brought her own silverware because restaurant flatware, even at a good restaurant, didn't have the right weight. Aunt Grace, when she heard this from Hadley, would later say, "I've no doubt it was the Gibbs family silver. Solid and stamped, and she's got all of it, right down to the grape scissors!"

Lavinia waved her large menu as if fanning us across the room and into our seats. I could tell Hadley was embarrassed; she walked quickly, with her head down, and glanced surreptitiously around the room to see if other tables were watching. Spencer, on the other hand, seemed delighted by all of it: Lavinia's ridiculous hat with a spray of feathers sweeping off to one side, the dog panting over a place setting like a very old fat man, missing only the cigar, and the buzz of waiters, circling like dark birds, dipping in and over the table, white napkins flapping against the crisp black uniforms.

She was smaller than I imagined, and at the same time, more imposing. But her expression suggested a certain ironic humor, as if her presentation was part of a role she was playing that did not depend on an audience although her amusement might be increased by one.

"The desserts here are famous," Lavinia stated, snapping a bread stick in two and feeding it to Mr. Phipps. Because of the dog, we were seated in an alcove in the rear of the room, near the kitchen, which I could tell irked Hadley. She didn't like dogs to begin with: they always smelled, or slobbered, or rubbed their parts against her leg, and this one was staring at her in a particularly unnerving fashion, with bold, bulging, round eyes.

"The uglier the dog, the nobler the name. It should work that way for men too," Lavinia was saying.

"She's demented," Hadley whispered to me. "Uncle Ambrose was right."

There was an awkward moment during which we occupied ourselves with the menu as though it were a challenging riddle that must be solved before conversation could begin. My tastes tended toward the proletarian so I chose the roast chicken, while Hadley skimmed the menu for the most elaborate and expensive entrée, running her finger down the side of the listings like an accountant going over figures, her brow slightly furrowed, determined to make the best of an opportunity that seemed to have little promise. Spencer was delegated to choose a wine for the table while Lavinia ordered a cup of consommé for Mr. Phipps.

Hadley selected the stuffed lobster and Lavinia said, "Have it if you like, but it's terribly rich and will probably give you gas," which made Hadley blush, the tips of her ears burning with fury, something I hadn't seen since the days when we had teased her into tears by calling her Stumpy. I could see that she was trying to decide which would be less humiliating, choosing another entrée, which might lead our smiling young waiter to believe that she was prone to flatulence, or letting the order stand, which might suggest she didn't care about the consequences.

"Don't worry," I whispered to her, "we can always blame it on the dog," which made her pinch my leg fiercely under the table. But if she had wanted to change her order, she missed her moment—the waiter had taken all the orders to the kitchen and was now busy fussing over Mr. Phipps.

"The French are fools for dogs," she said when the waiter was out of earshot. I looked over quickly to Lavinia, but she and Spencer had become engrossed in a discussion of the Rosenbergs that had them both leaning over the table, Lavinia's hands gesturing extravagantly. Hadley sighed and wadded a piece of bread into a ball under the table. We had been taught that it was impolite to discuss politics at the table, a taboo that at least in our family was easy to respect since those discussions, when they did occur, were predictably dull. Besides, it had been months since the execution, so the topic had grown cold even for the debating club at Renwick. Hadley tried to catch Spencer's eye, but he was illustrating a point with his fork, drawing the tines against the white linen tablecloth, as if writing in invisible ink. She was left with no choice but to talk to me.

"Mummy says she's arranging for you to have a tutor to supervise your studies since it's too late in the term to place you in another school."

"How kind of her."

"Well, what did you expect, Gabriel, just to lounge around reading detective magazines and smoking cigars? Your English teacher sent a list of books you ought to read and apparently they're all fat ones."

"What do you mean, fat?" I asked.

Hadley snickered. "Let me put it this way: *Moby-Dick*, *Bleak House*, and *War and Peace* are not exactly slim little novels you can read between bonbons."

Lavinia turned to her, with eyebrows arched expectantly, and said, "It's rubbish, don't you think?" Hadley smiled blankly.

"The hysteria about Russia and spies," Lavinia continued, "utter rubbish."

"Are you a Communist?" Hadley asked, putting down her fork. Lavinia and Spencer both laughed.

"If I were, don't you think your uncle Ambrose would have already given my name to Mr. McCarthy?" Lavinia retorted, with what seemed oddly like delight.

Mr. Phipps put a paw on the table and whined for another bread stick, looking longingly at Hadley, his head cocked to the side in supplication. Hadley took a bread stick out of the silver basket and ate it with sadistic slowness, while Mr. Phipps watched covetously, his jaw sagging with anticipation.

Spencer raised his wineglass and toasted: "To Aunt Lavinia, the Pimpernel of Paris."

Lavinia smiled and bobbed her head with a quick, birdlike motion, as if a certain kind of pleasure made her shy. "You forgot the Scarlet part," she added dryly, and I realized that her renegade status was a means by which she snobbishly distinguished herself.

But it was not a club into which she was going to grant me ready membership.

"A good education is not something to squander lightly, young man," she said, turning her attention to me. "Ambrose told me about your expulsion, and I don't like to dispense advice, especially when it's not welcome, but self-indulgence is not the same thing as rebellion. If you are going to sacrifice yourself for a cause, you should choose it with care, make it worthy of whatever you might lose as a result, or you risk accumulating regrets, becoming bitter, a most unattractive attribute, absolutely crippling for the soul."

I was stunned into silence: no one, except the minister at church, discussed *the soul,* and certainly not over lunch. I couldn't help wondering if she had regrets about her choices, but I was afraid to appear rude by asking. The lunch had gone fairly well so far and, besides, Spencer was regarding me with a cautionary look. Aunt Lavinia concluded her admonition: "Momentary pleasures are merely that, momentary." She let the word expand in her throat, lingering on it, before continuing, "Now on the bright side, I should note that many interesting and talented men have overcome obstacles far more impressive than an expulsion from boarding school."

There was something about her businesslike manner that appealed to me although I could see that it might be off-putting to others. She appeared to have no interest in humiliating me, which I appreciated, and while I felt she didn't know me well enough to give advice, at least she took no pleasure in it, seeming as uncomfortable delivering her message as I was in receiving it.

She continued, after pausing to feed Mr. Phipps a bite of her brook trout, addressing all of us now: "I'm not much of an aunt, as you already know, so we'll just have to decide whether or not we like each other's company, blood be damned. I think you're all old enough to populate your lives on the basis of merit rather than happenstance. You'd have to be a fool or very frightened to take unquestioningly what fate allots you. But that is, of course, only my opinion."

This last morsel of philosophy was delivered with the desserts, like a final homemade confection, a lopsided pie or crusty cake, offered without any further enticement or apology. I later wished one of us had been able to offer outright the acceptance Lavinia had been so long denied as to have lost interest in its arrival, but we were silent. Mr. Phipps had crawled under the table, and I could hear him now snoring gently at my feet.

Having learned early on that most people would rather be amused than understood, or because he felt that the silence might be taken as a rejection of our hostess, Spencer segued smoothly into a rich anecdote about a weekend in Paris he had spent with Albert Beckwith and Clayton Prather, his roommates from Yale. It was a story I had heard parts of before but in this rendition Spencer imitated Beckwith's nervous twitch and Prather's Southern drawl, and he introduced several new details that gave the account more dash and humor, culminating with Lavinia clapping her small hands, like a child unable to contain her delight at a magic show. I decided right then that I liked Aunt Lavinia and would somehow make her like me.

When Lavinia had finished her meal, she organized the remains tidily on her plate like a still life: one new potato, one spear of asparagus, a spent wedge of lemon, and the delicate skeleton of fish, fossilized in a gelatinous dollop of béarnaise sauce. Then she flicked a few crumbs from the table and said, "Spencer, I hear you sold all the family portraits, including the Sargent painting of Reginald Gibbs."

She wasn't looking at Spencer, whose face contracted with alarm, because she was peering into the dark mouth of her handbag in search of her compact, which she found and snapped open, releasing a tiny puff of powder.

Spencer sighed. "Yes I did," he said, folding his napkin with military precision. His face was serious now; he had been widely criticized within the family for what had been seen as a ruthless, irresponsible, and mercenary approach to heirlooms. Hadley's mother had typewritten a four-page letter on the subject.

"Well," Lavinia said, dotting her face rapidly with scented face powder, "I approve. The Gibbses have had an almost Shintoist reverence for their ancestors, most of whom were monsters. Those paintings only prove that our men have been wearing neckties for two hundred years, whereas a noose would have been more appropriate in most instances." Lavinia closed the compact with one hand, clicking it shut like a castanet. "Besides, they were yours to do with as you chose. Had they been left to me, who knows? I might have burned them just for the pleasure of it. They would have made a splendid bonfire, I'm sure."

Hadley was shocked. She lifted her wineglass and drained the last of the Pouilly-Fumé too quickly; it went down wrong. Her face brightened to a deep carmine as she choked behind her napkin and Spencer patted her back ineffectively.

"Take some water," Aunt Lavinia said, gesturing to the waiter for the check, "or count backward—no, that's hiccups. Spencer, dear, give her a dinner mint before she dies."

I offered Hadley my water glass but she waved it away. Spencer took out his handkerchief and dabbed at a tear on Hadley's right cheek. "You'll be fine," he said, "just take little breaths and think of England." Hadley sputtered out a laugh and rested her head on his shoulder. "I am fine, really," she gasped.

"Good," Lavinia said, "I hate for anyone to get more attention than me, especially when I'm paying the bill." She smiled broadly and leaned forward, letting Spencer light her cigarette. "Now let's get out of here. It's time for me to take Mr. Phipps for a walk. He needs fresh air—you see how he's wheezing?" Her bracelets jingled as she rubbed the dog's head, and again as she waved away our chorus of thanks. As we stood to leave, our waiter brought Aunt Lavinia her silverware, which she wrapped in a napkin she lifted from the place setting of an adjacent table. "Washed but not polished," she noted as she tucked the bundle into her large alligator handbag. "Next time," she said, as she was lurched forward by the leash connecting her to Mr. Phipps, "we'll talk about something *really* interesting."

The first weeks of my freedom were joyless, an undifferentiated yawn of long hours I had neither the inclination nor the discipline to organize. Late winter had scabbed the streets with patches of soiled snow and the heavy skies reflected the sooty drabness of the buildings. Spencer had written up a list of museums I should visit, but I had no energy for art. It was understood without his having said a word that he would prefer me to occupy myself outside the apartment while he was working—though his work, from what I could observe, took place less at the typewriter than on the Chippendale sofa where he stretched for hours at a time, smoking cigarettes and waiting for exquisite phrases to come to him.

I don't mean to suggest, however, that he was loafing: unlike my own hours on the sofa or in the chintz embrace of the armchair, Spencer's face registered supreme concentration. It was clear that he *was* actually working, even if he was in a supine position, even if his eyes were fixed, like a cat's, on a barely discernable speck on the ceiling.

I was miserable in my liberation and squandered my time in lethargic rambles along the frosted streets, kicking cans into alleys or watching tiny whirlwinds of debris spin crazily across an empty lot. Sometimes I window-shopped, staring greedily at merchandise that under other circumstances I would have scorned. I had lost my gloves and on windy days my fingertips would start to sting with cold but I couldn't bring myself to spend my meager allowance on anything as utilitarian as another pair, especially with only another five weeks left of winter. To get warm I would duck into a diner every few hours, sit at the counter over a coffee or, if I were flush, the breakfast special. My favorite diner was on Seventh Avenue, a few blocks down from Spencer's apartment. Originally named Lucky's Diner, the *L* was long gone, as was the optimism that must have chosen the name. That was a large part of why I liked it: the red vinyl booths had gashes that had been mended with duct tape, leaving large, silver, Chinese-looking ideograms on the seat backs. On the wall next to the booths, a clumsy seascape mural was painted, its waves cresting in a series of little white dabs, like a diminishing ellipsis the artist had brutally foreshortened, while three hovering *V*s flapped endlessly over the grease-stained foam of the Mediterranean.

Other than the garish depiction of the Amalfi Coast, the decor at Lucky's was bland and nondescript. The walls were a putty-colored stucco that matched the Formica counter, behind which Spiro, the owner, sat supervising. Spiro smoked a particularly pungent brand of Greek cigarette that had blackened his teeth over the years, making his smile, which was rarely bestowed, memorable.

His nephew, George, was the waiter. When George wasn't

serving a customer, he would hunch over the counter with the sports section of the *New York Mirror*, a toothpick flicking up and down in the corner of his mouth. Lucky's was a comfortable place to while away thirty or forty minutes, but by the arch of the afternoon I was usually driven into the stale darkness of movie theaters for overheated matinees, half price, where from the balcony I watched the haze of smoke swirl in languid calicos through the beam of the projector, the illuminated shapes changing form like bacteria under a microscope. The actual movie itself was inconsequential; by the time I had emerged, blinking into the dazzle of winter light, it was forgotten, replaced by the shrill penance of wind, pushing me back downtown and making my eyes tear more bitterly than any celluloid heartbreak.

It was at the Chelsea Art theater that I ran into Aunt Lavinia again. I had been dozing through the feature, a mediocre whodunit starring Dorothy McGuire, when the lights came up and I was distracted by a commotion in the front of the theater. The picture had been sparsely attended, with most of the audience scattered in the first ten rows. On the aisle of the third row, a commanding figure in a large hat was struggling with something under her seat. There was a low growling followed by a sharp yelp and I knew suddenly that Aunt Lavinia had brought Mr. Phipps to the movies. I watched her for a moment before coming forward to help her. Her coat was bunched up in the back and her hat was askew as she bent awkwardly between the rows of dingy velour seats trying to tug the dog out from the spot in which he was wedged, eating kernels of popcorn from the floor. There was something about her posture, at once archetypal and poignant, that reminded me of figures bending in a field, the harvest imagery that comes out at Thanksgiving to make you feel guilty and grateful.

When Aunt Lavinia turned around and saw me, she registered no surprise. "Just in time," she said, as if she had been expecting me. "Go down that row and push from behind while I pull. I was about to get an usher, but they're absolutely useless at anything but wielding a flashlight in your face."

"Aunt Lavinia," I said, following her instructions, "I don't think dogs are allowed in here. Did anyone see you bring in Mr. Phipps?"

Lavinia looked at me impatiently, as if I were mentally limited. "Of course, my dear. You don't think I'd be foolish enough to try to sneak in a canine as large and impressive as Mr. Phipps, do you?"

"But, Aunt Lavinia, how did—"

She interrupted with a gesture that flicked all her bangles into a bright jangle of resonant tones.

"Nothing could be simpler; I bought him a seat. The manager was easily persuaded by the eloquence of the greenback." Lavinia lowered her voice to a confidential whisper, adding, "I told him Mr. Phipps was my Seeing Eye dog just to make him feel less corrupt."

She had taken out a cigarette case that she now snapped open, offering me one of her private blend. I lit both our cigarettes as we proceeded down the narrow aisle, with Mr. Phipps trailing behind, nosing at the dropped candy that littered the floor here and there.

"If you are not rushing off, Gabriel, join me for tea. I am mad about the finger sandwiches at the Plaza, though we'll have to suffer through those syrupy Strauss waltzes."

The afternoon light was thin and yellow, casting a sickly tone on the sidewalk and buildings, and the temperature had dropped, making the air seem slightly bitter as we walked up to the avenue. I hailed a Checker cab for us and sat in the jump seat, while Lavinia and Mr. Phipps spread themselves almost voluptuously across the bench seat. Lavinia rolled down her window and stared out into the shock of rushing air. Her hair was whipped into a frenzied tangle and the wind brought tears to her eyes, but she remained oblivious. I didn't know if I should make conversation or wait for her to pull her head back inside the cabin of the taxi.

As the cab stopped for a light at Central Park South, Lavinia finally spoke: "You know, I'm actually too fatigued for tea. You'll forgive me if I ask you to accept a rain check on the tea. Where is the best place for me to drop you?"

I was disappointed out of all proportion. The idea of tea at the Plaza, now that the offer had been retracted, suddenly seemed emblematic of the kind of days I should have been having: vaguely aristocratic, full of purpose but carefree, elegant yet relaxed, engendering the expansiveness of thought a luxurious setting invites. A lump welled in my throat.

"No matter at all. This is fine right here," I said, jumping out of the taxi just before the light changed. Aunt Lavinia's face, as the taxi lurched forward, was a small oval of surprise. Central Park loomed across the street, naked trees and muddy paths and a string of empty park benches, weathering. I couldn't face its bleak prospect, so I started walking east, pulling up the collar of my coat and hunching my shoulders against the wind.

As I walked along the walled edge of the park, I studied the honeycomb pattern of paving stones. Across my path a flock of dirty gray pigeons wobbled, urgently pecking at bread crumbs some fool had scattered. I assumed, correctly as it turned out, that the source of the bread crumbs was a heavily shrouded woman slumped on a bench, beside a dented baby carriage. She looked rather disheveled for a nanny, and as I passed before her, scattering the pigeons, my footsteps sending them flapping in all directions, she seared me with her gaze. Two things jarred me badly: the intensity of hatred she leveled at me with a mere squint of her eyes and the fact that the baby carriage was occupied by a very ancient cat, lying on a folded pink baby blanket. The cat could barely raise its head, and its eyes glowed white with cataracts.

By the time I reached the carpeted steps of the Plaza Hotel, I had already decided to have tea alone, no matter how much pocket money the gesture required. At the time, I was deeply concerned with appearing sophisticated, and the gilded glamour of the hotel lobby, the crisp uniforms of the bellboys, and the grandiose bouquets of flowers buoyed me against the deflation that still lingered, the sadness that threatened to settle like a shadow on my day. As I wandered through the corridors, pretending I was a guest, I was aware of the looks I was eliciting from the staff. I followed a staircase up to a second level where the rooms had a sweet, stale smell, like Christmas fruitcake. No one was about so I palmed an ashtray from a side table and put it in my pocket: an offering for Spencer, a souvenir from the limbo of my life. It would, of course, be broken in my pocket long before I had a chance to present it to him.

Passing a men's room, I ducked in and examined myself at length, adjusting my corduroy jacket and combing my hair under the watchful eyes of an old Negro attendant, who smiled at me with what seemed like such genuine affection that I stuffed all the change in my pocket into his hand when I left. Unfortunately it was more change than his wrinkled palm could hold and it spilled noisily on the tile floor. My last glance before the door swung shut saw the old man bending over, picking up the coins with a trembling hand. It was this kind of incident that I think Spencer had in mind when he warned me about the city: "It will break your heart a thousand times a day."

I felt a little jittery, as if a bird were trapped in my chest; I sat down in one of the oversized Queen Anne chairs that lined the hall and realized I hadn't eaten since breakfast. Spencer had a cavalier attitude about meals. If he was caught up in work or reading or the last aria of a broadcast, dinner could easily be several bowls of cornflakes, or baloney sandwiches, or Ritz crackers with peanut butter. Nor did he mind having the same meal several times in a row.

On the other hand, when Spencer was miserable he would go to the market and spend hours palpating fruit and sifting spices from the wooden barrels in the Middle Eastern shop. Then the small kitchen would be filled with the scent of ground lamb or wine sauce, or glazed plums, tangy and sweet duets of flavor, the counter space dazzled by still lifes, a striking palette of succulents and savories, from the sweet, oozing gold of imported pears to the inky, purple eggplant skins. Spencer would concoct wildly ambitious meals, exotic and delicate couplings of taste, offerings appropriate for the most capricious emperor.

In these efforts, I was the galley slave and sous-chef, but I didn't mind. Helping Spencer in the kitchen was like being in an alchemist's lab. He liked to listen to Dixieland jazz or ragtime while he cooked, and we bowed before the kitchen gods after every meal: the cardboard likenesses of Aunt Jemima and Uncle Ben that Spencer had cut from their boxes and set in a silver frame whose double ovals had formerly held photographs of our mother and father.

"Hey there, Gibbs," someone said.

I snapped my head up and looked around. I am always uncomfortable being recognized in a public place, uneasy that I might have been moving my lips or had a slack, foolish expression on my face. On the subway, I saw any number of examples of this, which only fed my self-consciousness. Clayton Prather, one of Spencer's roommates from Yale, was striding down the hall toward the bank of elevators. Clayton had spent a few weekends with us at the house on the Cape just before Father sold it. I had always been amused by Clayton; he was so solicitous of Father, and Father was so contemptuous of him.

Clayton's family came from Tennessee but moved to our town in Connecticut while Clayton was still a teenager. The Prathers had bought a very large imitation chateau in the western part of Greenfield, in an area which was inhabited by "new money." His father was known in certain circles as the Cockroach King, having made a fortune in the extermination business. It was generally agreed by all the people we knew that Mr. Prather was a vulgarian. He was ostentatious about his money and he had married three times, the last to a starlet twenty-five years his junior, who was strikingly beautiful until she drank herself into a size sixteen.

Mr. Prather called everyone Darling or Sugar or Baby, unless they were male, in which case he called them Chief or Boss. But I think what irked people most was that the Prathers seemed to enjoy their money in a way that was unthinkable to the rest of us. Once when I was driving with Aunt Grace in her station wagon, we were passed by a speeding yellow convertible driven by Mr. Prather, who had in the passenger seat a pet cougar, wearing a thick leather collar and looking bored in a large feline way. Aunt Grace had almost swerved off the road, but when she steadied herself she said primly, "Don't look. It only encourages him."

Once when we were coming out of McCann's Pharmacy, we saw Mr. Prather staggering beneath a jeroboam of champagne he was carrying to his car. Aunt Grace gave an involuntary shiver as she commented: "That man has a face that makes you want to slap it. Heaven help me, but it's true." My cousin Hadley pulled a Good Humor Creamsicle out of her mouth to blurt out, "They've got two television sets, and a radio in the bathroom, and Mrs. Prather believes in ghosts and she's seen them, but only with the help of gin." Aunt Grace wheeled around and spoke sharply to both of us. "I don't want to even know where you would hear such trash."

Perhaps because of his odd upbringing, Clayton was always angling for approval. He ingratiated himself with Aunt Grace by arriving for the weekend laden with delicacies, tins of tea cake soaked in liqueur, candied fruits, hazelnuts, and Swiss chocolate, all from a famously overpriced gourmet shop. Even I was courted; Clayton invited me to be his partner at tennis knowing that I had a hopeless backhand, and even after I had stepped on his wooden racket press and cracked it, he let me drive his car down the long dirt road that led to the swimming pond. That was more consideration than I was used to receiving from Spencer's cronies.

"Hello, Prather," I said, my voice oddly high and thin.

"You here with Spencer?" Clayton asked, peering over my shoulder as if I might be hiding him.

"No, actually. Spencer's at work. I'm waiting to meet my aunt," I lied.

"Your aunt Grace?" Clayton asked, amazing me with his memory.

"No, my aunt Lavinia," I explained. "You wouldn't know her. She's lived in Paris all this time."

Clayton Prather laughed and playfully jabbed at my shoulder. "I hope she's very pretty, this aunt of yours."

His misinterpretation of the situation flattered me, so I let it go uncorrected. Only later did I realize he was humoring me.

We had by this time reached the lobby; a cluster of smartly dressed women had just arrived and there seemed to be some kind of commotion over their luggage, which was mounded in front of a potted palm and looked like a large wounded animal. Prather snapped his fingers for a bellhop and asked for a telegram form, but changed his mind almost instantly, telling the boy to skip it but tipping him anyhow. He seemed distracted and only marginally aware of me as he ran his hand gently through his sandy-colored hair the way you might pet a large animal.

Suddenly he said, "Why not come up with Spencer for the weekend sometime? I bought a house in Pawling, you know. It's pretty lively on weekends and I'd bet good money and bad that the Gibbs brothers could use a holiday. Here's my card. You're both welcome anytime. Let me know what train you're on and I'll send for you at the station."

It was an elegant card, cream colored, on heavy stock, with

his name in the kind of type I'd seen only on wedding invitations. I thanked him and slipped his card into my jacket pocket, next to the ashtray. Prather checked his watch again and glanced toward the revolving door.

"Do you have time for a drink?" he asked. He looked suddenly forlorn, like a child lost in a department store.

"Sure," I said, following him into the bar. The room was dark by contrast with the lobby and almost empty. A dark smell hung in the room, as if the bitterness of whiskey and tobacco had steeped the dark wood and deep green upholstery with its sharpness. Small round tables were set before large leather reading chairs and on each of the tables there were small bowls of mixed nuts, mostly peanuts and smoked almonds. As we walked to the back of the room, I reached into one of the bowls and grabbed a handful of nuts, quickly palming them into my mouth, making a slight snorting noise as I attempted to chew and swallow before we reached our table. If he heard anything, Clayton didn't turn around to investigate and I was able to drop into a chair and, with the back of my hand, wipe some salt from my mouth without Clayton's having even looked over at me. Normally I would have picked the cashews out and left the rest, but I was starving.

The barman came around from behind the bar and, rather pointedly I felt, refilled the bowl I had just emptied. Then he stopped at our table and took our order. He had a weariness that was impressive. Had I been alone he would have made me uncomfortable. Prather asked for a bourbon. I ordered a Bloody Mary and a club sandwich and then I bummed one of Prather's Pall Malls. It occurred to me that Prather would pick up the check, even if I offered to split it. I exhaled a huge rush of smoke through my nostrils, feeling the tingle of air move through my nose hair, which was vaguely disturbing, like rubbing your eyebrows in the wrong direction. Nevertheless, I was determined to smoke the way Belmondo did in the art movies.

Then I leaned back in the leather chair and stretched out my feet. The afternoon had finally achieved some stature. Prather tapped his cigarette on the table before lighting it, a gesture I intended to add to my collection.

"I would really love to see Spencer," he said with an audible sigh. "I'm in a bit of a spot right now and Spencer would know just how to handle it."

I couldn't imagine a situation in which he would defer to Spencer's judgment, unless of course he was having trouble with an obscure meter or trying to render a pun faithfully in another language. Clayton Prather had made a fortune by his twenty-fifth birthday, partly in stocks and partly by taking over businesses his father had neglected. Occasionally he was mentioned in the society pages of the daily newspaper; Aunt Grace would periodically comment on his progress and it was from her that I had heard about his recent divorce and the nightclub in Havana he was rumored to have bought. At twenty-seven, Clayton Prather could safely be called worldly. It was hard to imagine him having any problems, much less ones that Spencer had mastered. I nodded sagely and bit into the sandwich that had just arrived.

"I'd really like to get Spencer's view on this situation," Prather repeated. His thin fingers drummed lightly on the armrest of his chair. He seemed distracted. "You know how well he puts things—I've never been able to do that. In fact," he continued gravely, "I remember describing a girl to Spencer as 'swell' and he practically winced. He said my vocabulary was anemic." Prather removed a fleck of tobacco from his lip. "He's probably right, for what that's worth."

I waved my hand dismissively. I'd almost finished the first half of my sandwich, and a calm was settling over me like a sweet fog, making it hard for me to keep up my end of the conversation.

"Yup, that sounds like Spencer," I agreed, perhaps overvigorously. "He doesn't think much of the way I use language either."

Prather shifted in his seat and then lifted his glass, jiggling the ice before taking another sip. He didn't say anything and I realized that a man like Clayton Prather probably would not be relieved by a comparison with myself.

"Does your father still have the cougar?" I asked.

Prather looked at me. He had long lashes and his eyes were a pale brown that lacked resolve. I could see how he would be popular with a certain kind of girl: he was good looking in an almost cartoonish way. It was the kind of face you knew wouldn't age well—under the weight of middle age his features would seem flaccid and effeminate. He picked up his gold lighter and toyed with it, clicking the lid up and down with his thumbnail.

"Oh God no. Trixie mauled the pool boy within a matter of months. My dad had to pay a huge settlement even though we had a witness who saw the incident and said the fool had been prodding the cat with the end of his cleaning net. Dad has one of those giant poodles now, in Florida."

Prather stubbed out his cigarette and looked at his watch again.

"So what happened to the cougar? Did your dad give it to a zoo?"

Prather repressed a yawn, closing his lips tightly over his even teeth.

"No, I think that turned out to be a huge bother, so in the end the animal hospital took Trixie away. I wasn't especially broken up by it. She was a mess to feed; Dad had the butcher send us huge hunks of meat every day, and you can't imagine her breath. Still, she was a beautiful beast."

I had finished my sandwich and most of the nuts on our table, but the drink was still having an unexpectedly powerful soporific effect. I was tempted to ask Prather about his problem, not because I was particularly interested, or thought I might be of some help, but because I wanted at this point to do nothing but drowse to the sound of a voice, and my experience at Renwick had taught me that once you ask a fellow to tell you his troubles, he usually does so exhaustively. But before I could offer my ear, a tight knot of businessmen spilled into the room, talking boisterously, their bodies assuming the stylized postures of gaiety that belonged to a choreography as intricate as Chinese opera but which had nothing to do with the social pleasures it mimicked; rather, it was part of the serious work of concluding a deal. Behind them, weaving his way among and then past their ebullience, a bellhop not much older than I but with considerably worse skin carried a message for Clayton Prather on a black plastic tray.

Prather handed the boy some change and took the folded note from the tray. I could see from the way his jaw muscle flinched and one eyebrow arched that the news was not happy. I wondered fleetingly if it had to do with the problem he had alluded to earlier, but before I could ask, Prather stood up and pulled a few crisp bills from his wallet and put them on the table.

"Sorry, kiddo. I've got to go—but then I'll be seeing you and Spencer for the weekend."

I started to rise, awkwardly sputtering out my thanks, but Clayton Prather put his hand on my shoulder. "Stay, please. Have another sandwich if you like."

Once he had left the room, I called for the bill. Even after tipping the barman what seemed like an insanely generous sum, I still had money left for a taxi ride down Fifth Avenue and a Cuban cigar to smoke with my feet on the jump seat and my arms folded behind my head while the driver's radio played "I Love Paris" and "Stranger in Paradise," both tunes I considered girly but which I enjoyed nonetheless.

W hen I got home, Albert Beckwith was lying on the Chesterfield holding a large glass of scotch to his forehead while the phonograph swooned the final aria of *La Bohème*.

"He's gone out to get more ice," Beckwith said, his eyes dark slits behind horn-rimmed glasses. "Also your aunt Grace rang up. One of you has to call her this evening." Beckwith rolled his corpulent body against the back of the sofa and propped himself up on an elbow. Ever since our phone service had resumed, Beckwith had been dropping by more frequently, although he never called ahead, of course, or asked if he could use the phone for the lengthy, sometimes long-distance conversations he conducted from the living room couch. I had never understood why Spencer was friends with Albert Beckwith, but Spencer was oddly loyal to the most inexplicable types.

I sat down in the armchair and kicked off my penny loafers. I started to say something but Albert held his hand up and his face strained toward the phonograph as if he were himself shuddering out the final notes. This was a facet of Beckwith that irritated: he encumbered others with his sensitivity, as if he were one giant nerve ending all aquiver and the world was merely an audience for which he had contempt. But Spencer said he was good at chess, and he was just about the only other person I knew who read the obscure books that Spencer bought from the secondhand shops. Another thing about Beckwith—he had certain words he used excessively. Everything was either *ghastly* or *sublime,* and he liked to end a thought with "et cetera," as if he was just too pressed to go through the bother of finishing the sentence. Certain subjects, however, got him quite worked up, pontificating to the point of white foamy saliva specks appearing in the corners of his mouth, especially when he had been drinking. Moreover, Beckwith seemed to feel that his powers to enlighten entitled him to mooch shamelessly: his visits endured until he had consumed all the alcohol, cigarettes, and comestibles in any one location, for which he never expressed gratitude, thank-yous and thank-you notes in particular being a form of bourgeois subjugation.

Spencer banged in, holding bulging paper bags in each arm.

"Give me a hand, Bucko," he said.

"Bucko" was a nickname I'd had as a child, and because it was rarely used anymore, it had an odd power when it was invoked. Beckwith had replaced *La Bohème* with baroque harpsichord music, which filled the room now with its peculiar dark sparkle, and he had poured himself another drink, but he in no way bestirred himself to help us unload the groceries that Spencer had clearly bought for him.

As I helped Spencer in the kitchen, I tried to apprise him of the day's events. I could feel myself failing, like those dreams in which I want to run but find my feet leaden. The adventure I had imagined myself recounting withered on my tongue, turning dull and monochrome, without any of the fizz and dash that I had hoped to convey.

"So," Spencer recapitulated, "you ran into Aunt Lavinia at the movies, where you actually were instead of the library where you were supposed to be, and she offered to take you to tea but didn't. Then a lady hobo gave you the evil eye, which sent you reeling into the Oak Bar, where you ran into Clayton Prather, who bought you a sandwich and beseeches us to join him for a bucolic revel on some subsequent weekend." He drew deeply on his cigarette, making the paper burn quickly and with an audible sizzle.

I could see the day had lost some of its snap in translation. He was probably disappointed by my lack of progress on the assigned reading list. Beckwith coughed gingerly.

"Clayton *Augustus* Prather? Scion of the poison-powder fortune? Suspected member of Skull and Bones? Machiavellian mogul extraordinaire?" We both turned to look at him.

"I saw him the other day at Ashton's Cafe, making capitalism look bloody attractive. Or maybe it was just the woman he was having lunch with who looked so attractive. She was not, I can assure you, his usual fare. For one thing, she looked remarkably unimpressed by the whole shebang, the fawning waiters, the pretentious food—the insect slayer himself. She was positively *sublime*: the almond-eyed Madonna, you know the type—luminous skin, an air of sophisticated sadness—delicate but not in a *ghastly* hothouse way. She seemed completely oblivious to the splendors on offer. But don't get me wrong—this was not the posturing of a spoiled debutante—she was as thin as an orphan, her shoes were cheap, and the sleeves of her dress were too long and only days from threadbare. Still, those were just details. She looked sensational, you know, all style, no money.

"Those types are usually the first ones to fall for empty industrialists like Clayton Augustus Prather. If I could only get more gals like her to show up at the meetings, we could convert the country by the end of the year," Beckwith concluded wistfully, stubbing out his cigarette.

Albert was involved with the Communist Party and I was not supposed to know about it. Spencer shot Beckwith a glance and changed the subject. The pork chops he had coated in a beer batter now started to burn, creating a huge belch of smoke that filled the room instantly. We all scurried to open the windows—even Albert was roused from his supine position on the couch.

A rush of air dropped the temperature in the room by several degrees and carried in, like a wave depositing its detritus and treasure in a tangled heap, the sounds of the world: a dog's frantic barking, the slam of a metal gate echoing down a sullen alleyway, a car downshifting, and farther, a reedy child's voice singing a beautiful, taunting refrain, all of which contrasted jarringly with what now seemed the sterile prissiness of the harpsichord. Spencer went back into the kitchen to examine the damage.

It was my fault. I was supposed to be watching the chops while Spencer made my favorite: garlic whipped potatoes. A flash of shame seared through me, coagulating in a ball at the back of my throat. Of course Spencer didn't say a word of reproach, which only made me feel worse.

Since my father's death, I had started to collect failings, as if in his absence it had devolved to me to curate my inadequacies as they made themselves manifest. Events therefore carried with them not only the import of their own circumstances, but the accumulative weight of all preceding ones, the way in any collection the whole is more impressive than the sum of its parts and the slightest entry gains significance merely by inclusion and proximity.

Thus the burning of the chops, a minor, almost routine act of negligence in itself, was freighted with my indolence concerning schoolwork, the expulsion, a series of ludicrous lies Spencer had caught me in, the three dollars I had stolen from his wallet, and so forth, back to the summer when I was five and supposed to feed the box turtle Spencer had rescued from a gang of drunken locals who were kicking it back and forth across the white line dividing Randall's Road. When Spencer returned from sailing camp at the end of that summer and found the turtle, already starting to stink in its wire enclosure behind the barn, he wept.

Watching him now, tenderly scraping the black char off the pork, I wanted to explain to him once and for all that I was an absolute bust, a ne'er-do-well, bound to disappoint, and he was a fool for expecting otherwise, and I couldn't bear his kind forgiveness anymore. But Albert Beckwith was hovering over my shoulder, trying to see if the chops were still edible, squinting at the skillet from behind his thick glasses, breathing heavily through his mouth.

With Albert there, I couldn't even bring myself to apologize so I excused myself instead, saying I wanted to have a quick review before dinner of the Latin vocabulary cards Spencer had made for me. He must have known this was yet another fabrication, for even as he nodded his approval I could discern a flutter of a sigh pass his lips, which were registering a somewhat strained smile. As I shut the door to my room, formerly a maid's room and no larger than a monk's cell, I could hear them resume the conversation about Clayton Prather; Beckwith was counseling against accepting the weekend invitation. It occurred to me, as I sank with a detective magazine into the sprung coils of the mattress, that Albert Beckwith was almost girlishly possessive of Spencer. There was a kind of creepy aspect to the way Beckwith would puff out his already pendulous lower lip in judgment of others with whom he was jealous or competitive. I was especially annoyed that he was trying to queer the weekend with Clayton Prather and I churlishly comforted myself with the thought that Beckwith would never be having lunch with a woman like the one he described seeing with Clayton Prather, and, on some level, notwithstanding his extraordinary powers of illusion and self-inflation, Beckwith knew it too. Just before the wind slapped shut my door, I heard Spencer ask, "So what's the name of Prather's prize?"

"Lillian," Beckwith answered gravely. "I didn't catch the last name: I was in a ghastly rush; there was a terrible din, and the acoustics were appalling."

Spring arrived overnight with a flamboyance that was contagious: pallid clerks, sporting bow ties in boisterous colors, crowded the streets at lunch hour. Secretaries doused themselves in perfumes with names like "Paris Surprise" and "Midnight Madness," scents that lingered in empty elevators and lobbies and left the trace of gardenias and jasmine and oak moss blooming along hallways, weaving floral tapestries as intricate as an Oriental rug.

Fleets of Silver Cross carriages, with their navy hoods folded back like accordions, exposed infants to the cerulean expanse of sky while nursemaids crowded park benches, chattering like agitated sparrows.

In the park, fountains gushed the hyperbole of renewal, softening the air with the moist breath and lulling fall of water, attracting pedestrians who stopped to muse in the drowsy dazzle of light. Courtyards of tenements filled with the tinny blare of transistor radios playing sentimental songs, though now and then the broken edge of an argument drifted across the cracked cement from which sprouted a few hopeful stems of bindweed or quack grass. Air shafts echoed with the reverberating gargle of pigeons, and there were days when the light on the gray rise of buildings seemed almost like a cadmium wash, brightening the striations of soot with a yellow glow that buffed even the dullest stone.

It was in the busy confusion of one season yielding to another, in the green clamor of hope and resolve, that Lillian Dawes took root and began to bloom in my consciousness. I would later spend years haunted by the question why. Certainly I was ripe for the experiences into which I was launched by my infatution, and it is also true, I suppose, that first love is a canvas on which we paint our own desires. But nonetheless, there is the inextricable pull that certain people have: she was a woman who left an indelible mark on the imagination.

In a matter of weeks, Lillian Dawes started to make the papers. At first, it was just a caption under a photograph, showing her at a charity cotillion, dancing with a blurred escort, her head tilted slightly toward the camera, as if the strong curve of her cheekbone was leading, rather than the indistinct arm clutching the small of her back.

A week later she appeared twice: first stepping into the sheen of a highly polished car, its elongated curves suggesting an animal crouching, poised to remove her from the tedious festivities of a gallery opening. In the following photograph, she was throwing rice at a wedding, the straw confection of her hat brim casting a giddy veil of shadows, ornate as lacework, giving a vaguely Moroccan cast to her face, as if implicit in the composition was a delicate system of discretion and disclosure. Too fashionably attired to be a bridesmaid, she was listed simply as "guest."

A fourth picture, taken at the end of the month, showed her standing in the winner's circle with Clayton Prather, whose horse Golden Laurel had just won the purse at Saratoga. Golden Laurel was in the center of the photograph, wearing a necklace of roses, looking into the camera with an expression of outrage, probably having more to do with the flashbulbs than the necklace. On the horse's left, Prather's grin bespoke such satisfaction you'd have thought he'd run the race himself.

That, in fact, most of his victories were earned by the labor of others in no way diminished his sense of accomplishment. He was unencumbered, I was to learn, by the quotidian shackles of shame or duty, embracing the languor of his father's motto: "honor without effort." Clayton's definition of a gentleman, and here his Southern accent would be exhumed, was "one whose hands were clean," and here he would wink, "even if occasionally his conscience was not."

Lillian Dawes did not, however, look dazzled to be in the winner's circle. Her expression, where it was not hidden by tortoiseshell sunglasses, was one of patient resignation, as if she understood that standing in the sun for a group of reporters was required by the situation, but that it was nonetheless a rather steep price to pay for the club seat she had so briefly enjoyed.

I understood instantly that she was the woman Beckwith had seen with Prather, and in that moment of revelation she became my grail: I looked for her everywhere. Now that the weather had turned, I was even more restless than usual. Besides,

Spencer had arranged for me to earn pocket money by working for Aunt Lavinia, and one of the chores I had been assigned was Mr. Phipps's afternoon walk.

I would take the Lexington line subway up to Seventy-seventh Street, and walk over to Fifth Avenue, down streets conspicuously devoid of young men my age, until finally I stood before the great sandstone mausoleum which was her building. Entering Lavinia's lobby was always slightly disconcerting: it was impressively patrician and depressing at the same time. The ersatz living room decor reminded me of rooms in a neglected wing of Citizen Kane's house, grand and unhappy and underlit. Cadaverous doormen in creepy, dancing school white cotton gloves lurked in little alcoves of the sprawling marble entrance hall, and there was the vague smell of old skin in the dim air.

It was a great relief (I sometimes found that I had been holding my breath without realizing it) when the elevator would arrive, and the mahogany door would open to reveal Mr. Phipps, seated on the elevator banquette, drooling on the cushion, filling the small chamber with his heavy breath and dog dander.

The swoon of daylight and street noise when I was ushered back out into the world was a giddy reprieve, although it annoyed me that on these occasions Aunt Lavinia never invited me up or brought herself down. But she had been almost insultingly clear on that point. "Never mix business with pleasure or family."

To be fair, she *had* taken me out to lunch twice and bought me some shirts at Brooks Brothers, as well as a very sleek portable typewriter which I was too enamored of to actually defile with paper. It sat on my desk like a very large paperweight, shiny and ornamental, testament to my uselessness.

When I was being honest with myself (a demanding posture I generally avoided), I knew that I would have chafed terribly under the imposition of having to socialize with Aunt Lavinia before and after each walk. So I didn't bother to complain to Spencer if she treated me like a messenger or delivery boy when I went to her building on weekday afternoons.

Only once did I go up uninvited, and that was when urgency overrode protocol: I had stopped at the Delphic Diner on my way uptown and enjoyed perhaps too freely their all-you-can-drink coffee policy. Aunt Lavinia was on the telephone and she waved me impatiently across the room, dismissing me into the half bath the size of a phone booth, wallpapered in a very lively print that was dizzying in close proximity. From the toilet, you could comfortably wash your hands without stretching, that's how small the space was.

Hung to the left of the sink were two hand towels with Lavinia's initials elaborately embroidered in scrolling loops of gold thread. I was afraid to touch them; there was no way to use them without spoiling the starch that seemed to hold together the delicate gauze of the fabric. Still, I knew Lavinia would comment if she thought I hadn't washed my hands, so before I left, I let the water run in the sink for a moment, wondering if all guests secretly did this.

Aunt Lavinia paid me generously for "giving Mr. Phipps his fresh air," which meant that Mr. Phipps and I were assured of our series of rewards, which began with a frankfurter from the perpetually crowded Orange Julius on Lexington and Eighty-sixth, and usually ended, depending on the trajectory of our adventure, with a box of Cracker Jacks at the sailboat pond in Central Park, only blocks from Aunt Lavinia.

Our excursions varied with my mood. Sometimes I would take a book to the large meadow behind the zoo and let Mr. Phipps off his leash, allowing him to chase pigeons and squirrels until he wheezed and snored so loudly that passersby would inquire with alarm about his health. I never sat on the benches, but always positioned myself in the field so as to have a view of them. Once, I saw two men kissing behind a tree. When they came back onto the path, the older man looked over his shoulder nervously, touching his forehead with his handkerchief, and the younger man, a thin fellow in an expensive tweed jacket, had the saddest expression—a look almost of grief.

On another occasion, I followed Mr. Phipps into the brambles that crowd the unpathed stretch between the reservoir and the stone castle (in actuality a weather station). Deviant in its lack of landscaping, this area seemed the most thrilling—wild and slightly threatening after Olmstead's green restraints and gardening conventions—the kind of place where you might find a body, and I did. Following Mr. Phipps into the underbrush, I came straight upon a man's body lying under some shrubs, facedown. He was rank; his filthy clothing emanated a stench that was like a hard slap, making my eyes water and my head flinch. I felt a wave of terror pull me out, thrashing, back to the bridle path. He might have been unconscious or he might have been dead; I never thought to find out which.

It was also in those wilds, that strange paradox of steel

horizon and darkening primal foliage, that I first saw Lillian Dawes.

She was in a tree. She was wearing a riding habit, draping herself like a strand of scarf over a yoke of branches. I wouldn't have even known to look up had I not seen the horse, tied to a lamppost, grazing on a sickly azalea bush. Mr. Phipps ran ahead of me and started darting at the horse's heels, barking and snorting, agitating the animal into a rearing lather.

"Hey you! For god's sake," she called down to me. "Do something about that rabid little piece of sausage, will you?"

Before I could reply, she had thudded to the ground and was halfway to the horse. She managed to pull loose the reins, boot aside Mr. Phipps, and mount the horse in one continuous motion, so gracefully and swiftly accomplished that the white of her jodhpurs seemed to blur in the sweep of movement.

"I'm very sorry," I called out, gathering Mr. Phipps in, tightening his leash in my hand. She was calming the horse into a loose but controlled canter, switching leads every few paces so that from where I stood the animal seemed to be skipping.

"Your dog's supposed to be leashed."

I nodded foolishly. I didn't want to sound contentious so I didn't mention that she was not supposed to dismount, or to leave the bridle path, or, for that matter, climb the trees. She circled me a few times before she smiled.

"I won't tell on you if you don't tell on me," she said, and then she crouched forward on the neck of the great chestnut beast and the two of them glided over a park bench, clearing its backrest by several feet. I watched, mesmerized, as she receded down the leaf-thick lane, clots of black earth being kicked up in the anapest meter of a gallop. Though I would return to the brambles often and pace the various loops of the bridle path with regularity, I never saw her riding again.

On my way back to Aunt Lavinia's, I ran into Hadley. I hadn't seen her since our luncheon the month before, and wasn't sure if enough time had elapsed for me to be civil. She was walking with her ex-roommate and fellow graduate of the Miss Porter's school, the diminutive but aspiring poetess Eileen Lawrence, with the hyperthyroid eyes of a Pekingese dog. Hadley had spoken of her often, complaining that she borrowed lipsticks and returned them flattened, was tight about groceries, wore an "I Like Ike" button, and had broken the clasp on Hadley's satin evening bag. None of her discontent was evident now, as the two walked arm in arm along the park in animated conversation.

I could feel Hadley's eye on me, but there was no indication that she intended to acknowledge me. At Sixty-fourth Street, she parted from Eileen at the crosstown bus stop and hurried her step to catch up with me. I pretended not to see her as I trotted briskly up the avenue, tugging at Mr. Phipps, who was slowing our escape with his intractable curiosity.

"Gabriel," Hadley called after me, loudly enough that I had to turn and feign surprise. "Hello Hadley, isn't there a sale at Lord & Taylor's you should be attending?" I asked, pursing up my lips to peck her outstretched cheek. She was momentarily thrown by my greeting; her eyes narrowed almost imperceptibly then she relaxed into her first barb: "So how's work? I hear Lavinia gave you a paper route or something equally challenging."

"Challenging," I replied, determined to give her no satisfaction. Then it occurred to me: Hadley had been a bridesmaid at the same wedding that Lillian Dawes had attended as "guest."

"Say, Hadley, do you know a girl named Lillian Dawes?" I asked.

"Lillian Dawes?" she repeated, rolling the name on her tongue as if to taste its merit. "Nope. Should I?" she answered.

"I don't know," I said. "I saw her picture in the paper from that wedding you were at."

"Oh, her!" Hadley quivered with recognition. "Nobody even knew who she was! I was maid of honor and no one took *my* picture," she complained, her voice edged with indignation.

I merely smiled. I had struck a rich vein and had not even intended it. I could hear the giddy organ music of the carousel, tinny and old, like a music box opening the lid of unshaped memory, drifting up the hill to where we stood beneath some ancient locust trees. The music made me feel a sudden tenderness for the world, one so capacious and full I unthinkingly reached out my arm to include Hadley in its embrace. She bent forward at that moment, lighting a cigarette in the cup of her hands like a sailor. Aunt Grace would have been appalled.

"I hate that damn circus music," Hadley said in her exhale. "It makes me think of some smelly old monkey all dressed up, hopping around and touching its privates like they do."

But even Hadley could not dull the fluttering pleasure I felt, a permeating warmth buzzing through my veins like the vast twilight glow of alcohol on an empty stomach.

My afternoon quests were inspired in part by the curriculum devised by my new tutor, Albert Beckwith. Whether Spencer had recommended him to Aunt Grace, or Aunt Grace had somehow dredged him up herself, I was none too pleased with the arrangement. Three mornings a week, from nine-thirty until twelve-thirty, I met with Beckwith at his apartment.

Beckwith lived in the basement of a bulky soot-blackened building on the Upper West Side, near Columbia University. I gathered from the types I'd see going in and out that the rest of the building was populated by university faculty and their families. The elevator always smelled of sweetish pipe smoke, and the women for whom I sometimes held the door were a humorless lot, often bespectacled, always preoccupied, and authentically "academic" in the choice of book they had tucked under their arm. Their shoes were aggressively ugly, boxy and low, usually several years old and somewhat deformed by use—as if asserting the insignificance of material beauty in an all too insistent way.

For the most part, I felt sorry for them. They seemed very

good examples of what Beckwith described in his discourses as the "educated empties," drudges who "implemented the intellectual bureaucracy" against which he fought with his peculiar blend of ideology and unpublished poetry. At any rate, they made possession of intelligence seem an impressively burdensome gift in an entirely new way than that which was exemplified by my father or his prominent Yankee cohorts.

Beckwith's rooms, across from the laundry room and next to the furnace, were actually the super's quarters, but the superintendent of the building, Mr. Ramon Aguilla Alcazar, lived instead in Queens with his mother and rented his apartment out to Beckwith for a modest fee to supplement his paycheck. Beckwith had furnished his "two rooms and a hot plate" with *objets trouvés* he had salvaged from the curb or with items he had "borrowed" from the storage bins of some of the tenants.

His cupboard was conspicuously empty—with the exception of items lifted from restaurants and hotels: bars of soap and packets of sugar bearing the insignia of their establishments, after-dinner mints, bags of oyster crackers, and cellophaned pairs of saltines. About the only thing he spent money on, as far as I could see, were books. His apartment was filthy with them; columns lined the walls and there were small piles accumulating on the few available surfaces. They crowded the floor creating miniature labyrinths, and here and there a stack supported a reading lamp or a radio, or held a dirty cup.

It gave his rooms a vaguely surreal quality, having coupled the drabness of a library with the sinister encroachment of a jungle. Most of his books were broken-spined affairs no one normal would ever read, but he had as well all the requisite works of European literature to satisfy Aunt Grace's notion of "well-rounded." It was with that epithet in mind that the two of them had devised my course of study, a gentleman's tour of Western civilization, from Homer to Hardy, highlights only.

Beckwith's political paranoia infused his literary criticism; he demonstrated his ability to read a theme of class struggle and subjugation into almost any work we discussed.

"It's a metaphor that subsumes all other metaphors," he said if I complained about the singleness of his insight. Still, he was receptive to other interpretations, in fact, goaded me into finding them if only as a relief from the monotonous message he extracted so easily from our assigned texts, like a parlor game, lifting philosophic implications from a phrase or image, with no greater effort than plucking hors d'oeuvres from a platter.

In the evenings, Spencer helped me research my "thesis composition," a twenty-page paper Beckwith had assigned either to impress Aunt Grace with the rigors of his pedagogy or because he had begun to confuse the overheated chambers that pulsed and vibrated from the furnace like the engine room of a large ship, with the wood-paneled classrooms in which his neighbors taught. I had never been asked to write more than fifteen pages, and that only once, by Mr. Ardsdale, a very pretentious visiting professor of history at Renwick. Almost no one signed up for Ardsdale's course second semester even though he was, by any measure, a generous grader—we all felt that fifteen pages was beyond the pale. So it was with less than the best attitude that I had embarked upon "The Significance of the Quest: A Search for Meaning in the Works of Homer, Chaucer, and Malory."

But in the course of my discussions with Spencer, often taking place in the bathroom, where he spent huge amounts of time lounging in the claw-foot bathtub, a glass of sherry in one hand and a cigarette, held just above the waterline, in the other, I became suffused with his enthusiasm. I would sit cross-legged on the closed lid of the toilet, with a notebook in my lap, jotting down illegible phrases that Spencer tossed off in his waterlogged ruminations. He had become proficient at maneuvering the faucets with his feet, and had mastered the art of keeping his cigarette ash out of the bathwater, although he had no qualms about using the soap dish as an ashtray.

The steam that rose from the tub wrinkled my skin, misted the mirror, and warped my notepaper into a series of narrow ruled waves that buckled against the speckled cardboard cover. I had wanted to use the spiraled reporter's pads that littered Spencer's desk, feeling that the black-and-white composition books that had accompanied me through elementary school were too juvenile a venue for the thoughts I was now recording, but I was too embarrassed to actually petition Spencer for this upgrade.

It was in one of these damp sessions that Spencer first introduced me to the notion of "archetype" as a way of categorizing the various people who populated my somewhat restricted world, and the concept dominated my thinking for the next several years. It was also a way of harvesting an additional layer of meaning from the works I was reading with Beckwith, and the reason I came to read Plato, and Frazer's *The Golden Bough*, a text Spencer had been urging on me for several weeks but which I had until then resisted.

I had given it a quick perusal and dismissed it immediately on the following grounds: it had an epigraph in Latin that was untranslated, which seemed both pretentious and arrogant on the part of the writer; it was much too massive a text to be held comfortably in one hand, which I took as a personal and unforgivable imposition; and finally, there was the opening sentence, "Who does not know Turner's picture of the Golden Bough?," to which my limping ego shouted, "Me, and what of it?"

However, stimulated by references Spencer made to Maori taboos, fertility rites, and the worship of trees, I made a second attempt. In my paper, which was becoming impressively crowded with footnotes, I was juxtaposing the motifs of the wanderer with those figures of femininity that beset him: the siren, the enchantress, and the maid. It was a heady revelation, and one which provided me with a new way of regarding the world.

Previously I had attempted to dismantle the mysterious facade of the female by devoting my attention to the sedulous examination of her footwear. The scope of my investigation was mostly limited to my subway commutes, during which I avoided eye contact, having been harshly rebuked early on by a pale girl in a private-school kilt and Peter Pan–collared blouse, who loudly demanded to know, "Just what are you staring at, buster?," a question that engaged the rest of the car's concern and necessitated my getting off three stops early rather than withstand the withering glances of my fellow passengers.

I had therefore attempted to augur the intricate secrets of the women fate threw into my path by the study of ankles overflowing their leather confines like rising dough, or the open toes of pointy pumps revealing a flash of crimson nail lacquer, as disquietingly sinister and intimate as it was bold. I catalogued the scuffed loafers, the shiny patent leather party shoes, the sling backs that exposed red, calloused heels, or occasionally the haunting flash of delicate anklebone, yoked by a tight strap to the open grasp of a sandal.

Spencer had taught me the trope of metonymy, by which one part represents the whole, and I had found that its application in this circumstance rendered a nearly poetic understanding of the poignant hopes and vainglorious suffering reflected in the choices of heel height, color, and toe box. Now, however, I was armed with the intellectual means with which to synthesize the component parts and contemplate the whole: I turned my focus upward, to the monthly offerings of Miss Subway, slicing through their virginal personas with my newly honed analytic skills like the high priest at a ritual sacrifice. Aspiring actresses and accomplished secretaries were stripped of their dissembling veneers like bark from a sycamore, according to the principles of mythical attributes they embodied. Their hobbies alone were ample fodder for my classifications.

It was a source of great satisfaction, for example, to be able to identify Hadley as the witch that she was, the debilitating if not outright dangerous sneak, the Morgana figure in Ariosto's *Orlando Furioso*, Morgan le Fay in Malory's *Morte d'Arthur*, both of which I had read by now. When I shared this aperçu with Spencer, he dismissed it:

"I think you misread Hadley if you ascribe to her such beguiling powers. Consider her dating history and you may be inclined to revise your theory. She strikes me as a much more banal figure entirely, made slightly more interesting by her desperate plight to find a husband who will release her from the talonic clutch of Aunt Grace."

Of course, Spencer was right, though I was reluctant to acknowledge it.

"I think Valery is a more suitable candidate for the role of vixen," he went on, referring to the woman who worked at the dry cleaners and wore capri pants with stiletto heels: she had a surly kind of beauty that was absolutely wilting. Delivering a weekly bundle of soiled clothing to her was like going to confession empty-handed; my lackluster life was tallied on the green receipt she was handed back with a wry smile.

She was in love with Spencer: twice she had scrawled her phone number on the back of his laundry ticket, and once she had tucked into his suit pocket a folded sheet of typewriter paper that bore a lipstick kiss in the center and was so heavily scented with vanilla that Spencer had to hang the jacket in front of an open window for days to let it air. She led a fast life and had almost been fired by the owner when a fistfight between her admirers broke out in front of the establishment and left blood on the sidewalk, which Mr. Marcuso said was "bad for business."

I had been treated to more than one of Mr. Marcuso's diatribes on the subject, as he was often to be found at the lunch counter of Bigelow Pharmacy, fomenting about the unfair competition from "the chinks," or the ruinous policies of Mayor Wagner, or the problem of tailoring cheap suits. It was only the superior quality of pistachio ice cream at Bigelow's soda fountain that brought me repeatedly into the circumference of Mr. Marcuso's tuna-breathed rants, and I often left the pharmacy feeling as if he had talked the starch right out of my shirt. Even so, I was never able to muster more than a dollop of sympathy for his underpaid siren, who would routinely roll her dark eyes at his wild imprecations. Of all the females I deemed worthy of my attention and critical scrutiny, only Lillian Dawes escaped classification.

It would have been easy to be distracted from my quest by the balmy, almost sweet air or the green glow of trees, their thin ribs outlined by the pale knobs of buds, the tight pincurls of leaves itching to open like fists relaxing in the sun, exhaling through the moist bark the dark tang of fertility vaguely reminiscent of clay.

But my guiding sense of purpose had become inexplicably linked to the slim girl whose pale visage I had memorized from newsprint, grainy photographs which nonetheless captured a fleeting candor, haunting with the very intimacy it belied.

Throughout the last ravages of winter, Lillian Dawes had upstaged every other figure of devotion in my personal pantheon of goddesses, which included Grace Kelly and Eleanor Hackett, who had let me kiss her at her debutante party even though I hadn't been invited. I saw Lillian everywhere, in tantalizing fragments: the upward slant of a neighbor's eyes, the angle of a chin through the window of a passing bus, or even in the resigned poise that illuminates the figures in the paintings of La Tour, or

Vanderhaven, images I now sought eagerly in the halls of the museums I had previously shunned.

This ill-defined mission, ineluctable as the migration of birds, propelled me into odd corners of the city. I discussed it with no one, although I ached to tell Spencer but feared that if I were to couple myself with a notion as improbable or romantic as this, his wonder would have been tempered by the taint of pathos; I hated to liken myself in his heart to the human strays whose futile causes he championed out of a welling kindness that was undeterred by the stink of desperation that clung to them, like a vapor, dooming them to the realm of quixotic charity.

If I had told Beckwith, he would have dismissed it as some-thing cheapened by loneliness: the sophomoric desire to stand on her corner and maybe, if I timed it right, see her step out of her door, pause on the stoop to adjust her gloves or pin her hat before launching herself down the street like an expensive, sleek craft designed to skim briskly to the pleasures that awaited her in other parts of the city.

The second time I saw her was on a rainy Saturday; I had been sent by Spencer to an Argentine restaurant on Ninth Avenue to buy from the cook a half pound of roasted poblano peppers, which for reasons more intricate than interesting Spencer had developed a powerful need. He had been up for almost two days straight, pacing the apartment, smoking cigarettes between bouts of sporadic typing, the staccato clicks tapping out a Morse code of feverish urgency followed by erratic arpeggios of waning inspiration.

I was pleased to have a reason to leave the house: watching Spencer thrash his way through the difficult revision of a final draft was excruciating, like watching a pigeon batter about a room into which it has erred, blindly trying to find a way out.

It was late in the day when I finally reached Emilio's. Needing more solitude than the subway afforded, I had decided to walk, despite the intermittent showers. When I was feeling particularly restive, I could pass an entire afternoon moving steadily from neighborhood to neighborhood, watching the evolution of a slum or the accoutrements of affluence redefine a row of houses as gentrification spread its bright polish down another block.

Wedged between two other restaurants, an Indian establishment with festive depictions of elephants and monkeys painted in bright primary colors, as if drawn by a child armed with only a few bold paints, its tattered pink awning proclaiming in soiled, yellowing letters "Bombay Star," and a seafood joint, suffocatingly swathed in nautical themes, coils of rope, swags of fishing net, a rusty anchor, and a steering wheel all competing for decorative prominence, Emilio's looked a little drab by comparison.

Other diners must have thought so too, for on its unadorned black door was taped a little note, barely legible now that the rain had run the ink into dripping blue tears that stained the paper, exaggerating the forlorn nature of its message: "Closed Due to Misfortune."

I stared dully at the door for a moment, examining my defeat. The rain had devolved to a fine mist, swelling the air already heavy with moisture. My jacket was soaked and hung like a woolen weight from my stooped shoulders, and I was tired by the long walk, but the prospect of bringing home nothing but disappointment to Spencer was a greater burden than I was prepared to bear. I remembered passing a few Cuban dives on Eighth

Avenue that might be worth checking for Spencer's roasted chilies, and there was a Chock Full o' Nuts on the corner, whose date-nut-and-cream-cheese sandwiches now spoke eloquently to my hunger.

Through the plate-glass window of Chock Full o' Nuts I saw only one woman customer sitting alone at the far curve of the counter, which tightly serpentined across the large room. She was talking with what seemed like forced animation to the nearest of several waitresses. The waitress, I could tell even at a distance, was one of those "warrior women" types, solid and fierce, thick ankles and a crushing grip, hearkening back not to lovely Diana the huntress, but to Camilla, Virgil's fighting maiden who battled Turnus. Unlike Camilla, so swift of foot that she could run through a field of corn without bending a single blade, this warrior looked decidedly slow.

I kept walking. The truth was not that I was in any rush but rather that a peculiar shyness had overtaken me: I was reluctant to enter that overtly female environment—even the date-nut sandwich suffered by association, seeming suddenly too dainty, an effeminate choice. I crossed the street and headed downtown, keeping a lookout for the street vendors who sold hot dogs and pretzels, hearty food I could eat on the street like a workman.

A few blocks below Times Square, I found a little sliver of a place calling itself "Havana Cabana." It was a long, narrow restaurant with no more than twelve tables, each set with a formerly white tablecloth, red napkins fanning out of the water glasses, and a wilting yellow rose in a bud vase. The walls were covered in the kind of faux wood paneling usually reserved for basement transformations. It looked like the kind of place people came to for stingers or martinis or maybe a gin fizz at the long Formica bar, its dinner crowd culled from those drinkers who stayed out of inertia and the need for something to soak up the alcohol before they wobbled home.

The room was empty, but from behind the red bead curtain, separating the kitchen from the dining room, came the brassy throb of Latin music straining the batteries of a cheap transistor radio. As I approached the bead curtain, I could see a small circle of waiters clapping to the music and hissing encouragement at the two dancers in the center of the kitchen coiling around each other like snakes, undulating across the small space between the stove on one wall and the sink on the other, dipping and swirling without ever dropping the napkin that was pressed between their hips.

The music was interrupted by an advertisement, a rapid yet unctuous barrage of words abruptly silenced by a stocky busboy in a soiled uniform who clicked the radio off and began thumping out the rhythm of a tango with the heels of his palms, drumming on the greasy butcher block, singing with his eyes closed a song of such dark intensity I felt a catch in my throat as its throbbing syncopation moved through the dancers.

I suppose it is a cliché to say that the dance was sexy; what I hadn't realized before was that the object of the dance's seduction was the audience, not the dancers, who were gravely complicitous, focused in their mutual goal. They swirled by the curtain and I saw that the man's face was badly pocked and his black hair was stiff with scented brilliantine. He dipped his partner over his thigh and slowly bent her away from him, as if only the intensity of his eyes were holding her up from the floor. Then he snapped her back to him and spun her around him so swiftly her hair burst like spontaneous combustion into the long auburn whip that slashed the air as they flashed their bodies in and out of taut knots and sinuous angles. The girl threw her head back in an arch as they neared the curtain again and I saw it was her. It was Lillian Dawes fighting back a smile.

I must have gasped, for the room instantly reassembled. The busboy broke off his song in the middle of a tremorous phrase and quickly picked up a tray of glasses; the waiters flooded into the room filling it with agitated Spanish and I was quickly guided away from the beaded curtain by the male dancer, now transformed into a slightly annoyed bartender.

"We open at five. Come back then," he said, moving me toward the door with the same firm lead he had moments ago used with Lillian.

"Please," I said, almost desperately, "I need some poblano peppers for my brother." I had, in fact, almost forgotten the peppers, but the words flew out of my mouth serendipitously, prompted by my need to stall rather than my desire to accommodate Spencer. The bartender's face, a fierce jumble of sharp features, now softened into a smile. He snapped his fingers for one of the waiters and said something in Spanish that made the waiter laugh as he ducked behind the curtain, letting it clack like rosaries in a hundred nervous hands.

I wished I had chosen Spanish as my second language at Renwick instead of French. I imagined chatting wittily with the bartender, charming him with the velvet fluency of my tongue.

"What was that?" I asked, gesturing toward the kitchen with my head.

"It is not important," he said firmly.

"You're a hell of a dancer," I offered encouragingly, but he had turned away and was busying himself behind the bar, rearranging bottles and cutting limes into pale half-moon wedges.

A moment later, the waiter came back, again setting off the curtain into its plastic chimes.

The waiter handed me the foil-wrapped package and I reached to pull out my wallet but the bartender waved his hand dismissively.

"Our gift," he said.

I started to sputter out my thanks. Lillian had still not appeared though I had heard the rising lilt of a woman's laugh and the radio had been turned back on and was playing very softly now.

The bartender had moved to the door, holding it open for me.

"Bye-bye," he said, looking down at the worn threshold.

There was nothing I could do but leave. I glanced back over my shoulder at the curtain one last time, just in case.

"Thanks again, really," I said, but he was already closing the door behind me, slipping a plastic "Closed" sign over the inside doorknob.

Two days later, I called Clayton Prather. I was basically exploding with the need to talk about Lillian Dawes, and as far as I could determine, Clayton was my only conduit to the particular thrill that comes from hearing spoken the name that has been resonating in the mind of the besotted. I remembered how greedily Spencer had listened to the family's discussions of Lady Ambrosia Kenthy the month before he began his disastrous affair with her. A bluestocking with a wild streak, she had been sent to the States for a summer job at the Dowling House, an undistinguished museum in our part of Connecticut, on whose board my father and uncle sat as trustees of the small, eclectic, and generally second-rate collection of early American art and handicrafts.

I'm not sure how my family knew hers, but I know that the romance that briefly flared between Spencer and Lady Ambrosia engendered extravagant speculation and foolish expectation on the part of Aunt Grace, who was almost as distraught as Spencer when the affair abruptly soured. Hadley told me, although I was never able to confirm this with anyone else, that Aunt Grace had even suggested to Spencer that he expedite matters by "awakening Lady Ambrosia's domestic urge."

Ambrosia was charming in a way that I had childishly assumed was required of anyone with "lady" in front of her name. I was in sixth grade at the time, and she was my first aristocrat, so naturally I was willing to forgive her almost anything, although it was apparent even to me that she was unusually careless with everything, from borrowed cars to confided secrets or admiring hearts. I don't think she was cruel, just self-absorbed and maybe a little willful. She had a way of presenting herself, though, as merely spontaneous and carefree, turning her betrayals into caprices the wounded were just too stodgy to understand.

Naturally Beckwith hated her, and she returned the sentiment tenfold, referring to him as *Piglet* and, sometimes, with feigned respect, as *Sir Pig.* With almost everyone else, she flirted with abandon, including our ancient gardener, a Negro of diminutive proportion who had been called "Mister Boy" ever since he'd come to work for my grandfather. The way the story goes, Grandfather Gibbs saw him working in the yard pruning the mock-orange and called down to him from the bedroom window, "Boy, I planted that bush myself and there is nothing you can do to it that would be an improvement on what God has already done with it."

"It's Mister Boy to you, and if this is the best your God can do, I'd see about getting me a new church right quick, 'cuz I already made it better and I ain't half done yet," Mister Boy is supposed to have retorted. At any rate, Mister Boy and Lady Ambrosia got on fabulously: she used to let him sip sherry from the shagreen flask she carried in her handbag and that was given to her by Mrs. Churchill for her "coming out."

Maybe it was the insouciance with which she discussed Freud, or that she had memorized the entirety of *Eugene Onegin* in translation, or maybe just the fact that she was lovely and troubled that made Spencer fall in love with her. I was hiding in the dumbwaiter when he proposed to her, so I heard everything. He asked her to marry him, and she said, "Give me one good reason why I should."

"Because I love you."

"That's not enough. Lots of men are wild about me," she replied coolly.

"I'll be finished with law school in a year. I'll make scads of money for you, and I don't care how much you drink," Spencer continued with astonishing candor.

"I don't really care so much about money," she lied, "and I only drink because I'm bored. Give me another reason," she coaxed.

"Well, I come from a long line of founding fathers, including two signers of the Declaration of Independence."

"Oh, so that means you have good genes?" she asked.

"No, good heirlooms," Spencer said, and they both started laughing hard. Nothing more was spoken, but I could hear the telltale rustling that meant they were doing things that nice girls shouldn't. I had supposed it was all settled, but she was gone in the morning; it was only weeks later that we found out about her weekend with Clayton Prather, or how she had left him too, locked in a motel room without his clothes.

Even after the shabby way she treated him, you could tell

Spencer was still eager to hear her mentioned, no matter the context, as if her name alone could evoke some elusive pleasure, or conjure up a chimerical presence and temporarily subdue the pain of her absence.

Now that I too had become a beggar for the crumbs of conversation that would bring Lillian into the intermediary world of words, I deeply regretted the way I had tortured Spencer at the time, initiating the subject of Lady Ambrosia only to curtail it with teases like "Oh never mind" or "I guess there's nothing more to say, is there?"

I had waited until Spencer had gone to the library before making the call. My nerves couldn't have been more frayed had I been calling Lillian herself. I had rehearsed various conversations in my mind and I had assembled by the phone the paraphernalia I deemed necessary to accomplish the deed: a pack of Lucky Strikes pilfered from Spencer's desk, a large, clean ashtray, a glass of ginger ale in case my throat went dry, a half-eaten box of Whitman's chocolates (the Sampler collection), and a pin.

The first time I dialed, the line was busy, an eventuality I had overlooked in all my careful planning. I went into the bathroom and combed my hair. I examined my face in the mirror with particularly harsh scrutiny and practiced my smile. I smoked a cigarette and then tried the line again. Prather answered on the first ring.

"Hello, Clayton," I said, "this is Gabriel, Gibbs, Spencer's brother," I added, identifying myself furiously, "from the Plaza, remember?"

"Of course, how are you?" he said, betraying no surprise at hearing from me. "How's Spencer? How's the masterpiece coming? Are we almost rich and famous yet?" he asked, jovially.

I was glad Spencer couldn't hear this. It would have irritated him no end, that kind of patronizing goodwill. I deflected it with a bland flutter of, "Fine, fine, he's fine," answering only the least rhetorical of the questions. "Rhetorical questions," Spencer had told me, "are a fool's attempt at verbal mastery. They are not meant to be answered, so don't. They deflate in the smallest silence."

"Are you two coming up?" Clayton asked. "I can always use a few extra rascals on the weekend." I could hear him sipping something in which ice cubes played a role.

"You'll have the time of your life, kiddo. I've cornered the market on fun; someone had to do it, right?" he asked, waiting for confirmation.

Spencer had taught me to be suspicious of people who advertise their own happiness, but I wanted deeply to believe in Prather's powers.

"Sure," I said, answering both questions at once, an economy Prather's style of conversation prompted. "We'll come at the end of the month." I figured it would take at least until then to placate Spencer for having committed him to an engagement he had no desire to keep. I took a gulp of ginger ale, which by now had gone flat.

"Listen," I went on, trying to take control of the situation, for I feared if I didn't get to the point soon, I would lose the chance, "I was wondering about Lillian Dawes . . ."

"Oh God," he sighed, "Lillian," as if I'd struck a nerve. His bon vivant posture withered audibly on those three syllables. "That's not her real name, you know."

"Oh?" I said, sitting down on the couch and fumbling with a box of matches, which I clumsily scattered on the floor.

"No. It's the craziest thing," he continued, as if it were the most natural thing in the world for us to be discussing her, "I ran into someone at the Knickerbocker Club who thinks he met her in Venice, for god's sake. Traveling with some Italian no-count count, calling herself Lisa Dainwell. There was some stir at the Ragazza Palace Hotel, but he can't remember the particulars. I've had a man on it for a month, forty bucks a day plus expenses, and he hasn't turned up a damn thing except, I'll tell you this much, neither one of them exists. He's checked birth records and telephone directories, the works."

I scrambled for the chocolates, stretching the cord around the couch to the table where I had lined up my supplies. My heart was hammering in my chest and I wished I had poured myself a real drink instead of the now warm ginger ale. I snatched a handful of chocolates, hoping to find a caramel or a coconut center in the pile. We had long since lost the chart that accompanied the box, and now the only way to tell which ones you were eating, besides chancing it, which was too expensive a way to find the good ones, was to insert a pin into the bottoms of the chocolates and see what color oozed out in a tiny bead. That way, you could put back the ones you didn't want, like the ones with marzipan cream inside, for instance, with no one the wiser.

"You're kidding," I said, pushing a chocolate-covered nougat to the recesses of my cheek, where it bulged uncomfortably.

"I wish I were, kiddo. I wish I were. I can't figure out if *any-*

77

thing she says is true. I've talked to Dr. Pimm about her; at thirty-five an hour, he's useless too. He's not German. I should have gone to a German, maybe. They invented all that stuff," he said, lifting his glass again. "Always get the best you can afford. That's what my dad taught me and he was right, by god."

I could tell now that Prather was drunk. I could hear him rummaging on the other end of the line. He struck a match and inhaled.

"Whoever she is," he said on the exhale, "she's got me twisted up like a corkscrew. That's a first, I'll tell you. I don't even think she *likes* me, and I have such big plans for her."

I was afraid he was going to get maudlin. It wasn't even two in the afternoon and he was soaked, and I didn't think I could negotiate the social complexities of self-pity, especially when I was depending on him in ways I didn't understand, but knew intuitively could not support any further revelations of a self-deprecatory sort.

"Sure she does," I said. "You've cornered the market on fun, remember?"

"Yeah, that's right," he said, perking up, as if I had reminded him of an indisputable fact. "We'll have a great time, you'll see." He was switching subjects but seemed to have regained his composure, to have reclaimed the confidence with which he had begun the conversation. Much as I hated to terminate the call, I knew this was a good moment in which to end our chat: he had restored himself in my eyes, and I worried he might lose his balance again if I gave him a chance. Moreover, I was worried Spencer would return any minute, and not only did I not want to be found on the phone with Clayton Prather, I had had a small accident with one of the liqueur-filled chocolates, which had left a sugary red gob of a cherry center on the couch.

"I can't wait," I said, and in point of fact, I spoke the truth. Who knew what news he might have of Lillian by then, or if she herself would be there, the ultimate pinnacle in his hostly offerings.

"Let me know if you need directions or anything else," he said graciously and then we both hung up.

The doorbell rang a sharp series of bleats that sent me into a panic. It was unlike Spencer to forget his keys, and we rarely had visitors, except for Beckwith. I hastily threw a cushion over the stain on the couch and emptied the ashtray before answering the door. The bell continued to ring with urgent insistence. I was tucking in my shirttail as I opened the door to find Aunt Lavinia on the stoop, her finger still firmly pressing the buzzer.

"It would behoove you to bestir yourself," she said majestically, sweeping past me with various bundles that indicated she'd been shopping. "I come bearing gifts you don't deserve." She paused briefly before the hall mirror, examining the umbrella collection in the brass stand as if she were contemplating a trade but thought better of it. As she proceeded on to the living room, I struggled to catch the coat she had shed while moving purposefully toward the armchair.

"I'd love some tea," she said. "I couldn't find a Schrafft's anywhere, and my word, you boys never mentioned that you live so close to the Women's House of Detention. Are the 'ladies' always so vocal or is it just visiting time? Don't let your aunt Grace find out about your neighbors—she'll drag you back to wholesome Greenfield in her station wagon without stopping for the traffic lights! Now, where is Spencer? I have matters to discuss with him."

"He's at the library," I yelled from the kitchen, where I was trying to find a clean teacup and had set the kettle to boil.

"Come in here," she demanded. "I can't have a conversation without eye contact, and I want to give you this. I was feeling generous today."

As I stood in the doorway, she pulled out of a large shopping bag a box marked "Abercrombie & Fitch." She pushed it at me and then turned away imperiously, as if I were relieving her of something distasteful. Her awkwardness, at once both maddening and oddly endearing, made her seem like a small child whose misbehavior one humors because it is so amusingly transparent. I sat cross-legged on the floor in front of her and tore through the veils of tissue paper obscuring my gift. Aunt Lavinia had bought me a pith helmet. I was enormously pleased and put it on immediately. That it was slightly too large for my head in no way diminished my delight.

"Thank you, Aunt Lavinia," I said.

"It was very expensive, but you don't need to thank me," she bristled, but I knew from Spencer's careful tutelage that meant *Thank me more, thank me harder*, so I did. She began to blush, and to hide it, she strode nervously around the apartment, examining things. She wiped a tonsure of dust off the head of an ivory Buddha that sat in the bookcase between Chekhov and Cicero. She picked up a stray glove of Spencer's and idly tried it on. She found the Whitman's Sampler box and removed the pleated paper cups

I had so recently emptied, crushing them into tight wads that she held in her hand while she continued her inspection.

While I was rummaging in the kitchen for a tray on which to put the teapot, Aunt Lavinia found a notepad on which I had written Lillian's name about a thousand times.

"Lillian Dawes," she exclaimed. "I know her. In fact, I've been meaning to look her up. But of course that's not her real name so I didn't imagine she'd be listed."

I bumped the tea tray down on the coffee table in front of the sofa, sloshing some Earl Grey tea out of the pot, which I had to then sop up with my sleeve.

"How, Aunt Lavinia, do you know her?" I asked, dumbfounded.

She poured herself some tea and sighed, as if she were being asked to explain something perfectly obvious. Aunt Lavinia waved her hand at me, summoning an ashtray as she extracted from her cigarette case one of those Egyptian cigarettes she smoked, though she had dispensed with the holder now that they were being manufactured with a filter.

"I'm always on the lookout for intriguing people," she said. "I like to think I am especially good at finding them, even in as unlikely a place as the upper deck of the S.S. *Rotterdam*." Aunt Lavinia exhaled grandly, expelling smoke from her nostrils like a stoked engine.

"I had noticed her earlier, of course; she was the only other woman traveling alone, except for the dowager countess who smoked cigars and sent everything back at meals. I kept expecting her to join us at the captain's table. I was getting desperate, you see, for a decent conversation. I had been badly bored two nights in a row by a dreadful man from Hartford who actually wore a seersucker suit to dinner. That's not why he was dreadful, of course, though it didn't help."

She was becoming expansive in a way I might have appreciated more had I not been so intent on keeping the focus on Lillian. "So how did you find her?" I asked, trying not to sound impatient.

"Well," Aunt Lavinia continued, "she wasn't on the passenger list. I checked. Naturally that only made her more intriguing, so when I saw her heading up to the skeet-shooting match, I followed. I usually don't bother with noisy entertainments but I made an exception." Lavinia pointed at her empty teacup, prompting me to serve her without breaking her narrative flow.

"It was one of those embarrassing situations—an ugly competition had evolved between a brash American officer and an elderly British gentleman. Among the spectators there was an awkward silence. You could hear the wind snapping the skirts and head scarves of those mousy ladies shivering together behind the skeet trap, waiting for an opportunity to clap. All of a sudden, Miss Dawes took off her sunglasses and approached the rail. She hoisted one of the ship's shotguns to her shoulder, and yelled into the wind, 'Pull.' To our astonishment, she proceeded to hit sixteen out of twenty clay pigeons. I should mention that while she did not win the tournament, she certainly won the boisterous admiration of the deckhands."

Lavinia paused to light another cigarette and rearrange herself in the chair. I emptied the ashtray to have something to do with my hands. I was jittery with excitement, and watching Aunt Lavinia puff her way through the story like a determined caboose made me itchy for a cigarette of my own.

"So I confronted her in the library. 'When you've dressed, come to my stateroom for a drink and we'll go down to dinner together,' I said. I think it went without saying that I meant the second seating. She told me she was going to skip dinner. Can you imagine?" Aunt Lavinia raised her eyebrows and waited for me to shake my head before continuing.

"I reminded her that we were having Belgian artichokes and steamed lobster. I have always believed in getting my money's worth, Gabriel. I suppose that makes me a Gibbs after all. Besides, it is very nouveau riche to pay for something only to have the pleasure of wasting it."

"And what did she say, when you reminded her about the lobster?" I prompted.

"Oh, you'll never guess," Aunt Lavinia chortled. "She said she thought it was too complicated. She had never had lobster before and didn't want to be intimidated by an oversized crawdaddy. She said it was bad enough having to wear secondhand evening clothes; she didn't want to appear any more hardscrabble than she already did. So I told her anyone as plucky as she was shouldn't let a heap of shell get the better of her. I volunteered to talk her through the protocol. I don't usually extend myself in that way, but I was touched by her honesty."

Aunt Lavinia was quiet for a moment and then she mused, "It was odd, the way she'd be so candid about one thing and then lie outrageously about another." She turned her head to the window, talking more slowly now, as if unsure of how much to say.

"I've never made a fetish of the truth, my dear," she reflected, turning back to me to pinion me with her eyes. "I mean, let's face it, the truth is overrated. It's the refuge of the dull and unimaginative, and most of the time it's a big disappointment, while a lie worth telling or well told is, well, a kind of gift. I know most people don't see it that way. But then, most people are idiots."

I was, I admit, a little shocked. My uncle Ambrose, her older brother, was a judge after all, and in our house this kind of talk was heresy. Moreover, I wasn't sure how to respond. What if she was testing me, or if it was a sophisticated joke I was too naive to appreciate? I laughed nervously, and tried to shift the subject back to Lillian.

"So did Lillian end up eating lobster after all?" I asked. I sounded young and slow-witted, but it was the best I could do at the time.

Aunt Lavinia looked at me and sighed. I could hear the irritation in her sigh, and I knew that I had failed her.

"Lobster? No, darling, I don't think Lillian ate any of the lobster. She hardly sat down long enough to eat a grape! You see, by dinnertime she had developed quite an impressive bruise where she had put the twelve-gauge to her shoulder. More kick than she remembered, or she hadn't braced the gun snugly. She said she didn't want to put all the fine people off their feed. Her evening gown was strapless, mind you, so the bruise was exposed and, my word, it did look nasty. 'Thirty-seven shades of ugly' was how she described it. Don't you like that expression?" Aunt Lavinia asked without waiting for an answer.

"I advised her to drape a scarf over the discoloration and wear some jewelry to distract, but in the end she walked into the dining room wearing it like a purple heart. A little bourbon goes a long way when you have no heft. She was much too thin and I told her so, but I don't think she was paying much attention by then. It seemed like all the ship's officers were lining up to dance with her, so I left her to it. I've danced with enough of them in my time. They're too polite and they never know how to lead."

I stood up and stretched. The light in the room had changed, darkening into the amber hours of late afternoon. The tea had gone cold and the air had grown heavy with the bitter smell of Lavinia's dark tobacco. "Did you see her after that?" I asked as I gathered up the tray.

"I certainly did. We became friends, in our fashion. She accompanied me when I took Mr. Phipps for his morning walks, usually along the rail of the lower decks, where he was protected from the salt air. Once or twice we played backgammon together. I think she tried to hustle me, but I don't really remember."

I could tell Aunt Lavinia was getting ready to leave: she had stubbed out her last cigarette and was digging in her bag for her lipstick, her thin lips already puckering up in expectation.

It was in those last few minutes, as Aunt Lavinia distractedly emptied her handbag into her lap, that I found out an odd jumble of things Aunt Lavinia had come to know about Lillian Dawes. She loved root beer, crushed ice, and pralines. She bit her nails and bought her clothes at thrift stores and Goodwills. She was bored by flattery, and she stole the way a crow does, mindlessly, pocketing small items, glittery things of no particular value. She painted watercolors of clouds, spoke French, and had recently been very ill. There had been rumors about Lillian and the head steward, but those had been discounted by Aunt Lavinia because she did not like the man's mustache, and could not imagine Lillian "subjecting herself to the bristle of male vanity."

"But how did you know that Lillian Dawes is not her real name?" I asked Aunt Lavinia as she pulled on her gloves.

"Simple," she said. "Because it didn't match the initials on her luggage, which were all from the wrong end of the alphabet—xyz or something equally unfortunate."

"Then what's her real name? And why did she change it?" I asked, taking off my pith helmet and putting it back in its box.

"There are some things you just don't ask, my dear," Aunt Lavinia said, gathering herself up, indicating an imminent departure.

"I can't wait any longer. I'm sorry to have missed Spencer. Tell him to give me a ring tonight. I'll be home. And tell Lillian my coordinates, when you speak to her next. Mr. Phipps was seasick the day we docked. I never got to say good-bye."

The rich harvest of information about Lillian Dawes the day had yielded overwhelmed my thoughts, suffused them with a giddy thrill that surged through me whenever I reviewed the facts, savoring each detail like a miser fingering a stash of newly minted bills, repeating to myself particular phrases and choice adjectives until I had worked myself into a state of near swooning and could only think to climb into the claw-foot tub, where recumbent, I could drift into the dreamlike stupor available only to visionaries, opium smokers, and hapless romantics.

That was how Spencer found me, lying in a wiltingly hot bath wearing my helmet on the off chance the steam might shrink it.

"Great hat," he said.

He had the day's mail in his hand, which he shuffled distractedly. "Was Lavinia here? I thought I recognized the scent of her tobacco." He looked over at me.

"Yup, she came by for tea. She said for you to call her tonight. You know, she's kind of amazing, in a way."

Spencer dropped the lid of the toilet and sat down.

"We need a proper chair in here if this is where we are going to gather," he mused, riffling again through the bills. Then he smiled. "You're right about Aunt Lavinia. She's a remarkable woman. I'm glad you two are getting along; I suspected that you might."

"Spencer," I said, "you know, it has nothing to do with the hat. I'd have said the same even if she hadn't brought me a present."

"I know," he answered.

I reached forward to pull the plug out of the drain and Spencer handed me a towel and lifted the pith helmet from my head with exaggerated deference, like a manservant whose superiority is only increased by his humility.

"They're so completely different, Aunt Grace and Aunt Lavinia, no wonder they can't stand each other," I mused, wiping the steam from the mirror so that I could comb my hair, which was in need of a haircut and had matted in a feverish mess under the hat, adding a tropical authenticity to the look.

"Yes," Spencer agreed, "it gives credence to the notion of changelings and incubae." He patted his pocket for matches and lit a cigarette.

"Beckwith is very impressed with your progress, by the way. He thinks if you improve your calculus and add a term of chemistry, you have an excellent shot at a college like Haverford or Williams or even Dartmouth, which would please Aunt Grace no end. She's been fretting fiercely over your prospects for higher education and Hadley's prospects for marriage. I think she's written me off entirely, thank god."

I recognized this as a windfall opportunity: I hated to take advantage of Spencer's good nature but I knew I couldn't sustain a position of merit. Now was the moment to appeal to him about the weekend.

"Spencer," I said, "there are only two things I really desperately want in this world. And I'll work on my calculus, *I promise*, really, if you'll just let us go for a weekend to Clayton Prather's house. Please." I had descended to begging, letting my voice catch slightly on "please." I was suddenly reminded of an incident at school, the recollection oddly surfacing now, months later.

My last semester at Renwick I had shared a room with a pathetic sort of fellow by the name of Hastings. Robert Hastings was a year younger than I and new to the school, having transferred from a Swiss academy that had closed due to a scandal involving the headmaster. At least that's the rumor I heard. Hastings was painfully earnest and poor at sports, and some of the upperclassmen teased him about his beauty mark, all showing up at dinner wearing imitation beauty marks, drawn on with a black marker in just the same position on their cheeks. I had simply ignored him as much as possible. One evening just before lights out, he asked to read me a poem he'd written. It was about a squirrel; the poem culminated in the couplet "Munch and crunch, among the golden leaves / When the acorn is gone, the furry creature grieves." It was not the prosody of the poem that now came to mind, but rather the memory of how proud Hastings had been, the tremulous voice in which he had read it, and, after, the long pause in which he waited, like a lapdog, for praise.

I felt the queasiness of regret rising up like a sharp taste that can't be swallowed away; I resolved to send him a postcard of the Empire State Building and to replace the monogrammed handkerchiefs that had gotten mixed up in the laundry and which I had used to clean my pens.

Spencer was looking at me a little sadly. "What's the other thing?" he asked, a certain caution evident in his tone.

"A white linen suit." And then shamelessly I added, "And white bucks."

He looked at me quizzically for a moment, as if it wounded him that these were the things I coveted. Then he said yes, as simple as that. He was walking out of the bathroom, a thin wisp of smoke from his cigarette trailing behind him, when he added, "But don't let's make it an exchange for the schoolwork. I've never liked to think that virtue can be bought. Or at least, not from us."

Spencer had sent me to Tripler's, on Madison Avenue, for my linen suit. I was grateful that he had not felt it necessary to accompany me. I had found Aunt Grace's presence on shopping expeditions exasperating; she had a way of discussing me with the salesclerks that ranged from infantalizing to sheer embarrassing, and she was not above barging into the dressing room to "see how I was doing." Moreover, she liked to shop in the boys' section at Depinner, hoping to save money.

Spencer had given me a signed check, having established budgetary parameters that were more than generous for the purpose, and I had spent the better part of a morning on my acquisitions. A salesman had tried to steer me toward a rack of seersucker suits, but I was steadfast in my resolve: I had the first of three fittings with the tailor before leaving the store. My timing was impeccable. Spring had suddenly evaporated in the onslaught of blinding, sullen heat.

The ornamental pear trees lining our street had barely shed their confetti petals before the streets were bathed in a starker white, a withering blanket of light bleaching the pavements, scalding the lampposts, and glinting off the polished chrome of parked cars like the gaudy flash of scattered diamonds, throwing random sparkle into even the drabbest neighborhoods.

Beckwith suspended our lessons: he had removed himself to the Jersey shore to the house of a "comrade" until the weather broke, a decision with which I had no quarrel. The idea of venturing into the inferno of his underground warren under these circumstances was unimaginable. Even Aunt Lavinia had decamped for the shady comfort of a country rental in Sharon, interrupting my employment indefinitely.

"The heat," she said, "wreaks havoc on Mr. Phipps's sinuses. He has enough trouble just breathing the caustic city air, never mind having to fight all the dangerous germs that incubate in this kind of tropical hothouse situation." During her absence, she was having air-conditioning installed throughout her apartment. She was also having her floors sanded and restained. "Carpe diem. The uses of adversity. These are important concepts, my dear," she had concluded, leaving me without the resources to escape to the frosty chill of the Loews afternoon double feature.

I stayed indoors during the heat wave, carefully positioned in front of the fan I had propped up on a stool, perched on a stack of phone books, its small circle of wind directed at my back while I hunched over the card table that had become my temporary desk.

The radio was full of reports of record temperatures and the greengrocer on Bleecker Street had doubled the price of ice. But by late afternoon of that Thursday, I began to feel cabin crazy; the house was heavy with silence. With the radio off, I could hear the hum of our refrigerator reverberating on the new linoleum floor, and the faint sound of studio laughter from a television in an upstairs apartment. I had no choice but to close my textbooks and take to the streets until after dark, when Spencer would return from the cool entombment of the public library, making his leisurely way down Fifth Avenue with his schoolboy's satchel of books slung over his shoulder.

I turned off Seventh Avenue, noticing that the side streets were no longer vacant and lazy; clusters of women gathered to confer in the low, thrilling tones of gossip, and men sat on stoops drinking beers or reading the paper, and now and then the sharp screech of a child pierced the blue weight of the evening. As I walked by, heads would look up to appraise me, either nodding dismissively or ignoring my presence altogether. I was used to that. I had an air of familiarity that rendered me invisible, unlike Spencer: people could tell that he was marked for a different purpose.

A group of children burst into laughter as I approached, their light cries rising and scattering like sparrows, but I pretended not to notice. I hummed self-consciously to myself as my right hand dug down into the pocket of an almost outgrown summer jacket, fingering the key to the apartment, rotating it against the soft, frayed lining. Just before I reached the end of the block, someone whistled at me and I turned to see a rubber ball bouncing down the uneven cobblestones of the street. I intercepted the ball before it rolled under a parked car and threw it back to the pudgy boy who waved at me, calling, "Hey, mister, over here, mister."

I stopped momentarily to stare through the chain-link fence

surrounding the empty corner lot. It was an overgrown bramble of weeds and cans jeweled here and there by the glittery shards of bottles thrown against the targets of an abandoned stove, or the rusting carcass of an automobile, permanently stalled, its hood thrown open, gushing out vines and greenery. There was something oddly comforting about the sight, the way the car burst with vegetation, as if nature were composing something lovely from even the crassest form of man's debris.

It was a sign, just as Lillian Dawes appearing in the paper had signaled the beginning of something whose portent I could not decipher. I have always been able to recognize the looming symbols that dot our immediate horizons, though I cannot always read them, putting me in a more awkward and less sympathetic position than the much-aggrieved Cassandra of Greek mythology. Spencer said once, in one of the bathtub sessions, that it is a feature of modernity to be handicapped not by our abilities to do, but by our abilities to see, in the grand sense that renders the fulfillment of meaning. Hence the frustration that leads to decadence, paralysis, and futility, or at least ironic self-awareness. In this regard, I am a thoroughly modern man.

When I asked Spencer if there was a cure for the modern condition, he thought for a moment, taking a deep drag on the damp cigarette he had just relit, sliding his torso down in the water, his knees rising sharply above the lip of the porcelain tub. "Yes," he said, smiling mysteriously, "literature and love. They both come from the same impulse—to know and be known." Not surprisingly, I didn't really see what he meant. I am, after all, modern, and Spencer's a writer, so *of course* he would promote the improbable power of the word.

When I rounded the corner and approached Lucky's Diner, I saw the photograph of Lillian Dawes, Golden Laurel, and Clayton Prather taped to the window. It had been up for a few weeks and already the sun had yellowed the paper and curled the edges of the Scotch tape. It came as no surprise but rather as a confirmation of the quirky logic of coincidence that allows for any number of events to be construed as related, so I entered and made my way to the farthest booth, under the mural of the Amalfi Coast.

I ordered the meat loaf special without the slightest worry that it would diminish my appetite for dinner. I was experiencing a persistent hunger these days that no amount of food seemed to dull. It amused Spencer to watch me finish a box of cornflakes, or the end of a loaf of bread an hour or two after a large meal. "I had no idea you'd be such a gargantuan guest," he'd say to tease me, or sometimes he'd offer me an espresso, saying, "Maybe it's time to stunt your growth." Once I had asked him if he thought it was abnormal to have such an insatiable appetite. He had shrugged and asked, "What's normal? And do we even want it?"

I listened to the men at the counter chat among themselves. It was mostly about the races—Spiro played the horses, and behind the cash register, next to the worn five-dollar bill that was taped to the wall, were photographs of horses that had won the big stakes races. Occasionally a tiny man, circus size, with a fierce, vulpine face would stop by, transforming the establishment with the theatricality of his shiny vests, large jeweled cuff links, and patent-leather wing tip shoes. Zip Kilkenny liked to say he had "a flair for flash," and he would be the first to tell you, "A short man's gotta make an impression or all's they remember is you're short."

Zip's skin was as coarse and shiny as an orange rind, contributing to Zip's oddly mesmerizing effect: half magician, half loan shark.

As soon as Zip slid into the front booth, Spiro would become instantly unctuous, his large body unfolding itself from a slump behind the counter to hover anxiously over his guest, attentive as a sommelier, producing liquors for which the diner had no license, bottles he held to the light before pouring, as if to check the quality before he filled Zip's tumbler.

Zip had been a jockey and by most accounts, a good one. It was unclear what exactly he did now, but I guessed that he ran numbers or sold tips because when Spiro finally collapsed into the front booth, across from Zip, there followed a period of hushed, agitated conversation that could not have been interrupted even by a kitchen fire. After a while, Zip would excuse himself and go to the men's room. When he returned, he would chat with customers, working the room with a politician's ease, his diminutive hands darting wildly, like pale, trained birds pantomiming his crude words, transforming his advice, sartorial, romantic, or financial, into a haiku he sculpted in air. Zip was the first man I had met whose hands were professionally manicured.

"Whatsamadda with you?" he asked me, without waiting for a reply. "You don't got a problem Zip ain't had worse, believe me. I'll bet it's a broad. All right, I'm gonna give you a tip you'll thank me for before the night is done. Forget the candy and the flowers: what a dame wants is a laugh. You get a girl to laugh and you got her halfway to the bed, you see what I mean?"

I stared, afraid to eat while Zip stood by the table. My dinner roll was leaning in the gravy and soon it would be too soggy to eat. I nodded at Zip nervously.

"So, you good with a joke? You need some howlers? I got jokes I swear will get you laid," Zip went on, fishing a toothpick out of his pocket and rapidly chiseling it between his teeth, "guaranteed."

For a moment I considered telling Zip about Lillian, but Zip turned and started talking about barbers with one of the busboys, explaining the intricacies of a good haircut. I ate another forkful of instant mashed potato and then pushed my plate away and spread out the evening edition of the *New York Mirror*. I skimmed the news quickly and then turned to the society pages, hoping to find Lillian Dawes mentioned again. I had taken to buying three newspapers a day, like a gambler on tilt who tries to multiply his chances of winning by increasing his exposure. Zip noticed the paper and grabbed it from me.

"Lemme have this a sec," he said, flipping directly to the sports page, where there was a photograph of a horse and jockey, and then in a small insert in the upper-right corner, a picture of the owner, Mr. Harold Zimmermann, and a tight cluster of friends, grouped around him in a horseshoe of admiration except for two women talking at the far edge of the photograph, almost evading the reach of the camera.

"Lookie here, Laurel Love, my triple crown. Sired Golden Laurel, of recent fame. Now that was a horse!"

Spiro lumbered over and breathed heavily on the picture. "Yeah, that one was a star," Spiro agreed, nodding, tapping at the horse. Zip and Spiro started to reminisce, walking together over to the register, where a glossy black-and-white showed Laurel Love in the winner's circle.

I was pretty sure one of the women caught in conversation

during the moment of hushed glory and flashbulbs was Lillian Dawes. It was hard to tell, the heads of the women were tiny and their faces turned from the camera. But it made a certain sense. After all, it seemed to be a crowd she knew, however peripherally.

"Excuse me," I interrupted, waving Zip over with the paper, "do you know these women?" Zip Kilkenny barked out a blunt laugh somewhere between derision and a cough and his slim hands quivered in the air. "You still on the broads? Okay, bud, that's what we call persistence, s'what makes this country great. The blond is Vanessa Demmerly, currently the consort of Mr. Harold Zimmermann, a.k.a. owner of Laurel Love. And she is a piece of work, my friend, a piece of work. Myself, I'd rather get kicked in the head by the horse than fall in with a gal like that. But Harold don't seem to mind. In fact, he can't get enough." Zip snorted again. "The other one, she's just a friend of the Demmerly dame."

I wiped my mouth on the paper napkin I had balled up in my palm. "Do you know her name?" I asked deferentially, my voice sounding painfully young and earnest, "the friend of the consort?" I repeated. The word "consort" resonated with a kind of extravagance that made my mouth want to pucker, the same way "aigrette" and "ormolu" felt awkward on my tongue, as if my mouth knew they had no business being there and pushed them out in a high staccato, like a child repeating a word whose meaning is still years away. I stood up and pointed down at the bleed of black dots that covered the newsprint converging into a gray image that would rub off on my fingers.

Zip paused and studied me. A thin veil of sweat shone on his brow and he had begun to shred the paper napkin I had dropped by my plate.

"Yeah, sure I know her name. That's Diana Liswell," Zip said contentiously. His ebullient manner had changed. There was a chill in his brown eyes that gave his pointed face an especially rabid look and his hands had come to rest. "What's it to you, sonny?" he asked. From behind the counter, Spiro called out nervously, "Easy, Kilkenny, he's a paying customer."

"I just thought maybe it was Lillian Dawes. It looked like her. That's all."

Zip clapped me overly hard on the back, relieved and generous again. "Naw, that's Diana Liswell. Trust me. She introduced herself at one of Zimmermann's parties. Didn't condescend the way a less classy broad would. Impressive knowledge about horses, too." Zip said admiringly. "I'll bet she was a tomboy at some point in her past. The best ones always are and you can quote me on that." Zip plunged one of his doll-sized, immaculately groomed hands into his pocket and pulled out a wad of new bills. He slapped a five on the table and said, "You go buy yourself a drink or two. You need to relax, son. You're seeing things. Should never let a woman get to you like that," he said kindly.

Zip's last-minute largesse was mildly humiliating, but I was distracted by the discovery I had happened on: another name, a new incarnation. I folded up the paper and dropped some change on the table for a tip, keeping my eyes down as I slid the five neatly into my wallet. I said a quiet "Thank you," and went to the register where I paid the check, watching it be impaled on the thin metal spear where the paid checks were piled. Usually I couldn't resist touching the tip of the metal shank, testing its sharpness, always to find it duller than I had hoped, but instead I reached into the bowl beside it and took out three mints, quickly, because I wasn't sure how many were appropriate and I didn't want to test Spiro's generosity. Then I swung the door open, making the bell on its hinge spatter bright coppery notes, round as falling coins, out into the violet evening into which I walked, as if it too were painted by the same hand as the mural.

We got lost three times before we reached the wrought-iron gates of the cockroach kingdom. Spencer had agreed to come; nonetheless, his ambivalence was everywhere evident. While I went to pick up my suit, he had undertaken the packing of a leather suitcase and a canvas valise. When I returned, he was still troubling over his selection of reading, having already packed two novels and a collection of essays. He refused, moreover, to take the train. That would, he felt, put us at the whim of a schedule and limit our autonomy, a circumstance he plainly found unacceptable. Instead, he had managed, after considerable procrastination, to borrow a car from a friend, a Studebaker scabbed with rust. Then he insisted that we make the trip exclusively on back roads, in search of exotica, architectural interest, or at least a scenic view.

During the drive, I was assigned the duties of copilot, which meant reading the maps, lighting cigarettes for Spencer, and changing stations on the radio when he became bored with the disc jockey's choice. When we had to ask for directions, I was the

one who ran through the muddy streets until I found a knowledgeable face. But I didn't mind any of it: in my hours lying on the
Chesterfield sofa reading detective magazines or doing crossword
puzzles at the kitchen table, my thoughts had returned to Clayton Prather and his invitation with a desperate insistence. The
more hopeless my situation seemed, the farther behind I fell in
my schoolwork or the more lonely and craven I felt myself to be,
the more Clayton Prather seemed my only hope, the deus ex
machina who could save me from the bitter fruits of my many
weaknesses. I'm not sure exactly what kind of divine intervention
I hoped for, although I'm sure it involved some measure of his
power and wealth being conferred upon me in a way that would
circumvent the necessity for college. In my fantasies, I was always
gracious to the point of cloying in my acceptance of his gifts, following in his footsteps with my head slightly bowed, like an
acolyte at the altar of Mammon.

It was somewhere outside Hartford that Spencer broached
the subject of our father. We had stopped earlier and had lunch at
a Howard Johnson's, where foolishly I had ordered the fried-clam
plate. They now sat heavily in my stomach, making the task of
digestion require my full concentration. I had turned up the volume on a station playing "Mona Lisa," and as the verdant fields of
Connecticut blurred by in a bright sweep of color, I was imagining what my chums at Renwick would be up to. I pictured them
on the soccer field, practicing spitting while they waited for
teams to be chosen.

Spencer had both hands on the wheel, at ten and two, just
like Mr. Hevner at Renwick had taught those of us who had taken
driver's training instead of shop.

"You know, Gabriel, Father was a complicated man," he said, turning down the radio.

"Uh-huh," I answered, turning the radio up again. Spencer turned to look at me and then he turned the radio off. We had the windows rolled all the way down and the sound of rushing air whistled through the cabin of the car, filling the void where moments before the velvet voice of Nat King Cole had throbbed.

"You remember our discussion of the dichotomy between appearance and reality, don't you?"

"Yeah, yeah, fruit and chaff, all that glitters is not gold," I said, not wanting to sully a day with such promise by the invocation of Father, with all the attendant queasy feelings his memory could conjure, the guilt and anger and failures melding into a confused, sickening sadness that cast a wide shadow on my thoughts if I gave it access.

"The point is," Spencer went on, struggling for purchase on what was clearly difficult terrain, "Father was . . ."

"A righteous old bastard," I filled in, desperately trying to preempt any further discussion. I thrust my arm out of the window, letting my fingers comb the cool air.

"Yes," Spencer sighed, "I suppose he was that too, but let's not forget the revered lawyer and honored philanthropist that he also was, which brings me to my point precisely: he was an interesting mix of divided ambitions and conflicting impulses."

"All right, he was fascinating, for a goody-goody," I said, closing my hand in a fist, trying to catch the wind in the small pocket of my palm.

"Actually, he wasn't." Spencer kept his eyes on the road, and for a moment there was silence between us. The fortnight of sweaty, oppressive weather had lifted with the recent rain and the air was sweet again, and balmy. I took a deep breath, almost tasting the emerald tang of cut grass that scented the lawns on either side of the road.

"What do you mean?" I asked cautiously, looking at his profile, envying the easy accord of his features, a kind of offhand handsomeness that began casually in the arch of his eyebrow and swept down the lean angle of his jaw. I resembled more closely our mother, whose features were softer and had diffused their charms in replication, so that my face, when I encountered it in surprised reflections from a storefront glass or ill-placed mirror, seemed to me to be objectionably unremarkable.

"I had debated the merit of broaching this at all—but Aunt Lavinia helped persuade me that anything less than full disclosure would be a disservice to you. She's been adamant about it. You see, she took Father's papers and journals, after his death, thinking to organize them into a body of documents that might be of interest to a library archive. I think she was motivated not so much by the hagiography of his public persona as by the possibility of a tax benefit. She's admirably practical in that regard. No one else knew quite what to do with his desk work; most of the correspondence is spectacularly dull, and Aunt Grace, who was one of the executors of his will, was, as you might imagine, relieved to be relieved of it."

"So what's the big revelation? Did he have a mistress? A bastard child? What?" I asked, feeling slightly dizzy. "Tell me quick, because I'm getting a little carsick."

The combination of twisting road and fried clams and nervous anticipation made me want to lean my head out of the window, like a big dog, facing the full force of the air we drove through, our speed creating a density that yielded to our mass like water opening around a diver.

"It seems," Spencer said, shaking a cigarette out of a pack and handing it to me to light, "Father did something heinous as a young man, and spent much of the rest of his life trying to make up for it."

"What did he do?" I asked impatiently. "What was it? Did he kill someone?"

Spencer laughed. "No, nothing like that. He embezzled."

"Oh," I said, relief flooding me, a palpable wave of calm moving directly down my esophagus. "That's not so bad."

"Yes it is," Spencer said, still smiling. "He abused his position as the lawyer of a large estate to basically steal money from the heir. That would be bad enough, but to make it worse, the estate he was representing was that of an old friend, a distinguished financier who had helped Father considerably when he left Doyle and Dunbridge and was starting out on his own. Look," he said, flicking the tail of his cigarette out the window where it skittered behind the car like a dancing spark, "no one knows this. Only Lavinia, you, and me."

"Well, I won't tell anyone, if that's what you're getting at," I said, a slight peevishness straining my tone.

"No, that's not at all what I mean. I suppose, in due time, I'll tell the rest of the family. Or you can, if you want."

"Nooo thank you," I interrupted. "I can imagine Aunt Grace's reaction and I don't want to be anywhere near when this bomb drops. She's likely to shoot the messenger, but it won't be me, that's for damn sure."

"Yes," Spencer agreed. "She'll be devastated. She's always set Father up as the pinnacle of virtue around which she's fluttered in her chiffon cocktail dresses with the sanctity of a temple virgin, echoing his august pronouncements. I think in another life she must have been a budgie or a parakeet—one of those small pastel birds that flit about as domestic ornaments, without any song of their own."

Spencer glanced at his watch and then shifted gears, pushing the car into fourth. "I don't mean to be cruel," he continued. "I *am* fond of Aunt Grace and I hate having to knock the perch out from under her; Father occupied the high moral ground with the ruthlessness of a conquering army. Uncle Ambrose will simply issue a vehement denial and then never refer to it again, or maybe he'll invent a Byzantine theory of conspiracy to explain away the defamatory revelation. But this will be hard for Aunt Grace. She'll need support," he said, looking at me again, as if I was already withholding it.

"So don't tell her," I suggested, opening the map again, spreading it wide on my lap.

"It's not that easy. You see, there is the question of returning the money."

I could feel my jaw go slack, like the hinged mouth of a ventriloquist's dummy. I have never liked that kind of corny entertainment; even at an early age, at birthday parties, I felt embarrassed for the interlocutor and found something disturbing in the little wooden mannequin on his knee. I snapped my mouth shut and swallowed hard.

"What do you mean?" I asked, letting the map crumple to my feet as I reached over to the driver's side of the dashboard, where Spencer's pack of smokes had slid. I shook one out, snapped open the glove compartment, and tapped the cigarette on its yawning tray, waiting for a response.

"As soon as Aunt Lavinia wrote me with her discovery about the embezzlement from the Whitcomb estate, I stopped drawing on our inheritance. We agreed that some effort should be made to try to find the heirs, and return to them what is theirs, after all. It raises the sticky question of your college tuition since you precluded the possibility of a scholarship with your ill-timed proclivity for Cuban tobacco products."

"Spencer, you've got to be kidding," I countered, puffing angrily on my cigarette. "What's done is done. It's our money now. It's mine, at least. You've already had your education. Easy for you to be big about it." I continued smoking in silence until I could feel the heat from the head beginning to burn my fingers. "It's just crummy, what you're doing, because I'm a minor, and don't have any say. Real crummy."

"Easy there, Bucko, nothing's been done yet. For one thing, we are not even sure there are any heirs. Why do you think I sold the family portraits, Gabriel? Why do you think we've been living so frugally? I've been trying to scrape together enough money to launch you into the world on my own, in case a Whitcomb heir turns up. What did you think? I was just cheap?"

"Yes," I said.

Spencer laughed again. "You can accuse me of many things, I fear, but not that. My own inclinations run in the opposite direction. I'm lazy and profligate by nature, and have expensive tastes by nurture."

I smiled at Spencer and shook my head. He was wrong. I was

the expert on lazy and profligate and Spencer didn't begin to qual-
ify. Still, I was pleased that he thought of himself that way; it
closed the gap I had assumed separated us in his estimation. He
reached out his arm and patted my head, as if I were a little boy.

"Don't worry about this. It will be fine however it works out."

This last gesture touched me more deeply than I would have
suspected. I felt almost choked with gratitude. I tried to think of
something to say but couldn't, so when he returned his hand to
the wheel, I stretched my arm along the back of the bench seat
and patted his shoulder in return, keeping my eyes ahead of me,
staring out past the dirty windshield.

We had come to a stop sign at an intersection. Sagging near
the crossroads in front of us was a dingy clapboard farmhouse.
The patchy square of lawn before the house was littered with
abandoned children's toys. A headless doll lay facedown in the
uneven grass, one arm outstretched. Near a balding patch of the
yard a red bicycle slumped on an inturned wheel and a chained
dog chewed on a bright yellow Hula-Hoop.

"Find out which direction takes us to Red Spring Road,"
Spencer said quietly.

"There's no one home except that dog. Let's go on to the
next town and ask there," I suggested.

"Go around the back."

There was no point in further discussion. I got out of the car,
leaving the door ajar, and crossed the road. As I walked across the
yard, the dog looked up at me, a mouth full of slobber stretching
into a wide, panting grin. Its tail thunked the ground hopefully. I
skirted the house, following the porch around to a back door in
which the screen had been punctured by something the size of a

baseball or a fist. Peering into the darkened room, I made out a kitchen that was more tidy than I would have expected. Something simmered on the gas range, so I called out hello several times, each increasingly loud and imperious.

"Cut the noise," a voice warned, and then a woman appeared holding closed a cheap nylon bathrobe, under which I could see part of a negligee in the same shiny rosebud pattern. Her hair was rolled up on puffy pink curlers like the ones Aunt Grace secretly used when she couldn't go to the beauty parlor. I could see the contour of the woman's breasts through the thin fabric. They were small and pointy, like a funnel. When she saw the direction of my glance, she asked what I wanted, making no attempt to conceal her irritation, or her chest. She was not particularly attractive, but I found I could not sever my focus as I repeated Spencer's question.

She pointed to her right, saying something about a fork in the road just past an Esso filling station. As she lifted her hand to point, the robe gaped wide and I saw the blunt edge of a nipple pushing against the slick sheen of the material; there was a small, darkening wetness there. She followed my eyes down her front and said wearily, "It's from nursing," as if she had long since given up the notion of her body as a source of wonderment, its magic, like the bedroom lingerie, nothing more now than utilitarian. Then she turned and went back into the dark depths of the house, stepping on a squeaky toy in her path.

All the way up the tree-lined drive to the house neither of us spoke. The foot of the drive had been flanked by a pair of painted cast-iron lawn jockeys holding small lanterns that presumably lit up at night. Spencer had not been able to suppress a snort at the sight of them, but now he withheld further comment. There was an unmistakable ostentation to the place: the approach was over-long, and the lawns stretching away on either side of the white gravel road were exuberantly lush, glowing green with a Technicolor brightness that made you want to squint. Picturesque plantings clustered around stands of mature trees that punctuated the landscape's soft rise, and here and there, with a strident insistence on old world charm, marble statuary had been placed almost randomly.

From the top of the small hill on which the large, Italianate mansion sat, you could see past the lawn to the edge of a small lake. A rowboat, crowded with guests, lurched across the still water, the sounds of drunken hilarity floating up to us as we parked the car next to a collection of expensive vehicles, some of which had been left at odd angles of abrupt disengagement. A green Jaguar's trunk had been left open, revealing a solitary, high-heeled evening shoe and a jar of cocktail onions.

Spencer busied himself with our luggage while I surreptitiously checked my reflection in the side mirror, feeling self-conscious in my new suit, and nervously giddy at the same time. From within the house, we could hear music from a distant room. It was late afternoon, and Spencer stood for a moment with his back to the house, watching the light shiver on the twisting leaves in a large birch tree. Then he turned to me and said, "Shall we?"

No one responded to the bell so we let ourselves in. A series of rooms gave off the front hall, and having left our bags beside the newel post of the center stair, Spencer wandered into the empty living room, showing no inclination to follow the indications of activity that emanated from farther in the house, a swell of laughter and the hum of conversation that rose above the Duke Ellington tune, the long waver of a saxophone dispersing in the hall like a wisp of smoke. Spencer was drawn immediately to a large oil landscape hung over a console table set between two windows.

"It's Dutch," Spencer remarked. "Probably eighteenth century. Look at the handling of the sky." I agreed without looking. On the lid of the piano in the opposite corner, a clutter of empty glasses and an overflowing ashtray distracted me, evincing festivities that I had missed, and my greed for adult pleasures welled like a frustrated thirst, the longing a shipwrecked sailor must have when first sighting land from his miserable dinghy.

"Come on," I urged, "let's find Clayton and the others."

A door opened from the far end of the room and a woman

stumbled in, giggling. "Oops," she said, giggling again as she made her way around an upholstered chair and headed straight at me with her hand outstretched. She was pretty in a Kewpie doll way, dimpled cheeks and a bursting roundness her tight silk dress could barely contain. But there was a sort of bruised quality about her, like an overripe banana, sticky sweet and pulpy.

Spencer introduced himself, and then me. As she shook hands, she pumped vigorously within the double clasp of her small moist hands, as if she were priming a deep well. "Enchanted," she said without offering a name. She hiccuped and put a plump hand in front of her bright lips in a coy gesture, like a schoolgirl or a geisha. It was hard to tell which was the effect she wanted.

"The party's in there," she said, flapping her other hand behind her.

"Is Clayton presiding?" Spencer asked, reaching forward to steady her as she swayed on her heels.

"Clayton?" she repeated mindlessly. "I haven't seen Clayton for days. I think he's down by the lake," she said vaguely, casting about the cushions on the sofa. "I'm leaving just as soon as I find my purse. Have you seen the help anywhere?" I shook my head no.

"Oh well. They'll just have to send on whatever turns up in the morning. They do that, you know," she reassured us.

"Do you need a lift somewhere?" Spencer asked.

"No, sweetie, thanks. I've already got one," she said, winking at us both. When she left the room, Spencer flopped down on the sofa and ran his hand through his hair. "Let's face it," he said, "this was a mistake. I never should have brought you."

I sat down beside him, trying to marshall arguments, but

they were unaccountably elusive. I realized that anything I might say would only confirm his conviction to leave. "How about we try to find a bathroom and then a drink?" I suggested, trying to sound as reasonable and sober as I could, but the atmosphere was infectious and I felt half intoxicated by the gin breath of the departed woman as well as by the tingling sense of proximity to a happiness that had hitherto been denied me.

The double doors to the living room opened from the hall and an Asian man in a housecoat peered in. He carried a lacquered tray under his arm, and seeing us startled him. "You here long?" he asked, chewing nervously on his lip.

"We've just arrived," Spencer said, rising from the sofa.

"I getting Henry. You wait," he said, and then before he left, he scurried across the room and gathered some of the dirty glasses on his tray, bobbing his head at us from the hall.

"You wait," he repeated before closing the glass-paned doors behind him, a maneuver that he accomplished with difficulty now that his tray was full. Minutes later a butler appeared. He had probably been hired out from an agency on short notice. There was something almost alarming about his size. He had a large, awkwardly bulky body that looked as if he had been painstakingly packed into his uniform by means of an extruding device: no amount of last-minute tailoring would ever get the cloth to hang in a natural way, and as a result he resembled a human cannoli. He stood very straight and thrust his chest forward like a pigeon, a tuft of white shirt threatening to escape the buttons of his vest, which strained almost audibly.

"I've put your suitcases upstairs, in the guest suite to the right of the landing on the second floor. Mr. Prather is down at the boathouse, I believe, but he has been expecting you all after-noon. I can show you to your room now, or I can serve tea or cocktails if you prefer. Dinner will be served at eight-thirty and breakfast is buffet style unless you want a tray brought to your room. Mr. Prather doesn't rise until ten," he explained without inflection, as if he were auditioning for a role he had already resigned any hope of getting.

"If you need anything else, you can ring the bell. Ling will bring you whatever is required. My name is Twichell. Please let me know if you find anything unsatisfactory."

"We'd like cocktails," I piped up. Twichell raised an unruly eyebrow.

"Here or in the music room, with the others?" he asked, addressing himself exclusively to Spencer, I noted with annoyance.

"Here would be fine. A scotch and soda and a ginger ale," Spencer said, but feeling my furious nudge in his back, he relented. "Make that two scotch and sodas, one in a tall glass with extra soda."

Twichell left us and we both burst out laughing. "Where do you suppose Prather dug up Twichell?" Spencer asked, his features relaxing now around his boyish grin. "He's straight out of a Hal-loween parade, or Sing Sing." Now that it was clear we were stay-ing, I felt no need to rush Spencer into the other room, where Benny Goodman had replaced Ellington, and judging from the scuffling sound of feet on the parquet, people were dancing.

Ling brought us our drinks and a small porcelain bowl of smoked almonds.

"Little foods in the other room," he said, setting down the almonds. "Cheese and cracker and salmon mouse." Spencer pressed his lips together so as not to smile but when Ling withdrew, Spencer's smile burst forth mischievously. "Salmon mouse— neither fish nor fowl!" he said. "We'll eat well here, at any rate," he said, smiling, and we lifted glasses and clinked.

"I know you'll find this tiresome," he continued as I took my first gulp of the very tall drink I held, "but I feel the need to dispense some brotherly counsel. I know you've been drunk before, and I know you'll be drunk again, and very soon it will be none of my damn business, but you're on my watch now, so I'm asking you to be measured in your indulgences. Pace yourself, and don't get greedy, and you'll be fine. It's better to go to bed wishing you'd stayed a little longer and had a little more than regretting that you did. Especially when you're sharing a room with me. I think you'll find," he said, lighting up a cigarette from a silver urn on the coffee table, "in a variety of experiences, that more often diminishes the enjoyments provided by less. There are some notable exceptions, of course," he concluded.

"To notable exceptions," I said, lifting my glass again.

We finished our drinks and went upstairs to inspect the room. Spencer insisted we wash up and change for dinner. He had taken the precaution of packing for himself a dinner jacket "in case Prather went pretentious on us," and for me, the dark wool suit in which I had attended my father's funeral. I had not been thinking, and had foolishly assumed I would wear my white linen attire throughout the weekend, changing only into more casual wear if sporting events were arranged. The twin beds in the room had been turned down and our bags had already been unpacked. The funeral suit, newly pressed since our arrival, was hanging on the door of the armoire. Spencer's clothing was hung in a closet in the small adjoining sitting room. I was pleased that Ling had mistaken the hierarchy of our wardrobe, and teased Spencer about it, but he was unconcerned. His attention had been diverted by the astonishing amount of toile the room contained. The curtains were toile, the bedspreads were toile, as were the lamp shades and the boudoir chair.

"This," he said, gesturing broadly with his arm, "is a perfect example of what I was referring to: toile is not a notable exception."

I let Spencer shower first while I poked around, riffling through the drawers of the desk and the bureau, where I found a forgotten pink garter belt, possibly the property of the only guest we had yet met. When he emerged from the bathroom, I could see he had shaved again, although his beard was not particularly heavy, and he had availed himself of the aftershave that was among the toiletries lining a glass shelf above the bathroom sink. I was surprised by this: Spencer was not the type to use scent and the musky citrus fragrance that wafted from him was my only indication that he too was touched by the occasion. The laughter and perfume had managed to permeate his initial reticence, and the thrill of unseen possibilities had not been entirely eclipsed by their circumstance.

It was twilight when we went downstairs, and a group of guests had gathered on the terrace. Others were arriving by car, and more straggled in, having only just torn themselves from the various diversions offered by Prather's extensive facilities. The bathing suits and tennis whites in which a few couples hurried upstairs announced the pool and court we would later find on our ramble through the grounds after dinner.

I grabbed two glasses of champagne from a tray Ling was carrying out to the terrace, and we followed him through the loose knots of conversation, listening for one we wanted to join. I was younger than this crowd by five to ten years and suddenly my social inadequacies were plain to me: without Spencer I would have little chance to infiltrate the web of mingling that stretched effortlessly before me.

Tea candles lined the perimeters of the flagstones, illuminating the boxwood borders enclosing the guests from the vast sweep of lawn, and torches had been lit along a path leading down to the lake. The world had turned a cobalt blue, shading the crowns of trees in indigo shadows, as if a wash of ink were seeping into the air. In the gazebo at the near end of the herb garden, a jazz quartet was setting up; the guitarist was tuning his instrument while the trumpeter flirted with a few women in evening dresses.

Yellow pools of light spilled out of the open French doors to the dining room, where the caterers were preparing a long buffet table draped in starched white linen, which glowed against the encroaching night with a stark incandescence. Spencer was chatting with a statuesque brunette whose teeth were as white and square as Chiclets. She was complaining about how difficult she found it to walk across the grounds. The thin spikes of her heels kept sinking into the moist earth.

"See," she said, lifting up the skirt of her dress and pointing a shapely ankle in his direction, "they're ruined already. Brand new too. And imported, and dyed to match."

We were rescued by Clayton, who came up behind the brunette and put his hands over her eyes. She shrieked with delight and swung around to confront him.

"You are very naughty," she said to him with evident pleasure. "I've been looking for you everywhere."

Clayton looked almost dashing; he was wearing a dinner jacket with a satin shawl collar and his bow tie tilted rakishly—I was sure he had skewed it deliberately to achieve that particular touch of insouciant elegance.

"It's a thankless job being host," he responded with a bright smile. "No rest for the worldly . . ."

He turned the beam of his charm to us. "I see you've met Margaret, so there's no use issuing caveats now. I hope Twichell has made you comfortable?" he asked, without the slightest allusion to the intervening years in which his friendship with Spencer had been in hiatus, dislocated but not severed. I think he took for granted Spencer's vast capacity to forgive, his nature tending to find, like a dowsing rod, even the most obscure merit buried within people, and to overlook the sometimes brackish qualities that were more readily apparent.

I was able therefore to allow myself the illusion that Spencer was as pleased with our situation as I was. We were joined in our little circle by a number of other guests, all of whom, men and women alike, competed for Clayton's attention, so we detached ourselves. Spencer went to find a drink for Margaret while I wandered down in the direction of the lake. The band had begun playing and their music sparkled over the lawn, tinkling like dew between the thin blades of the darkening grass. I wallowed in contentment, staring up at the first stars as they began to throb in the sky like one more enchantment Clayton had designed for our pleasure. I had forgotten the sources of my earlier discomfort: my youth, the itchy wool of my funeral attire, and the nagging doubt that perhaps I should have purchased a tuxedo as the most recent supplement to my scant closet.

As I approached the wooden dock of the man-made lake, I could see up the bank a cluster of men gathered in a circle under the boughs of a large maple tree. There was some kind of genial commotion; it was hard to tell what, from where I stood, for the darkness rubbed the contours of the scene, soft as fog smudging the distinguishing features of the event. The circle kept rearranging itself to accommodate an activity I couldn't see in its center. I went to investigate, nursing the last of my champagne as I walked.

As I neared the outer edge of the circle, I could see a girl in the center. A chiffon scarf had been wrapped around her eyes and she was being spun around, as if to play pin the tail on the donkey. She was barefoot under a gauzy evening dress that swirled around her thin frame like a green mist. Her head was tipped back and her arms were spread for balance and she was laughing.

"It's no fair if you try to make me dizzy," she said, and the two young men who were twirling her at the waist only spun her faster.

"What's going on?" I asked a fellow puffing a cigar, watching from the outer ring beside me.

"It's a bet," he said without taking his eyes off her. "She must identify at least three different trees blindfolded, just by the sound of the leaves. She claims they each have different voices." In front of me, an older man with graying temples and an air of eminence threw back his head to drink from a bottle of champagne he held by the neck, swilling it like beer. He turned and offered us the bottle but we shook our heads, not wanting to be distracted.

The two men who had been spinning the girl now led her on a circuitous path in and out of the stands of trees, and well away from the maple under which I had joined them. There was a jostling among the spectators for the privilege of guiding her, holding her elbow or the small of her back when she seemed in danger of stumbling. I followed, trying to work my way closer to her. They stopped her under a magnolia tree but she stamped her foot.

"Don't patronize me," she said. "Even if I couldn't smell the spent perfume of the magnolia blossoms, I'd know these waxy leaves by their telltale clack. You might as well ask me to identify a pair of castanets. Do better than that, gentlemen, or I'll feel bad about taking your money."

There was a smattering of applause, some hooting, and voices shouted, "Try that one over there" and "No, let her try this tree over here." Once again, and this I think was more so that new arms could encircle her waist than because there was any question of needing to disorient her further, she was spun around until the outer layer of chiffon lifted like a sail catching wind, billowing at the ends in loose, sheer scallops. As the group reassembled under an aspen, there was a hush and we turned and shushed each other as she tipped her head, listening.

"Aspen," she said, and then she held her arms out before her like a blind man. "Next," she commanded. In short order, she proceeded to identify an oak, a beech, and, for extra credit, and because her admirers were reluctant to relinquish the access to her the game provided, a mulberry. I broke through to the interior of the circle tightening around her just as she pulled off the long blindfold of green gossamer, which revealed itself to be a thin sash of fabric matching the outer sheaf of her gown. She held it up over her head and waved it triumphantly, like a banner ribboning out a message of victory. Then she curtsied deeply to the men, who pulled out billfolds as they continued to marvel. "Gentlemen, thank you all," she said, collecting her winnings in the skirt of her gown, which she held out before her like an apron.

She turned in my direction and I said, "Lillian," in a choked whisper. She smiled at me, momentarily struggling to recall my face, but finding no memory to connect us, she merely nodded, and gathering her gown with both hands, ran quickly up the hill, back to the music and the lights.

I pushed my way past the dazzled throng, trying to follow, but my wrist was caught, and I wheeled around to see Spencer, with Margaret clutching his arm. He had a quizzical look on his face, but he was silent. It was Margaret who spoke. "Now wasn't that a spectacle," she exclaimed with breathless jealousy. "Next it will be juggling, I suppose." Spencer looked at her and opened his mouth to respond, but instead he lifted his glass and sipped his drink.

"What do you say we get something to eat?" he suggested, gently disengaging his arm from Margaret's grasp under the pretext of allowing her to precede him on the narrow path. My heart was pumping wildly, as if I had just run the feverish race that would have been necessary to catch Lillian before her back disappeared into the thickening mass of revelers who crowded the terrace, spilling out onto the dark edges of the lawn in a swelling tide of silk and sequins and cummerbunds.

"Sure," I said, reaching for Spencer's glass and taking a gulp of scotch that seared through me like a flare.

We plunged into the current of dancing couples moving in a vaguely clockwise pattern around the flagstone dance floor, though a few couples flailed in the corners, unable to join the flow, like fish trapped in an eddy between rocks. By the time we reached the dining room, the hall was congested with the first trickle of departing guests. A gaggle of colored maids in lace aprons had turned their attentions from the kitchen work to retrieving women's wraps and handing men their hats.

Twichell stood by the door, somberly handing out party favors from a beribboned wicker basket filled with key chains for men and compacts for the ladies, both of which advertised new concerns Prather had recently acquired. The brass key chains dangled a disk the size of a quarter, stamped with the motto "Sleep Well at a Sleep-Eaze Motel," and the shiny compacts were engraved, "For the Woman of Style, Try a Kane Cola Smile!"

"I want one of those," Margaret said, breaking away from a conversation I had tried to initiate with her. I followed Spencer into the dining room, where the buffet table was now a disordered jumble of picked-over platters. We assembled plates of food and carried them into the library, where Ling was clearing the debris of previous diners onto his lacquered tray. A couple sat together on the leather sofa, smoking. We took the armchairs in front of the fireplace and balanced the plates on our laps. I made two more trips to the buffet table before I felt sated, but I didn't see Lillian in any of the rooms through which I passed, taking the most comprehensive circuit each way. Spencer was still in the library; he had chatted with the couple briefly and now was examining the bookshelves.

"Look at this," he said when I returned, waving me over to him. He pulled down book after book, opening each to the flyleaf, on which effusive inscriptions by the author gushed out verbal embroideries of gratitude, concluding with phrases like "I couldn't have done it without you" or "With thanks to my most esteemed friend and critic." I was astonished by the number of literary giants indebted to Prather, until Spencer pulled down his own volume, *Apropos of Nothing*. "To my great friend, whose constant support and advice helped make this possible." I looked up at Spencer.

"It's not your handwriting," I said, a slight queasiness fluttering up above my thorax.

"No," he said, "it is not."

Spencer closed the book and placed it back on the shelf, among the other books, and then he began laughing, a runaway hilarity buckling his knees and bringing tears to the corners of his eyes. He tried to share with me the source of his mirth, but it came out in gasps, words degenerating into the hiss that announced another wave of laughter as he doubled over, struggling for breath and composure. Finally, he sighed deeply.

"Oh, Gabriel," he said, lifting his sleeve to his eye to rub away a final tear, "it's just that at Yale, the only books he bought, besides the required texts, were yearbooks. High school yearbooks from all-girl academies. Emma Willard, Concord Academy, Abbott, Brearley, Dana Hall, Garrison, you name it. He had a man who got them for him. We used to say, 'Well, at least he's reading something besides the financial statements his father forwards.' I guess this is his way of graduating to higher literature, and it's a doozy."

Shortly after two, the band stopped playing music and began packing up their equipment. The guests had thinned down to the last stragglers, party hounds who lingered by the bar or couples who had paired up cozily in corners of the terrace or by the pool. Like champagne too long uncorked, the effervescence of the evening was dwindling. A hush had descended over Clayton's kingdom, and you could hear the frogs from the lake trilling a symphonic weave of minor chords, in eight-bar intervals, making a mournful racket.

We had run into Clayton again as he was settling up with the caterers. There seemed to be some disagreement about the payment they were due, and he pulled us over to ask Spencer to lend him some cash. While Spencer went upstairs to find his wallet, Clayton put his arm around my shoulder, leading me away from the large women who were waiting in an angry group by the kitchen door. He began to tell me about the fabulous investment possibilities represented by two companies he had just purchased. He began to tout the benefits of buying stock now in the

Kane Cola Company, which he explained manufactured a spicy vanilla-flavored soda that enjoyed a devout following south of the Mason-Dixon line. It was his plan to introduce the product to New England and the Midwest, and he briefly outlined some of the advertising fanfare he had in mind. I was flattered to have his attention, though at first I thought he was teasing me with his salesmanship or, worse, had confused me with someone else for whom the complex investment strategies he outlined were actually intended. He was definitely drunk by now, but I began to realize that his inebriation was not what accounted for the gush of persuasive rhetoric to which I was treated. I think it was more subtle than that: he wanted me to repeat his pitch to Spencer rather than approach him directly.

Spencer handed over a sizable sum of money, which Clayton took with a few cursory remarks of thanks and went off to dispatch the station wagon full of weary serving women, whose complaints were just audible through the open window. When he returned, he led us into his study, where he pointed out with almost childish pride the imposing Rembrandt Peale portrait of Alexander Ambrose Gibbs, our great-grandfather, for whom our uncle Ambrose had been named. It had been reframed since the days when it hung in our father's law office, and now was engulfed in a hugely ornate frame, which Spencer would later note was not period correct.

"It cost me a bundle at the Sotheby's auction," Prather said, "but I figured, what the hell, might as well do you a favor."

"You've done me a great many favors," Spencer replied with pointed irony, but before he could elaborate we were interrupted by the arrival of Vanessa Demmerly, who banged open the door with a barrage of apologies for having been detained. She looked just like her photograph, but larger, swathed in furs that must have been sweltering on such a warm evening.

"I've got the brat in tow. Her nanny quit this morning," she declared, as if to preempt any rebuke that might have been forthcoming, but Prather seemed to have been unaware of her absence, indeed, he seemed not to recall having invited her. He blinked in confusion until Spencer asked, "Can we help you bring in your bags?"

"Yes," Prather chimed in gallantly, forcing enthusiasm into his voice, "yes, we must attend to you and little Gloria now that you've finally arrived!" He began his ministrations by helping her out of her enormous fur, which, because her hair was dyed blonde and swept up in an elaborate hairdo, combined to make her look like a Norsewoman, or a Wagnerian extra too slim to be a central character. Prather then busied himself with making her a stinger, for which she expressed a more urgent need than her luggage or her child, cumbersome details Prather conveniently left to us.

She had parked her Cadillac Eldorado directly in front of the house, blocking the driveway. I collected the sundry suitcases from the trunk while Spencer charmed the little girl, no more than eight years old at most, out of the passenger seat where she was kicking her skinny legs against the dashboard. He carried her piggyback into the house while I struggled with the assorted leather bags, sufficient, I would imagine, for a month's tour of Europe. But there was no question in my mind that Spencer had taken the more demanding burden upon himself, literally, for little Gloria was pulling Spencer's hair and beating him with her Raggedy Ann doll in her efforts to make him gallop.

Spencer delivered her to Ling, who had clearly been roused from slumber and was now wearing a maroon kimono over striped cotton pajamas. He muttered in Chinese what could only have been a series of curses, judging from his intonation and the way he took the child's hand and said, "You sleep now. Very late for little girl. No bad-bad, okay?" As he led her away, I could hear her whining attempts to negotiate.

"Mommy said I could have candy," Gloria repeated down the corridor, until finally a door closed on her exasperating voice. Vanessa Demmerly had slung herself over the arms of a club chair, her long legs crossed over the side, dangling a shoe from her toes in what was clearly a provocative pose she had struck before. She did not, to use Aunt Lavinia's expression, "bestir herself on Gloria's behalf," even to the extent of a quick good-night kiss. Instead, she swirled the chipped ice in her drink with her index finger and then licked it.

"I'll have to go to bed soon," she yawned, addressing the room at large, though it was only populated by Clayton and myself, and a plumpish fellow who had just wandered in, wearing tiny metal glasses that lent him an academic mien, undermined only by a loud, hissing laugh that wheezed out of him like air being released slowly from a balloon. Vanessa turned to observe him and then she said, "Listen, Poindexter, I'm glad you find me so entertaining, but there's nothing funny about beauty rest. It's a girl's one prerequisite, besides money, and an occasional massage." He hissed again in loud appreciation of her wit, his cheeks turning a vivid pink, making him look momentarily like a grotesque caricature of a cherub, his golden curls askew above his unabashed leer.

"My name's Gerald, actually," he said when he stopped hissing. Vanessa ignored him, and clicked open her cigarette case. Finding it empty, she snapped her fingers at her latest object of scorn. "Cigarette?" she commanded of Gerald, recrossing her legs.

Clayton glanced at his watch and left the room, stumbling slightly at the threshold. There was something vaguely unsettling about Vanessa Demmerly's feline demeanor, as if she could, on a moment's notice, spring like a panther on the nearest neck. She stretched herself languidly to accept one of Gerald's cigarettes and arched herself up to meet his lighter. I said good night and went outside to the gazebo. I wondered if Spencer had gone up to bed, or if I would find him among the last guests talking in a late-night hush by the pool, their voices floating out on the night in the thin cobweb of whispers.

As I leaned against the wooden rail and looked up at the studded night sky, I saw a shooting star traverse the black expanse, and then another, lower on the horizon. Out of the darkness, a voice spoke from the lawn below me.

"Do you think it's better to wish for the same thing again and again, to increase your chances of its coming true, or to diversify, wishing each time for something different, spreading out your chances?"

I peered over the rail and saw Lillian lying on the grass, one arm bent beneath her head.

"I don't really know," I said, forgetting to be nervous. "Half the time I forget to wish at all or I wish for something stupid, and waste it."

"Like what?" she asked, lifting herself up on an elbow and shaking out her hair so that it fell around her shoulders.

"Oh, I don't know. Like something that I really want at the moment, a slice of Horn and Hardart pumpkin pie, say, or something else dumb like that. Something you could have easily at another time but definitely aren't going to get now."

She laughed, and I felt myself smile involuntarily, as if my soul had seeped out through my heavy wool suit and were floating up into the ether of the thin atmosphere, where the glow of the stars touched me with their distant warmth. She was shivering, so I walked down the steps of the gazebo, down the curve of lawn to where she lay, and put my jacket on her shoulders.

"You know, your friend has arrived," I said, sitting down beside her.

"Who's that?" she asked.

"Vanessa Demmerly," I answered, pleased to know her name, for Clayton had not bothered to introduce us.

Lillian laughed again. "I don't think Vanessa has friends, just human accessories," she said matter-of-factly.

"You don't like her," I blurted out. Lillian plucked a blade of grass and put it to her mouth, making a sharp, razzy whistle. Then she cocked her head to one side, considering the statement.

"It's complicated. Actually, that's one of the things I *like* about her. She's not a sap. She doesn't go telling her sad story all over town. Everyone thinks she left Captain Demmerly, *the war hero,* because he came back damaged, missing a limb, right?"

I nodded knowingly, hoping she couldn't see in the dark how shamelessly I was faking familiarity with the subject.

"Well, that's a lot of crapola."

I had never heard a woman swear before, at least, not a beautiful one. Only Mrs. Austin, who used to get drunk at the Greenfield Country Club and talk in an increasingly fake English accent until her husband finally took her home, ever cursed openly, and then only as she was being stuffed into their white Cadillac. I was mildly shocked and greatly thrilled, and shifted my position on the lawn to conceal how stirring I found her words.

"The fact is," she continued, "the Peter Demmerly she was so wild about never did come home. His head injuries changed him and he just wasn't the same man she loved anymore. It had nothing to do with his being a cripple. It was things you can't describe easily: he didn't kiss her the same; he had a different sense of humor; he had a new personality. He was just plain different. And she didn't want to go through life pretending not to notice the switcheroo. I don't think that makes her the bitch people say she is. She's just unhappy in a big, empty way. You see," Lillian said, stretching her arms over her head, "I'm really a terrible snob when it comes to unhappiness. I do feel sorry for her—it's just that there's no nuance in her feelings. And in the anatomy of melancholy, nuance is the equivalent of soul. I think the real—"

She was about to continue but was distracted by a shadowy figure advancing up the hill. As the shape loomed closer, I could see it was Spencer. His shirt was off and he carried it with his jacket in a roll under his arm, his shoes and socks in the other hand. He was wet. Beads of water gleamed on his torso and dripped from his hair. He looked so classically beautiful at that moment, like a Greek kouros, that I felt a twinge of irritability, and wished that he would go away.

"I couldn't resist," he said as he approached us, shaking out his hair at a small distance from where we sat, like a dog shedding water from its fur. "No one was down by the lake and the water's still warm, with just a suggestion of mist on the surface. I even saw a few shooting stars," he added, looking up to scan the sky again. "Clayton certainly didn't stint on the enchantment angle. I half-expected to see dancing swans come out of the woods." He sat down beside me and drew a pack of cigarettes from his crumpled jacket and offered it to us. Lillian shook her head, but I took one, and for a few minutes we smoked in silence, watching the stars. Then he rubbed out his cigarette and stood up. "Good night," he said quietly to Lillian. "Don't stay up too late," he said to me, making me blush in the darkness.

I can't remember what I talked about after Spencer left, but it was just chatter, the odds and ends of what I would later recognize as cocktail conversation. Then suddenly Lillian sprang up and said, "Come on, I have just the thing for you, my friend." She reached down her hand and yanked me to my feet, pulling me behind her as she half ran back to the house. I couldn't imagine what she had in store for me, but she was giddy with the prospect of it, laughing as I stumbled behind her. She led me to the back door of the kitchen and shushed me. The lights were out, but she made her way quickly to the refrigerator and the arc of its illumination shone on her face as she bent forward, reaching into the middle shelf.

"Shut your eyes," she said. And I did, though I was sorely tempted to watch her, for at the moment, her face was radiant in the refrigerator light. I heard her opening drawers and cupboards and then a match was struck.

"Now," she said, "open them." The refrigerator had been closed and a single lit taper had been placed in a shallow saucer. Its small radius of flickering light cast huge dancing shadows across the room but revealed in its yellow glow the Formica table. There was a small plate on the near end of the table, almost obscured by a slice of pumpkin pie, a fork rising from its narrow prow like a metal mast. Lillian was watching my face, mirroring my delight.

"I found it earlier when I came in to have dinner. I was scavenging for sandwich meats, and the women were just lovely to me," she said, "because, for some reason, I just couldn't face eating with the rest of the guests. I'm not all that shy—it's just sometimes I have nothing to say to a bunch of strangers. I get that from my mother, I suppose. But then, she was socially eccentric, to say the least."

I ate the pie as she watched, a connoisseur, clearly, not just of unhappiness but of that rare variety of happiness which is akin to grace, moments in which one is so utterly and absurdly content that the world is suffused with the sublime, as if a vast and nonspecific infatuation was taking in its embrace the whole damn planet, warts and all. It was almost dawn when I said good night to Lillian on the landing of the stairs.

It was past noon when I awoke, and Spencer's bed was empty, the covers pulled up in a half-hearted attempt at tidiness. Despite my best efforts, I had managed to acquire a hangover of staggering proportion. This had evidently been anticipated by Spencer, who had left the toile curtains drawn tight against the sun, and had put on my bedside table three aspirins and his sunglasses.

I dressed slowly, sitting on my bed the whole time, like an elderly invalid. My clean shirt and the linen suit seemed blindingly bright, making me squint against their whiteness, but my need for coffee drove me on, compelled me to conjure with the shrill squeak of the sink faucet, the brutal force of the water pounding into the basin and echoing no less fiercely in my temples.

I held the banister and descended the endless stairs that separated me from coffee, and, perhaps, the kindly ministrations of Ling, in whom I now placed my hope for some ancient Eastern cure which could restore to me a modicum of well-being, some concoction I imagined as herbal and dark but highly efficacious. Ling was nowhere to be found; however, Gerald was very much in evidence, sprawling belly up on the living room sofa, snoring slightly as he clutched a cushion to his breast, his head on the verge of falling off the edge. I found Margaret, who was also wearing sunglasses, hunched over the abandoned breakfast table, contemplating the bottom of her coffee cup, and when she looked up at me and forced a smile to her lips, I could see a smear of lipstick on her top teeth. It was the kind of unpleasant detail that made my stomach churn, but I nodded to her at great personal expense, moving my head carefully so as to incur the minimum pain required by the exercise.

"Some party," she croaked in the desiccated manner of a deathbed utterance, only perhaps slightly louder and with less resignation. I poured myself a cup of coffee from a lukewarm coffeepot that sat on the sideboard, next to a plate of scrambled eggs that had obviously been out for several hours and became the second unpleasant detail to test my stomach.

I tried to focus on something else, breathing through my mouth to fight a rising wave of nausea that was swelling in the hollow desolation between my loins and my nose. Unfortunately, my mind was vacant but for one striking image that I could not banish, and that was the fury that Margaret would loose upon me should I happen to become ill at the table. I would have simply excused myself if I had felt confident that words and not matter emerge, but I didn't think I could just leave the table without explanation in the middle of Margaret's disquisition on *proper* party etiquette. She was still steaming about her shoes, it seemed, and the powder in the compact she had been given was a shade too pale for her complexion. Not enough dessert forks had been provided for all the guests, and the butter was salted. Some of the gentlemen had not stood up when a lady entered the room, and no one had helped her take off her bolero jacket when she became overheated from dancing. Margaret's standards were impressively unforgiving. It would be better to befoul myself there at the table and then pretend to lose consciousness, keel over and keep my eyes shut until some kinder agent attended to me. But before any of these exigencies came to pass, Twichell entered with a fresh pot of coffee and a slice of unbuttered toast.

"Your brother suggests that you start with this," he said, putting the plate in front of me. He stood there as if he intended to watch me eat it, but when I thanked him, he left promptly, whistling under his breath the popular tune "Whatever Lola Wants, Lola Gets," which I couldn't help but feel was a slight somehow directed at me. I managed to eat the toast, and by my third cup of coffee I determined that the stark sunlight of midday could be no more brutal a punishment than the prospect of listening to Margaret, so I made some blithe remark to her about facing the day, and putting on Spencer's sunglasses, pushed open the French doors to the lawn.

Ling was crawling around in the grass spearing cigarette butts with a bamboo skewer; it was a depressing sight, so I hailed him with extra cheer, making a point of complimenting his thoroughness. He looked up at me with undisguised loathing, so I changed the subject quickly and asked him if he had seen Spencer. He said he didn't know, which was pointedly unhelpful, and much more annoying than a simple no. I lit a cigarette as a sort of silent rebuke and wandered down to the pool, where a skeleton crew had assembled under a large striped beach umbrella.

The distinguished-looking older man whom I had seen swilling champagne the night before was in a bathing suit, wading gingerly into the pool from the steps at the shallow end. His chest hair was silvery, and though he was slim for his age, his pectorals sagged like dog teats. I waved to him and he waved back and then plunged into the aqua water, setting off a series of waves that splashed up on the flagstones, eliciting a chorus of squawks from the women shadowed by the umbrella. Vanessa emerged from under its shade and squinted at me. She was wearing a red-skirted bathing suit and a ridiculous sun hat, the kind of thing you might win at bingo in a resort in the Caribbean, bedecked with seashells and a fringe of palm fronds.

"Oh," she said, with disappointment, "I thought you might be Twichell. I need more ice."

"I imagine there's a ready supply in the kitchen," I answered. It came out sounding kind of snotty, which I hadn't actually intended. I looked past her, at Lillian, who was wearing a white cotton sundress with navy polka dots on it. Her sun hat was, by comparison with Vanessa's, austere: it had a low crown and a wide brim but carried no ornamentation, not even a thin ribbon or bow. It was a classy look, the kind of effect Hadley was always trying to pull off but never quite managed.

But Vanessa moved herself to block my view. "Yes," she snapped back at me, "I imagine there is, since that is one of the things Twichell's *paid* to do, keep ice in the kitchen and in our drinks."

I was momentarily stunned by the ferocity with which these last words had been spat at me. For the blink of a second, I actually thought I might cry. My hands were shaking with the raw humiliation that was registering in my body like a blow. I am not usually confrontational and have avoided fistfights where possible, having only had one set-to at school, which was a veritable record for Renwick, so I didn't have a lot of experience being decked, but I doubt it would have shaken me any more had I been physically struck.

Lillian smiled at me, but I turned away from her awkwardly. "Gabriel," she said, "I've been waiting to show you something. Will you take a walk with me down to the lake?"

I nodded, and pushed my sunglasses up on my nose, trying to calm down. She gathered a small straw satchel from under the glass table where she had been sitting and handed it to me.

"You can carry our accoutrements," she said, "while I find you a cornflower for your buttonhole."

I walked beside her silently until we had passed the gazebo. Then I said, "What a stinking rat and her teeth are too big," expecting full accord from Lillian, who I was fairly sure had contrived the walk to be alone with me. She surprised me, though, by saying, "You could have just offered to get her the ice and charmed her socks off."

"She could have gotten it herself just as easily," I replied, hearing the petulance in my voice but feeling too miserable to care about it now.

"A woman like that is used to a certain amount of attention, and besides, you're a guest," Lillian said, stooping to pluck a yellow daisy from the grass.

"She's a guest too," I countered.

"Yes," Lillian said, placing the daisy in my lapel and patting my shoulder, "but we're *good* guests. Our job is to counteract the bad guests, to make things easy and light. We are invited to diffuse, not create, friction, and therefore it is necessary to perpetuate the social fiction that we enjoy each other as much as our host enjoys us. It's not such a big deal really, when you think about what we are going to get in return. I mean, just look at that lake. And the willow over there, and the way the light is yearning for it all, and it's ours for the moment."

The light was glowing on Lillian's hair, highlighting the deep chestnut red with sparks of rusty gold, and I understood what she meant about the yearning of light, the way it was caressing her shoulders and playing off her cheekbones, and casting a brilliance on the tips of the trees and glittering on the water, and she was right, of course, I should have just gotten the ice.

Little Gloria was wearing a rhinestone tiara and a bright red bathing suit when we found her behind the boathouse. She was eating jujubes, stuffing them by the handful into a mouth ringed with a bright orange stain from an earlier bout with a Popsicle that had dyed her tongue a sunset hue. I know this because the first thing she did upon seeing us approach was to distend her tongue as far as it would go, displaying not only its astonishing length, but the half-masticated rainbow of candies that were cupped in its center. Then chortling to herself, a harsh, gargled sputter that sounded confusingly as if she was choking on a knot of jujubes, she ran off, stomping through the grass, thrashing at flowers with a reed she wielded like a thin whip.

Lillian called to her as Gloria rustled out of sight, dodging behind the thick growth of trees that edged the far rim of the pond. Gloria did not respond, although she did turn once and make an oblique gesture of disrespect in my direction. Lillian sighed and pushed a strand of hair back behind her ear.

"That kid has some major problems," I opined. Lillian's eyes were trained on the thicket from which a few birds rose noisily into the air.

"I think she's up to something, but I'm not sure yet what it is," Lillian said, her voice revealing an unexpected agitation she would not comment on further.

"Come on," she urged abruptly, skipping ahead down a steep section of the curved bank from which she could survey the collection of weathered rowboats, slanting up on the bank of the pond like large, dormant animals, wooden alligators sunning their winter-blistered hides. "This one," she said, stopping at the third boat. I was a little hesitant about embarking; I had had only enough experience rowing to discover my inadequacies at the sport. I remembered having difficulty keeping my strokes even, and found that my upper-body strength was quickly sapped by the effort. I did not have an opportunity, however, to disgrace myself. Lillian stepped lightly into the boat and seated herself on the bench with the oars.

"Push us off," she commanded, smiling childishly as I gave a shove and set her adrift. I was just barely able to hobble clumsily into the boat at the last moment, before her first stroke pulled the boat out of reach of the shore. Lillian pulled the oars evenly, making them click in their metal stirrups with the rhythmical precision of a metronome while I arranged myself at the back of the boat, enjoying inordinately the reversal of roles. With each stroke of the oars, I could see her breasts rise beneath the fabric of her dress, flexing taut against its fitted bodice.

"You need a sun hat," Lillian commented. "You'll burn out here on the water, dear boy, without one."

The sun was having a salutary effect on my general state, dissolving in its white wake the remnants of my headache and the sour disposition with which I had encountered the day. I was so taken with the tenderness of her concern, and the word "dear," that I forgave its coupling with "boy," which otherwise, and from anyone other, might have rankled.

"I have one, but it's at home, of course," I said, squinting at her from under the hand that I held like a visor at my brow. "But don't worry, the worst I'll get is freckles. I don't really burn," I assured her. "This *was* a splendid idea."

Lillian smiled and pushed her hair back with her wrist, letting the boat drift a moment. "Listen, there's a mockingbird."

"I wouldn't know a mockingbird from a crow," I said lazily. "I thought all we had in these parts was pigeons, anyway. But if you say so, I'll believe you. Besides, it has a certain ring, don't you think, saying, 'I heard a mockingbird today.' Like what Byron might say between drinks before dinner, you know, if there was a lull or something."

"I don't really think he had too many lulls," she said, trailing her hand in the water, and then she laughed. "And I'm not sure a mockingbird has enough panache to have registered with a roué like Byron. Even the vaunted nightingale might have trouble distinguishing itself in the realm of the truly jaded."

Her cheeks were glowing, and a breeze skimmed the placid water, puckering its surface. "Look, above that tree," I said, pointing. Lillian turned her head to follow the flight of the hawk. "A male sparrow hawk," she pronounced with authority. "See the gray on the wings? The females don't have that." It had dipped from view but Lillian continued to gaze at the serrated top of the woods, where the sky began. "A poet once described the flight of the hawk as 'the vagaries of the human heart rendered visible,'" Lillian mused.

"Lapadini," I said, happily recognizing the line from Spencer's translation. "My brother's translation was 'the vicissitudes of the heart made manifest.'"

"Yes, that's good," she said, smiling at me as if I was the one who had polished the words into a pleasing sheen.

"How do you know Lapadini?" I asked, unable to suppress my curiosity. "Spencer says Lapadini is 'the world's most obscure poet,' since only two manuscripts exist of his work, in Bibliothèque Nationale and the Bodleian Library. He only discovered Lapadini by following a footnote in a manuscript of Tasso."

Lillian rubbed her nose. "Tasso? I wasn't aware of that connection. Sidney refers to Lapadini's work in one of his letters. I liked the title: 'The Guardian of Sorrow.' I wasn't allowed to handle the manuscript. A very old man with white gloves turned the pages for me when I indicated with a nod that I was ready. He seemed himself like a guardian of sorrow."

The boat creaked like a hammock as it rocked, rubbing its wooden lullaby against the chafe of water as Lillian rested the oars on the frame of the boat, rotating them like a bottle of wine so that they wouldn't drip.

"What were you doing at the Bodleian?" I asked.

"I was at the Bibliothèque Nationale, and I wasn't really doing anything. Just killing time," she answered, clearly wanting to change the subject.

"Are you a spy?" I blurted out.

"If I were a spy, I couldn't tell you," she said, smiling at my frustration.

"You could tell *me*," I cajoled. "I have an excellent reputation as far as secrets are concerned. In fact, that may be the only damn thing my reputation's good on, so tell."

Lillian laughed and carelessly raked her hair to one side, changing her part. On the shore, a flock of yellow finches, attracted by bread crumbs, wobbled around Gloria, who squatted in their midst looking bored and stoically patient. Gloria tried to catch the closest one but her lurching grab scared them all off in a raucous fumble of flapping and scattering, only to regroup nearby.

"It's nothing nearly so glamorous, I promise you. No silk underwear with secret pockets. No pearl-handled pistol in my handbag. I've done lots of different things, but never espionage. Mostly, I get by doing a little of this and a little of that. I'm not too proud to take a paying job when I find it. Lately, though, I've just been a guest, which, as I've tried to explain to you, is more work than it seems."

Lillian laughed, her giddy rasp sounding like leaves being scraped into high, bright piles.

"Damn," she said, and I turned and saw Vanessa's hat floating along the surface of the water, making straight for us with the slick determination of a water snake. She was swimming the breast stroke, her black sunglasses resting on the surface of the water. As Vanessa approached the boat, she yelled, "Don't just sit there, young man, help me in, for Lord's sake. My hat is getting wet."

How much more preferable it was to be Lillian's "dear boy" than Vanessa's "young man," I thought as I hoisted her, dripping imprecations and water, into our now violated craft. From across the pond, I spotted Clayton, standing on the rise of the lawn in his tennis flannels, waving a martini shaker at us. It glinted in the afternoon sun like a beacon, flashing its irresistible message in slivers of light that radiated across the water to us in broken arrows of brightness. Vanessa stood up and clapped her hands, the boat swaying violently beneath her as she shouted, "Look, look, it's salvation! Just in time; all this water makes me thirsty." Lillian quickly reached out a hand to steady her friend. "Sit down and I'll take you there," Lillian said, dividing the sentence between command and coax.

Lillian rowed strenuously, each stroke seeming to pull her farther from Vanessa's chatter, which rose in the air like mist evaporating even before the syllables cooled, leaving behind them no wake but the swirling trail of oars creasing the green water. As Lillian relaxed into the lulling repetition of the oars rolling the pond under her in neatly paired folds, her face seemed almost holy as it tilted up toward the sky, where a few tattered clouds hung in ragged wisps.

Vanessa stopped talking in the middle of a sentence to stare. She had been discussing the air-conditioning in Harold Zimmermann's Chrysler when she finally realized Lillian had absented herself from the moment, her whole body transformed by whatever thought or memory she was visiting. She had relaxed into the loose posture of a gangly child. A small dot of soot smudged her cheekbone like a beauty mark and her face had the beatific expression of escape, as if she were playing hooky from the life she shared with the rest of us.

Vanessa scrutinized the girlish incarnation sitting before us, listening with cocked head to something far off, and unable to tolerate it any longer, Vanessa snapped her fingers loudly, cutting the still air with a sharp insistence.

Lillian looked up at us, her face dissolving like that of a dreamer waking to the contours of a room, and her eyes registered, for a brief moment, fear.

"I was just remembering something . . . ," she said, and her voice quavered almost imperceptibly.

I would have liked to ask her about it, whatever it was that had the power to so palpably move her, but we had arrived at the boathouse and Vanessa was clambering over me in her rush for terra firma, her mouth issuing directives with no less speed than her long legs covered the ground that separated her from the next event.

A small group had converged on the terrace, queuing up for Clayton's martinis and the club sandwiches that Twichell had arranged on a platter next to a bowl of potato salad and a pile of paper plates. A bouquet of plastic forks filled a wineglass and had drawn Margaret's censure. She lifted one up and wagged it at me, arching an eyebrow critically, as if to indicate a complicity between us of unspoken dissatisfaction.

Spencer came up from the tennis court deep in conversation with the older man I had seen earlier by the pool. I tried to catch his eye, but Spencer's attention was locked on the gray-templed gentleman who was leading him over to a pair of wicker chairs in the corner. Clayton hovered genially over the martini shaker, dispensing its balm like a priest administering to the needy throng that encircled him, offering with the olive or onion the occasional witticism, as final garnish to his hostly concoction.

Lillian sat by herself in the gazebo, arranging a handful of brushes in order of size. When I approached, she was just closing her box of watercolors; an unhappiness enveloped her, hunching her shoulders and bowing her head so that it hung like a weight from her long neck. I was accustomed to the notion of women having moods; I was practically raised by Aunt Grace, after all, and Hadley was no stranger to the hissy fit. But in my experience sadness was never among the emotions on display, and seeing it so undisguised made me feel ashamed, a voyeur, as if I were witnessing something I was not supposed to see, like Aunt Grace in her girdle.

"Hey," I said.

"Hey," she repeated.

"Can I get you some lunch?" I asked.

"Not just yet, thanks," she said, turning back to stare at the black enamel paint box. "I'll join you all in a moment," she added, forcing a smile, and I understood she wanted to be alone. I also thought I had gleaned the ghost of a Southern accent, a fraction of elision smudging the edge of breath dividing "you" and "all." But then, I don't have much of an ear for that sort of thing, so I had dismissed the notion by the time I returned to the terrace.

Spencer waved me over, introducing me to Mr. Wincett, who worked for the State Department. He shared, it seemed, an interest in French realist literature and the political history of the Roman Empire, and was knowledgeable about the customs of hill tribes of northern Thailand and the mating behavior of Indian elephants, all areas over which their conversation had already drifted. He nodded at me, and repeated my name before resuming his thoughts on the dialectical materialism of Marx and Engels.

I excused myself and went over to the buffet table, where I

lingered over my sandwich selection as a means of assessing the possibilities remaining for luncheon companionship.

The situation looked, on the face of it, rather bleak. Rather than subject myself to a further jeremiad on entertaining dos and don'ts from Margaret, who I could feel was signaling me to sit by her though I refused to look at her and become entrapped by the very laws of etiquette that she found so compelling, and of which she had such an encyclopedic grasp. Vanessa was discoursing on the new design of French brassieres with Gerald, who was still wearing last night's tuxedo and looked pretty wrung out as he sipped his martini, and a woman wearing what looked like a purple housedress, something Aunt Grace might wear at breakfast while her hair was still up in curlers.

For some reason, I couldn't bring myself to eat alone so I stood contemplating the choice of corned beef and tuna salad until Clayton slapped me on the back and said, "Take 'em both. No shortage of grub around here!"

I piled the sandwiches on my plate and followed Clayton over to a pair of lounge chairs, stepping on the heel of his shoe in my zeal to maintain a proximity which would demand his conversation.

"Easy there, kiddo," he said, dropping himself into the padded embrace of the reclining chair. "You're an eager beaver today, aren't you?" he asked, lighting a cigarette. I wasn't sure what he meant exactly but I agreed anyway.

"Your brother, on the other hand." He let the thought drift as he waved away the smoke from his cigarette. He started again, on a different note. "A damn good tennis player, when he wants to be. We played doubles this morning," he continued, chuckling, "but I made the mistake of pairing him with Wincett and the two of them tried to throw the game by talking like a pair of magpies about God knows what. Broke the concentration of my partner, but what the hell. There was no money on it, kiddo, if you know what I mean."

I nodded, waiting for him to refer to our conversation of several weeks ago, when I had called him at home. I was hoping he would take this opportunity to update me on developments in his investigation of Lillian, although, looking over at her sitting alone in the gazebo, I felt ashamed, as if I too were spying on her. But he showed no inclination to discuss her and I began to wonder if he even recalled our having spoken of her.

I was trying to think of a way to initiate the subject tactfully when an extraordinary thing happened: there was a scream, a long, painful slash of sound that brought us to our feet, and then we saw Ling running. He was holding something against his chest as he ran but suddenly it exploded into movement, flapping and screeching and over our heads flew a small, brightly feathered bird, dipping and rising crazily above us, like a kite yanked precariously by an unsteady hand. Several times the bird tried to land, dropping dark beads of blood on the pale stone of the terrace floor, but something was wrong. It was bleeding and a drop had hit Clayton as he stood, streaking his white shirt with scarlet.

Ling was sobbing, his face contracted in a gruesome manifestation of a howl that emanated from the core of his compact frame, and seemed to unravel him as it unwound, like a burning wire that lashed us all with its sharp edge. While the rest of us stood, speechless, Spencer put his arms around Ling and held him until he finally crumpled into the comfort of the embrace, keening in a hoarse wail, "My songbird, my songbird."

Lillian was the one who caught the bird and calmed it sufficiently to be able to examine it and pronounce the problem: its left claw had been severed. Mr. Wincett offered to drive Ling and the bird, now bundled in a tea towel, to the local veterinarian, while the rest of us speculated in hushed shock about the circumstances of the accident.

"It was not an accident," Lillian said, having gone down to the barn to examine the ornate bamboo cage which housed the bird. "I found this in the straw near the cage." She held in her palm Clayton's gold cigar cutter, which had been used to guillotine the bird's claw.

"Don't look at me," Clayton protested. "I've been looking for that since yesterday. I assumed someone lifted it at the party. It's from Dunhill's. My father gave it to me," he explained nervously.

"Relax," Lillian snapped impatiently, "no one is accusing you, Clayton. Gloria did it, obviously."

"How can you say that?" Vanessa objected defensively, looking around quickly for the child whose absence until now she had failed to notice.

"Of course she did it," Lillian repeated, more gently now. "She's been trying to catch birds all morning, but the wild ones were too quick. I watched her flush them from their perches when I was down by the pond. Besides, she's been practicing dismemberment on her dolls. Her little sailor is also missing a foot, and so is Raggedy Ann. It's a remarkable coincidence, don't you think?"

"We'll buy Ling a new bird," Vanessa offered quickly, "an even better one."

"That's not the point," Spencer interjected.

"I'm going to take care of this now," Lillian said, turning toward the barn, "before any other creature comes to harm."

"Don't hit her too hard," Vanessa coaxed, returning to her martini.

"I'm not going to hit her at all," Lillian answered without turning. "It wouldn't do any good. I have another approach I think will work much more effectively."

Spencer and I followed at a slight distance, fascinated by the confidence Lillian exuded in the face of a deeply disturbing situation. She walked briskly down to the boathouse and made straight for a young maple. She paused at the base of the trunk and removed her sandals, and then she shinnied up the trunk and hoisted herself up into the branches, out of our view. Spencer turned to me with raised eyebrows. "That was impressive," he said. "She didn't even stop to look for foot holds."

We crept under the canopy of the first bough and looked up. Lillian was sitting in the fork of a high branch, the skirt of her dress splayed up on snagged twigs, making a white ruff of her slip. On an adjacent branch slightly above her was Gloria, almost entirely obscured by leaves but for a patch of red bathing suit and one pudgy leg dangling down, toes curled like an angry fist.

"I know what you did to the bird," Lillian began. There was no answer, but Gloria shifted her weigh and the leaves rustled.

"Maybe you're just feeling mean and angry. I don't really know what you're feeling, Gloria, but I'll bet hurting that bird doesn't really change much for you. Not the way you wanted. I know that for a quick while it feels good to lash out, but in the end, it only makes your world smaller and meaner."

We drew ourselves closer to the trunk of the tree, where we

had a better view of the two of them. Lillian was standing on the limb now, reaching her hand out to Gloria, whose worried face peered down, looking unaccountably ancient.

"Here," Lillian continued, "here is the cigar cutter. Take it," she insisted, and Gloria reached out and took the shiny tool. Then Lillian did a chilling thing: she extended her hand, balancing herself on the shaking limb as if on a tightrope, and inserted her pinkie in the mouth of the cutter.

"Go ahead," she challenged. "If you want the satisfaction of hurting something, hurt me. I'm offering you my finger. Go ahead. Clip it."

The tension was sickening. Spencer started to make a move for the first branch but I put my hand out to stay him. I was afraid that any noise or movement might jeopardize the precarious safety in which Lillian delicately balanced. I don't think I was even breathing.

"Go on," she urged, "it's a good trade. My pinkie, right now, in exchange for your stopping this. Come on now and do it and then you can be done with it, okay? No more, ever. This is the grand finale."

For a moment, there was no sound but the rush of blood in my temples thundering like a swollen river and then there was a gasp and Gloria threw down the gold cigar cutter and started sobbing. Lillian climbed up another branch and wrapped herself around the shaking red bathing suit, rocking the two of them in the cradle of the tree, making the bough swing and the leaves weep down in raspy green syllables of relief.

Spencer was up the tree before I had drawn my first good breath, and he took the red bundle from Lillian, carrying the sticky, matted mess of sobs safely to the ground while Lillian followed, stretching herself down from branch to branch until she landed on the ground and silently put on her sandals. As we walked back to the house, Gloria took Lillian's hand and lifted it to her cheek before dropping it like a spent match and running off, pounding up the hill, shouting, "You're all a bunch of stinkers. I heard my mommy say so." But from that moment on, both Gloria and Spencer looked at Lillian differently. You could see it in the way their eyes followed her, like light yearning for the beauty of this world.

By evening the kingdom was deserted. Ling had quit and Vanessa had taken Gloria back to town, telling all of us repeatedly, "I don't really understand what all the fuss was about," but it was disingenuous—you could see she was shaken by the weekend's event. She kept lighting cigarettes while she already had one burning in an ashtray and her hands shook perceptibly when she put on her lipstick at the hall mirror before saying her good-byes. Margaret had agreed to drive them to the city.

She needed to return anyway, she said, the mattress in her room was too soft and she was desperate to get back to her own kitchen. Her stomach was very sensitive, she told me, easily offended by cooks too free with spices. I think she was cutting her losses, frankly. None of the single men remaining (with the exception of Gerald), was making himself available to her charms and she did not seem disposed to conversation for its own sake.

Lillian had gone with Ling in a taxi to the train station. She had insisted on accompanying him to town.

"I just think someone should go with him. He has so many bundles besides the bird and he's rather upset. Really," she told Clayton firmly, "I just have to go with him, that's all there is to it."

I walked her out to the car, carrying the empty birdcage, which had to be put in the front seat next to the driver, so full was the trunk with various boxes and packets wrapped in brown paper and twine. Ling seemed to eschew the convenience of the suitcase or satchel, relying instead on old linen pillowcases to carry the bulk of his possessions. His attention was now exclusively focused on the only bundle he would not release: the wounded bird staring blankly from tiny glazed eyes, still wrapped from the neck down in the soiled tea towel.

While Ling clucked encouragingly to the bird, I stood awkwardly next to Lillian.

"It's awfully nice of you to do this," I said.

She waved off my compliment with her free hand. "Not at all. I was ready to leave anyway. I always like the idea of this kind of thing more than the event itself. I should know better by now. It just makes me feel like an imposter, and, I suppose, I am."

I would have protested, but her face registered a weariness that forbade the fatuous gallantries I might summon. Instead, I asked, "How did you know Gloria wasn't going to snip your finger?"

"I didn't," she said, opening the door to the cab and folding herself into the backseat next to Ling and the bird.

"Oh," I said as the cab drove off. It was only later, in the gloom of twilight, that I realized I hadn't even said good-bye.

Clayton roamed the house looking vulnerable and bewildered, until finally he retreated to the safety of his study, where he remained for most of the duration of our stay, emerging between long-distance phone calls to report on the status of a deal or tip us to a stock he had been discussing. During these intervals, he would hover over the card table, where a bridge game was being played by the last few guests left to entertain themselves. He would turn up the record player, as if an increase in volume could somehow swell the quotient of pleasure we would derive from the music, and he cracked his knuckles as he studied our faces, making his discomfort audible despite the vibrating bass of his expensive speakers.

Twichell came regularly through the room, replacing the ice in the ice bucket, emptying ashtrays, passing around cocktail pigs-in-a-blanket. I watched some television with the woman in purple and then I went down to the pool and swam laps until my arms were shaking. As I was getting out of the pool, Spencer and Wincett arrived, drinking gin and tonics. Spencer had brought me a towel, which he tossed at an empty deck chair near my end of the pool.

"May we join you?" he asked, approaching the congregation of reclining deck chairs I had now spattered with water in my efforts to dry myself. Wincett had changed into a dark suit and looked ominously glum. I reached out for Spencer's drink without answering and he smiled.

"Take it," he said, "I'm already intoxicated. I have been all afternoon." He was beaming at me in a way that made my stomach lurch just as it did when an elevator stopped abruptly after a rapid ascent: I knew him well enough to know from his demeanor that he was not at all drunk.

"We were wondering if you knew Lillian's last name. Clayton is fabulously inefficient at introducing his guests."

"No," I said quickly, poking the lime in the glass to avoid looking at Spencer; his happiness was unbearable.

"No," I repeated after taking a long gulp that almost drained the glass. "As you said, Clayton is fabulously inefficient at introducing his guests." I handed him back the drink and pulled the towel around my shoulders. "I'd better get upstairs. I need to get dressed for dinner."

As I walked up the path to the house, I could hear the crickets rubbing away the last contours of the day, bringing down another night, though this one I felt already sure was as devoid of magic as the last one had been full. At the landing of the second floor, I stopped in front of the door to our room but did not enter. I went instead up to the third floor, where I found the dormer room in which Lillian had slept. The window was open and a breeze advanced, tentatively fingering items as if taking a random inventory. I stood on the threshold for several minutes, allowing myself only to savor the hint of her scent, which still traced her movements like an olfactory ghost, thrilling the air with the suggestion of her presence, in essence a broken promise sweetly alluding to the very thing it can't deliver. Then, hearing laughter rise up the stairwell from the card game, I entered her room and closed the door behind me.

The room had the sterility of most guest accommodations, all the familiar features of a bedroom uncomplicated by a resident personality, which invariably bestows a particular character to the space it inhabits. The theme of the room was white lace and seemed too frivolous and girly for Lillian's austere elegance. The bed was neatly made but the pillow still held the depression of her head so I lay down on top of the eyelet bedspread, put my face

into the pillow's center, and for reasons I did not then understand, I wept.

I think I was beginning to register intimations of what Lillian had come to symbolize for me, though I was still years from
articulating it. Yet my body knew, as it shook out its few paltry
tears, that she had become the repository, the vessel in which
were mixed that most potent recipe, loss and desire, a volatile formula in any combination.

It would not have occurred to me to rummage in any of the
enclosed spaces of the room, as I had in our quarters, but as I sat
on the edge of the bed, wiping my face with the beach towel I still
wore like a shawl over my shoulders, I noticed a piece of paper
that had fallen under the bedside table. I retrieved it, and without
meaning to crossed yet another boundary. It was a scrap of envelope, part of the gummed flap, on which were penciled the words
"Schadenfreude and Weltschmerz—my Scylla and Charybdis?"
On the other side of the paper was a list of Salvation Army centers
that had all been crossed off and the initials SRO and a question
mark. I put the scrap of paper on the table, next to a box of tis-
sues. After straightening out the bedspread, I took a tissue from
the dispenser and gave my nose the kind of vigorous cleaning that
Aunt Grace said was unacceptable in public, and then headed
back to my room for a shower.

Just before the door, I lobbed the wadded Kleenex at the
lace-trimmed wastepaper basket that nestled under the white
vanity table, but I missed the basket by several inches. As I went
back into the room to put the tissue properly in the wastebasket,
I found at its bottom a discarded watercolor torn in two. It was a
picture of the gazebo, looking up from the vantage point of the

pond, with the clouds above bleeding off into the white of the paper. It was very well executed, suggesting, as the medium is sometimes able to, considerably more than was actually shown. But that was not what surprised me—it was the signature at the bottom right: Elisa Linwald. I considered taking the painting, but decided not to add to my list of petty crimes by including among them theft from the girl whose absence wrung from me a greater sense of desolation than my father's death.

Downstairs, Wincett and Spencer occupied the wing chairs in the living room, sitting in front of a fire that Clayton had decided was necessary for aesthetic reasons even though the evening was too warm for a fire. Clayton had closed the windows and turned the air-conditioning on full blast, so that his guests moved instinctively to the hearth; even the cardplayers had reassembled around the fire. It was an inspired ploy on Clayton's part, for the unexpected cold caused his guests to contract into a small knot of animated conversation, creating the illusion of intimacy and affiliation that had been lacking before, when the warm evening had been allowed to seep dolorously through the house, dilating the social impulse, spinning guests off in tiny constellations of languid, isolated endeavor.

I wondered whether Clayton had thought up this solution himself, fortuitously stumbling on a reprieve to the deflation the house party suffered or whether he had gleaned it from the pages of advice offered by hostesses like Millicent Fenwick or her ilk. It didn't matter much; either way, my admiration for Clayton had been restored. I sat down on the leather fire bumper, facing a room now noticeably devoid of women, the last two female guests having gone upstairs for last-minute refinements, giggly tinkerings to their makeup and hair, the reapplication of powders and perfumes with which they galvanized themselves for dinnertime flirtation. The unmistakable atmosphere of a men's club pervaded the room, altering the humor of the quips that were exchanged, the anecdotes acquiring racier detail as the drinks became stiffer.

Clayton extracted himself from his study long enough to tell us about the casino in Havana he was considering as a possible investment, deftly fending off the obvious caveats about casinos and the dangers of the gambling world, which gave way to enthusiastic inquiries about the rate of return, the cigarette girls, cigars, and rum, but rapidly devolved to the inevitable requests for free anything. Wincett remarked that opposition to Batista was growing, and the potentially explosive nature of political unrest should inform any future investments in Cuba, but he was shouted down by Gerald, who wanted to know if it was true that Cuban cigars were rolled on the moist thighs of teenage girls.

Twichell entered and announced dinner. The ten of us took our places around the dinner table from which the extra leaves had been removed, creating again the need for guests to crowd together, elbows tucked at our sides as if to accommodate the expanding boisterous mood that swelled the room. The conversation had splintered now into a variety of competing subjects, each struggling genially to command the attention of the table. I was down at the far end of the table, with Spencer and Wincett and the older of the two women, a Mrs. Finley, who had a deep, smoky laugh and wore a peach cocktail dress with a plunging neckline. I watched her cleavage collect crumbs from the dinner roll she ate, until I felt a gentle tap on my shin and met Spencer's disapproving glance with a blush that scalded my cheeks.

I focused on my food, a canned tomato soup that I recognized at once as one of my personal favorites. By the time the roast beef and mashed potatoes were served, we had lost Mrs. Finley to a spirited debate that consumed the other end of the table, having to do with Hemingway, and the Nobel Prize versus the Pulitzer. As if by tacit agreement, Wincett and Spencer immediately withdrew into their own quiet discussion of Lillian, now that they no longer had to entertain Mrs. Finley, who was half out of her chair in her efforts to insert her opinion into a loud dispute that now raged like another bright fire Clayton had purposely set.

"During our chat about Verlaine," Wincett was saying, "I corrected her quotation of one of the lines. She shook her head and said, 'Pity. I prefer my version.' Later, when I referred to her as an intellectual, she corrected me, almost fiercely, saying, and I quote, 'I used to flatter myself that I was endowed with great abilities in this arena (doesn't everyone) but perhaps more to the point, I was cowardly about confronting worlds I knew only from literature. I held ideas up like a shield to protect myself. But now that I've actually met a few, no, I don't think I could rightly call myself an intellectual anymore.'"

"But surely anyone with your education . . . ," Wincett had protested, only to be corrected yet again.

"I've never had formal schooling, as improbable as that may sound. I'm an utter barbarian when it comes to the standard curriculum. I could astonish you with my great abyss of knowledge, things you would expect a child to have mastered, like multiplying fractions."

Spencer had not touched his food. He was, it would seem, so full of questions about Lillian there was no room for any other appetite to be appeased. Wincett shrugged off Spencer's myriad queries, continuing his account of the conversation.

"So I asked her if she was more comfortable being described as an artist and she just laughed. 'You mean because I paint? That's hardly a qualification.'" Wincett crossed his fork and knife in the European manner to indicate he was through with his meal and leaned back. "Maybe she's a war orphan—she never refers to her past; even when questioned, she's evasive. Maybe she doesn't have one anymore. I didn't detect any regional accent that would place her here in the States—it used to be a parlor trick of mine, identifying accents. Twichell, for example, comes from Cleveland, don't you?" Wincett asked as Twichell leaned over him to clear his plate.

"That's correct," Twichell said without enthusiasm as he lifted the dinner plate over Wincett's head.

"She knows a helluvalot about trees and birds and she's not a spy," I added, impulsively inserting myself into the discussion.

"What on earth made you think she might be a spy?" Spencer asked, his tone edging toward ire.

"Well," I began defensively, "she's used a bunch of different names: Diana Liswell, Lillian Dawes, and Elisa Linwald, and Aunt Lavinia said the initials on her suitcase were from the tail end of the alphabet, which doesn't match any of those names."

Spencer stared at me, his features wavering between incredulous disbelief and annoyed disappointment. I couldn't tell if this was because he now knew I had withheld information from him, or because I had lied earlier, or because he just thought my reasoning was flawed.

"Those are all anagrams of each other," he observed before focusing on the issue that seemed to stick in his side like a sharp thorn: "What has Aunt Lavinia to do with this, and why didn't you mention it before?"

"Who's Aunt Lavinia?" Wincett asked, but Spencer, in an uncharacteristic lapse of decorum, ignored the question, keeping his eyes trained on me, waiting for an explanation, or apology, or both. The odd thing of it was that while on the one hand I felt terrible remorse for having deliberately evaded his earlier inquiries, I felt no greater inclination to share with him now what little information I had about Lillian. On the contrary, I was seized by an overwhelming desire to withhold whatever facts I now possessed that he did not. It was as if I suddenly equated the surrender of details *about* Lillian with the surrender *of* Lillian herself, and I had never felt more possessive or territorial about anything than I did at that moment.

The more he pressed me, the more unwilling I became to answer. It was extremely ungenerous, after all he had done for me, not to mention childish. I believe I even crossed my arms in front of my chest in silent protest to his questions, confident I could imagine no torture capable of prying so much as a syllable from my thinly pressed lips, and I had visited the subject frequently in idle moments at Renwick, horrifying myself by envisioning, and even inventing, a wide range of cruel tortures.

Spencer exchanged a glance with Mr. Wincett and then changed the subject. Mrs. Finley asked me what I thought of

Pope Pius X being proclaimed a saint, and I took up the subject with a tenacity that surprised her and left her no possibility for retreat since I punctuated my opinions with the question, "But what do *you* think?," mercilessly holding her in a dialogue with me until Clayton scraped his chair back and rose from the table, signaling for us to join him on the terrace.

The moon was almost full, bathing the terrace in a thin, milky pallor that mirrored the anise-flavored liqueur being poured into thumb-sized flutes, so that the evening seemed to have already suffered the distortions of the luminous alcohol, or perhaps it was the other way around: the small glasses held some precious distillation of that white glow, casting everything into a heightened radiance.

"Damn good stuff, isn't it?" Clayton asked, pouring me another. "The French drink it for breakfast." I couldn't tell if this last remark was a fact or a witticism, so I laughed uncomfortably, searching among the guests for a clue, but their faces were opaque, registering nothing more than dull contentment.

Gerald and Mrs. Finley began to dance a fox-trot, which prompted someone to ask if they should put a record on, but Wincett opined that it was unnecessary, when we had the music of the spheres. I think that he was disinclined to dance, especially with the available female partners, and was trying to steer the entertainment in another direction. One of the men sitting in the shadows suggested that we all go to the drive-in, where there was a midnight show of *Rear Window*, starring Grace Kelly. It was an attractive plan from my point of view, since, like Mr. Wincett, I had no particular interest in dancing, whereas I was always available for the embrace of the wide screen.

Spencer was smoking a cigarette, chatting with the brunette who had been seated next to Clayton at dinner. Even from across the terrace you could tell she wanted him to ask her to dance. She was sort of swaying, as if gathering momentum to be swept up into a waltz or whatever the spheres were currently playing. He said something I couldn't hear, and the brunette threw back her head in laughter. I began to feel ashamed of myself, and I started over to join Spencer, whose company I now missed, watching another enjoying it, but I was intercepted by the contingent that had been agitating for an excursion to the movies.

"Come on," a tall fellow smoking a pipe said as he pushed past me, "we're taking Clayton's convertible, but we have to leave now if we are going to make it in time. Allen's filling a flask with scotch, but grab some beers anyway," he counseled.

I caught Spencer's eye for just a moment through the rush of guests milling across my line of sight, crowding toward the French doors as if caught in the vortex of a force that now spun them into uncertain action, the impetus to participate colliding with the desire to remain at rest. Mrs. Finley and Wincett stood at the threshold, debating the merits of joining the exodus, oblivious to the bottleneck they created by their stasis. I jostled forward and joined the rowdy surge that swept out to the cars, feeling, as I stumbled away from him, Spencer's gaze on my back like a warm hand.

Suffice it to say that after another two beers consumed en route, and the cozy crush in the backseat with Mrs. Finley on one side and the portly Allen Watts on the other, exhaling the dark fumes of the scotch he nursed from an oversized flask, I was asleep before the credits rolled across the towering screen. When I awoke to the sound of a car door shutting, we were back at the house and I was aware of only a groggy need to urinate. The others were already dispersing to their rooms, exaggerating their hushed efforts not to wake the dark house as they tiptoed through the hall.

Allen Watts was turning on the lights in the living room when I passed by. "Join me for a nightcap?" he asked, exuding an air of supplication in his half-bowed posture, but I shook my head and made straight for the bathroom adjoining our rooms. There I relieved myself in the sink so that I could avoid the embarrassingly loud plumbing noise that announced each flush to the rest of the house and made me increasingly self-conscious about my use of the toilet. Spencer was not in the bedroom, though the lights were on and several of the books with which he had armed himself for the weekend were piled on the floor beside the bed, as if he had been perusing them.

The sleepy dimness that had cloaked my thoughts was lifting, as if evaporating in the night air, and I went back downstairs to find Spencer. Allen Watts was still in the living room, flipping through an art book that had been left on the coffee table and which previous guests had used as a coaster—its glossy dust jacket was ringed with the sweat marks of various glasses. "Sorry," Allen said when I asked him if he had seen Spencer. The rest of the house was quiet; even Clayton's study was dark, the phone receiver finally sleeping in its cradle.

In the kitchen, however, I found Mr. Wincett seated at the Formica table with a large glass of milk before him. "Insomnia," he responded almost apologetically to what must have been a quizzical expression on my face.

"The scourge of middle age," he continued, staring unhappily at the glass of milk. "I used to scoff at such complaints when I was your age."

I didn't really know how to reply, so I joined him in his contemplation of the milk, hoping he would break the awkward silence that filled the kitchen. Instead, he picked up the glass and gulped down the milk like a shot of medicine. When he put the glass down, he had an uneven white mustache that he wiped away with the back of his hand. There was something heartbreaking about the moment, making him seem both ancient and juvenile at once. I thought about recommending for future libations the addition of a lot of Bosco chocolate syrup, but I feared he might think I was making light of his condition. I pulled up a chair, determined to offer, if not comfort, at least diversion.

"How was the movie?" he asked. "Hitchcock's never been one of my favorite directors, though I am aware of his great popularity. Jimmy Stewart's always good, at any rate."

I couldn't bear to tell him I had slept through the movie. I felt as if I would be disappointing him somehow, so I lied. For a good twenty minutes I invented a very dramatic plot combining elements of several Hitchcock thrillers I *had* seen. Maybe he had read reviews or heard about *Rear Window* from a friend. His eyes registered increasing disbelief as my plot careened wildly through spy rings, murders, and international intrigue. It was hard to balance the need for restraint with the desire to entertain. When I concluded, he said only, "Well, that certainly does sound exciting, if a bit hard to follow. Or do I mean swallow?" He winked at me and pushed his chair back from the table, taking care to rinse his glass and put it in the dish rack by the sink.

"I guess I'll go back and try again to summon Morpheus," Wincett said wearily.

"Do you know where Spencer is?" I asked, remembering suddenly his absence.

"If he's not upstairs, then no, I don't know where he is. Have you checked in the library?"

I nodded yes and he suggested that maybe Spencer couldn't sleep either and had taken a stroll. "I wouldn't worry about him," he said kindly, which had the unintended effect of making me feel foolish and clinging.

"I'm not at all worried," I hastened to assure him, "just curious."

"Good night then," he said, turning toward the door.

"What do 'Schadenfreude' and 'Weltschmerz' mean?" I asked abruptly.

Wincett paused and cinched tight the belt of his bathrobe. He looked surprised, even startled by my inquiry, as if he hadn't thought I had it in me to engage him on this level. I smiled while he rubbed his left eye and formulated his answer.

"They're both German terms," Wincett said after a pause, his back straightening slightly as he moved into a more didactic mode of discourse. "'Schadenfreude,' I believe, means literally shadow-joy. It's a word used to describe the pleasure derived from the misfortune of others, though in English the meaning is more toward the satisfaction of a just retribution. 'Weltschmerz' means world pain, and describes the overwhelming oppressiveness of existence, though it's often specifically applied to the pain of youthful idealism confronting the corruption of the world." He sighed audibly, as if he had just divulged a deep Masonic secret, and rubbed his other eye.

I was impressed with Mr. Wincett, and I nodded my head vigorously, trying to communicate a sage appreciation of his informed eloquence. He looked fatigued, and I felt as if I had taxed his late-night resources. "Anything else?" he asked, and I inferred from his tone the desire to be excused from further colloquy. He had begun to sag slightly, as if he had invoked

Weltschmerz by merely naming it, and now he too was burdened by the oppressive weight of the world. I said good night and turned off the kitchen light, sitting in the darkness remembering the previous evening's conclusion here, at the same Formica table.

Then I realized where Spencer was: with what amounted to a dazzling coruscation of insight, elevating a simple hunch to the level of a certainty, I knew that Spencer was swimming again, drawn back to the soft comfort of water, his head tipped back, waiting for a shooting star. I let him have the expanse of water and hope to himself, taking myself upstairs, where I put myself to sleep with the same image that buoyed Spencer, keeping him afloat in the dark pull of the night.

When I awoke, Spencer was whistling as he shaved, leaning his torso over the sink.

"Better get packed," he said when he saw I was awake. "We're leaving after breakfast."

I didn't protest: the weekend had been full enough. I understood now in a visceral way the lesson he had tried to impart at the beginning of our visit. If we prolonged our stay, it would only dilute the pure satisfaction of our encounter with Lillian. Once again I donned my linen suit, which had become an impressive weave of wrinkles, and was freckled on one sleeve with a spattering of coffee stains. As we took our places in the dining room, I noticed Clayton had conspicuously left a stack of business prospectuses out on the table, which several guests were reading in lieu of the Sunday paper. A quick glance informed me that they

pertained to the Kane Cola Company, "a product ripe for intro-
duction to new markets."

Mrs. Finley was wearing a white tennis dress with a small
pleated skirt; her lack of makeup and the unflattering morning
light conspired to make her look much older than the previous
evening. Looking around the table, it was as if Prather's kingdom
had aged all of us, like a strange reversal of the Shangri-la in *Lost
Horizon*. I ate extensively, fortifying myself against the unseen
forces of the coming day, returning to the chafing dishes of the
buffet three times before I was finished. Twichell, it turned out,
had mastered the art of eggs Benedict as well as the ever elusive
fluffy pancake. He admitted, when I cornered him in the
kitchen, that he had had a stint as a cook at the Wellington
Hotel, an establishment I had not heard of, but which I assumed
must be known among the discerning traveler for its breakfast
cuisine.

Our good-byes were brief; by the time we had descended the
stairs with our bags, most of our housemates had disappeared,
presumably having gone on to the various activities that beck-
oned outdoors. From the terrace, we waved our adieu to Mrs. Finley and Gerald, who were arguing at the net of the tennis court,
but interrupted their dispute long enough to exchange a farewell
with us. We didn't bother about the others, who were down at the
pond, wading in the shallows, nor did we wait for Allen Watts and
the brunette to return from their walk, although we could see
them in the distance, cresting the hill that rose from a neighbor-
ing field.

Mr. Wincett and Clayton saw us off. Clayton stood by the
door, looking vaguely impatient, betraying the fact that he had

other things he wished to do besides watch us load our luggage in the trunk of the car. Wincett just looked sad, like a child who has been left out of a trip but knows better than to beg. We shook hands all around, and Wincett handed Spencer his business card, urging him to call sometime for lunch or a drink in the city.

As soon as we turned out of the iron gates onto the county road, Spencer told me to find a station on the radio that I liked. He seemed relaxed, occasionally singing along when he particularly liked a tune, but he was driving faster than usual and I suspected there was an urgency fueling his desire to return to the city that had nothing to do with the collection of short stories he was trying to complete. We rode for more than an hour in silence, watching the evolution of a small rainstorm form and pass, barely necessitating the use of the windshield wipers. Twice Spencer asked me to light cigarettes for him, and I surmised that he was trying to include me in the thoughts that occupied him, moving across his features as visibly as the clouds we had watched gather and disperse on the horizon.

But I was content just listening to the stations fade in and out, feeling the buzzing hum of the car vibrate in my bones. I made no effort to talk. Finally he said, "Poor Clayton," and he said it without sarcasm, as if he really felt sorry for the man.

"I used to think he was just a genial fool, but now I realize he is neither. There's a kind of predatory ruthlessness motivating him, and it is at odds with what he most wants, which is still the almost shrill desire to be liked and accepted."

"What do you mean?" I asked, unable to restrain myself.

"Well," Spencer said, "it's in everything he does: he seems determined to prove his success long after the world has readily conceded it. It's as if he expects to be questioned on the threshold of exclusive clubs, and in compensation he has dutifully acquired all the accoutrements of privilege, in which he seems to take no particular pleasure save that they reinforce his position as a man of standing."

I was shocked. It was such a harsh indictment, and I was still in an almost tremulous state of gratitude; I didn't want to accept the truth of what Spencer was saying. It made me feel disloyal and seditious to be listening to Spencer expose Clayton Prather like a sentence being parsed, finding only faulty grammar, missing the light sparkle of the words. I began to protest, but Spencer put up his hand, presciently addressing my concern.

"There's something very likable about Clayton, and he's not without a certain charm, but he never trusts that it's enough; he's always hedging his bets, working an angle. You have to pity him, really, because in his effort to have it all, he ends up missing the point. You know," Spencer said, taking his eyes from the road to look at me, "Clayton confided in me his plans for Lillian."

My stomach fluttered uncomfortably. It was the same feeling of impending doom I had felt waiting outside the headmaster's office while the phone calls were being made. "And?" I prompted, wanting to get this over with as quickly as possible. If Spencer had some hideous revelation to unload, I'd just as soon not subject myself to the agony of incremental disclosure. I can spook myself halfway to a blind panic imagining the possibilities of a situation, which is why I don't ever walk under the El at night.

"He wants her to be the Kane Cola girl. Can you imagine?"

I'm not sure what exactly I had expected, but compared to the inchoate fear that had clenched me a moment before, this seemed benign. At least Clayton wasn't marrying her—anything short of that was a relief. Spencer lit another cigarette and smoked in a quiet fury. "It's just so crass," he muttered. "It's people like Prather who trivialize the world, turning a buck on whatever rare loveliness they can defile in the name of commerce."

"You sound like Beckwith," I said, and Spencer laughed and flicked his cigarette out of the window. "Do I?" Spencer asked. "I'm sure Beckwith would have plenty to say on the subject; he always does. But he would see Clayton as a mere pawn of the capitalist impulse to corrupt the individual by subjugating beauty to the industrialist desire to accelerate consumption," Spencer said, smiling at me.

I whistled my appreciation. "You do that so damn well it's scary. I don't know exactly what it means, but I'd say you've out-Beckwithed Bethwith at stringing together a bunch of words that flash out ideology like a tangle of blinking Christmas lights!"

Spencer demurred modestly, protesting my praise. "It's just foolish rhetoric, mostly. Orators have been using the same devices since the Greek Sophists to persuade the public to their position. Beckwith honed his skills at debating meets and in coffeehouses, and when he hits stride he could convince you the sky is red. But it's probably time to feed you something besides empty slogans. What do you say we find ourselves a town with an appealing name and a luncheonette with a decent cup of coffee?" He handed me the map, although I knew that both tasks were challenging and the two together were well-nigh impossible.

There was a note from Hadley thumbtacked to our door, an embarrassing missive she had not had the discretion to enclose in an envelope, which meant that all weekend our neighbors had been puzzling unnecessarily over our business. The message written in an angry script read:

> *Aunt Lavinia says she has been calling you for days. Why don't you answer your phone? I am not a messenger boy and will not continue to serve as such. PLEASE contact her immediately. Also, Mother has not been able to reach Albert Beckwith. WHAT IS GOING ON? She would like an explanation. We are all extremely put out.*
>
> *Hadley*

Spencer crushed the note into a tight ball in the palm of his hand and said, "Hadley has such a way with words. It positively makes you want to thwart her just to see what literary delights will follow," but seeing my readiness to implement this plan he added, "but we'll just have to resist that temptation for the moment."

After we had unpacked, Spencer dispatched me to the grocer to replace the perishables that had not survived our absence while he went to return the car. "See if you can find some more of those peaches," he instructed me as he handed over a wad of crumpled singles he had dug out of his jacket pocket.

I had only just put my parcels down on the narrow kitchen counter when the phone started ringing. I let it ring at least five times before I answered, just on principle, because I was not under house arrest after all, and because Spencer wasn't back yet to object. My efforts to assert myself were wasted, however, because the call wasn't from family. It was Leslie Lynd, who had been two years ahead of me at Renwick but was a pretty decent guy despite having a girl's name.

"Hey, you old fart," he said when I answered. "I've had a helluva time trying to get hold of you."

"I'm flattered by your persistence," I said coolly; I didn't want to betray just how true this was. "So how are you doing? How's life at Brown?" I asked.

"It stinks, like you'd expect," Lynd said. "But why I called is because my family was up last weekend for a crew race, and you remember my brother Larry?"

I said yes even though I didn't remember his having mentioned a brother. We were never very good friends, just shared a few jokes here and there, locker-room camaraderie mostly.

"Well, he's got a job teaching at St. Ignatius now, in the history department, and he told me about the faculty voting to take a kid next year from Renwick who got the boot. He asked me if I knew you. I was sorry to hear about your getting the boot, you old fart. St. Ignatius isn't so bad, but don't let them put you in Walker House. The master at Walker House is a real bastard, from what I hear. I felt it was my duty to warn you."

I thanked him for the information, and promised to take his brother's course on Asian civilization, even though it sounded like a snoozer, and the fact that Leslie was trying to drum up students for his brother's course was not a promising sign. I hung up feeling mildly depressed and peevish. St. Ignatius was not a terrible school per se; it was not, for example, one of those schools for morons or troubled kids, and it had an okay hockey team, and it wasn't a military academy, but still, I felt deflated.

I rummaged around in the kitchen cupboards until I found some stale Hydrox cookies, which I ate systematically, opening them up and scraping the sweet white filling off with my teeth, then letting the chocolate wafers melt one at a time on my tongue like a secular version of the host. I derived only a modicum of pleasure from this ritual because my thoughts kept returning to the prospect of a year at St. Ignatius. Spencer found me in a near stupor, leaning over the counter, unable to speak, with my palate caked in the thick residue of partially melted wafers.

"I guess you couldn't find the peaches," Spencer said. I pointed at the paper bag near the sink and coughed out some cookie crumbs.

"Have you spoken to Aunt Lavinia or Aunt Grace yet?" he asked, emptying his pockets of change into the small celadon bowl on the hall table, his back to me. "No," I said when I finally managed to swallow the final clump of sugary sludge clogging my throat, "and I'm not going to." Spencer turned around, perplexed by my vehemence.

"Aunt Grace is sending me to St. Ignatius. Did you know about it all along?" I demanded, squinting at him less because I believed he had been party to this outrageous development than because a sharp pain twinged in my lower abdomen.

"She mentioned it was one of the schools she was going to talk to on your behalf, but I hadn't heard they accepted you. Congratulations. It's a pretty good school," Spencer said evenly. "They have a good hockey team, if I remember correctly."

I stamped my foot because the pain was getting more severe. I was bending over now as I shouted, "I don't play hockey."

"Let's face it, Gabriel, with your grades, Exeter was not a possibility. You have to graduate from somewhere. One year at St. Ignatius isn't the worst scenario— Are you all right?" he asked, interrupting himself.

I was on my knees now, whimpering. "Gabriel," he said, squatting beside me, "don't get so worked up. We haven't even talked to Aunt Grace yet. Maybe there are other schools . . ." I waved him off.

"It's not St. Ignatius," I gasped. "It's my side. I'm dying or something."

"Are you sure?" Spencer asked, picking up the empty box of Hydrox cookies that had been knocked to the floor.

"I'm sure," I said, and as if to prove it, I vomited a dark streak of bile and chocolate across the linoleum floor. Spencer grabbed his keys and wallet and then hoisted me up and carried me the four blocks to the emergency room at St. Vincent's Hospital, alternating his patter between reassurances about my health and reassurances about my education. He was sweating about as fiercely as I was when we got to the admitting desk, and his shirt was fouled from where my mouth had rubbed against it, confusing the admitting nurse, who initially mistook Spencer for the patient.

But whatever debutante had thought Spencer would be hopeless in an emergency was dead wrong. He managed to get me on a gurney to the operating room in less than ten minutes, where my appendix was removed by a Dr. Singh, whose last words before I sank into the effects of the anesthesia were, "No, never have I heard of Ignatius, patron saint of the appendix."

When I awoke, I was in a ward room painted a battleship green. A thin curtain separated me from the next bed, and for a moment I thought I was back at Renwick, listening to John Vorhees's chronic hack. I sustained this illusion for only the briefest moment; no sooner did my waking mind begin to discern from the blur of sleep the contours of my new environment than I heard Aunt Grace's fluttery voice, thin and wispy as a paper fan agitating the air.

"Gabriel, Gabriel, are you awake?"

"Yes, Aunt Grace," I answered wearily. Her very presence in the room made me want to submerge myself in the dark chasms of unconsciousness.

"Gabriel, you frightened me half to death. I drove down in the dark, which is very disconcerting and dangerous, as I'm sure you know, and I haven't slept at all."

I was still disoriented—groggy and dehydrated, but nonetheless I understood that Aunt Grace wanted an apology, as if I had engineered my illness specifically to upset and inconvenience her. I put my hand gingerly on my side, trying to feel through my thin blue gown the stitches that were throbbing under a gauze bandage, while Aunt Grace continued to lament the ordeal she had been put through. It seemed she was displeased with the hospital Spencer had brought me to.

". . . knows better than to trust your care to a Catholic institution. Lenox Hill Hospital is very good, and the rooms are much nicer. I have a terrible crick in my neck from sitting in this metal chair . . . ," she continued.

I closed my eyes and enumerated the organs I would gladly sacrifice if I could be spared Aunt Grace's whispery voice, filling the room like a delicate fern spreading its lace in a suffocating grasp of all available oxygen.

"Where's Spencer?" I asked, finally interrupting her litany of displeasures.

"He had to go, dear. He's with your aunt Lavinia. He'll come back this afternoon when the doctor makes his rounds."

I groaned.

"Hadley said she would come too. She's bringing me a roast beef sandwich on rye. I can't eat the food in the cafeteria. I tried, I really tried."

I pretended to sleep, making little whimpering noises like a dog until the room fell silent but for the ticking of a wall clock and the irregular coughs from the other bed. Occasionally I heard Aunt Grace's chair squeak as she shifted her weight, and once she sighed a long, wheezy exhalation that filled the room with her peppermint breath which, I imagined as I drifted off, was blue and swirling like cold smoke.

When I awoke again, the room was dark, and I had the beginnings of a headache. I pulled myself up in bed and reached for the light.

"Hold it there, Bucko, you'll get me in a heap of trouble if the nurse catches me loitering after hours," the shadow in the next bed said.

"Spencer, it that you? What happened to the guy who was hacking up his lungs?"

Spencer swung his legs over the edge of the bed and lit a cigarette. The match flared like a tiny beacon, illuminating his eyes for an instant, and then I could only follow the glowing tip of his cigarette as it moved to and from his mouth.

"Don't know about your colleague. The bed was empty when I got back, and it looked awfully inviting. I thought I'd catch a nap until you returned to the land of the living. It's kind of cozy here, bunk to bunk. Like camp, but without the enforced fun."

I snorted out a derisive laugh and asked Spencer for a drag on his cigarette.

"Whoa, I don't know about that. You're still an inmate here and I think they might arrest me for that kind of breach of etiquette."

"Come on," I coaxed, "the movies are full of guys giving their buddies a last puff on the battlefield, and those guys are *dying*. I'm not even sick compared to those guys," I said, reaching out my hand in the direction of the orange glow.

"Okay," Spencer capitulated, "just one drag, but don't slobber on it, and for god's sake don't tell anyone what a softy I am."

I took a long, greedy suck on the cigarette, making my head spin and inducing a slight wave of nausea. I passed the butt back to Spencer and started formulating my questions while he took one last puff before he rubbed the cigarette out in the bottom of a wire wastebasket near the window.

"So did you talk to Aunt Grace about next year?"

"I did. Unfortunately, there were no other takers. So you've got your marching orders, or, maybe in this case, your religious orders. I hear they make you wear a brown cossack tied with twine as a uniform. And there are only two days a week in which you observe total silence."

I leaned over to punch at Spencer's arm. "Cut it out," I said, "it's not funny."

"Enlightenment never is," Spencer said, trying to maintain a somber tone, but I could hear his amusement crackle under the surface of his words, like a dry leaf ready to crumble with the slightest provocation.

"What did Aunt Lavinia say?" I asked, moving the conversation away from what Spencer found such a rich vein of humor.

"Well, you'll be surprised to learn that Ling is now in her employ. Which means, I'm afraid you're out of a job. Apparently Ling's duties include the constant care of Mr. Phipps, the clever canine that I understand has already learned to respond to several commands in Mandarin. So that just goes to prove you *can* teach an old dog new tricks."

"WHAT?" I barked, loudly and with incredulous irritation in my voice.

"Yes, amazing but true," Spencer said, sitting down on the edge of my bed. "It seems Aunt Lavinia and Mr. Phipps were returning from their country idyll at about the same time Ling and Lillian were escaping theirs, and the two forces converged in an unlikely meeting at Grand Central station, near a telephone booth, and I guess after the usual flutter of exclamations, Lillian explained that she was helping to relocate Ling, who was in need of a new job, and Aunt Lavinia took one look at the broken bird and hired him on the spot."

"What?" I repeated, wondering if I was having trouble comprehending this odd turn of events because of some residual drug that coursed through my brain, causing it to throb with the pain of each new epiphany.

Spencer patted my foot. "It's actually a very expedient outcome from all points of view, excepting yours perhaps. But I have news that might hearten you—as one whose pecuniary interests are at odds with the welfare of others. Aunt Lavinia has information concerning the Whitcomb heir. Vienna Whitcomb, otherwise known as Mrs. Willard Daniels, is dead."

I had just extracted an ice cube from the pitcher of water on my bedside table and inserted it in my mouth, so my reception of this news was a gargled sputter of delight.

"That's great," I said when I had repositioned the ice in my cheek pocket. "So it's over now and we can keep the money. Hallelujah."

"Not so fast," Spencer said, standing up as if to subliminally emphasize the moral stature of his position. "She had two children, one of whom is also dead. The other's whereabouts are unknown. But she would be the sole heir, assuming she can be found, assuming she is even alive."

"Well, how long do we have to assume? When can we consume?" I asked peevishly.

Spencer laughed. "Let's see your scar," he suggested suddenly, pulling back the cotton blanket. I showed him the bandage but we were both squeamish about removing it. "Answer me," I insisted.

"I'm not sure. A while longer. Aunt Lavinia and I want to give it a little more time, let her investigator see what he can turn up now that he knows who he's looking for. We want to feel that we made a good-faith effort. Right?" he asked.

"I guess," I said. It didn't matter. I was pretty sure now that it was just a matter of being patient.

"Oh, Gabriel, I almost forgot," Spencer said, smiling at me from the foot of the bed, his teeth glinting in the dimmed light of a street lamp so that for a moment they were a quick sparkle of white, like phosphorous in the night sea.

"Hadley brought this for you," he said, pulling out a Tootsie Roll and tossing it at my chest. I caught it with my right hand and ripped open the paper wrapper with my teeth, in one quick, fierce pull, as though I were yanking the pin on a hand grenade. "Tell her thank you," I said, biting off a nugget of the chewy candy, its turd-like shape not lost on me. "Tell her her generosity is truly touching. Tell her it's the most thoughtful present I've ever gotten. Tell her it makes it all worthwhile," I continued furiously, chomping noisily at the candy while I fulminated, but Spencer was already receding into the depths of the shadows and then a wedge of light from the doorway punctuated his departure.

Six days later, I was released from the hospital with a scar any one would be proud to display. It rose from my flesh, thick and pink, bordered by tiny black scabs where the stitches had been. There was something vaguely ghoulish about it that thrilled me, and I spent a good deal of time when I was supposed to be resting standing in front of the mirror that hung on the bathroom door, contemplating its savage beauty. Spencer said it would be almost as valuable an asset with women as a Purple Heart, and I entertained the notion of growing a beard, to make myself look older, and claiming it as a war wound.

Spencer had missed the war by a matter of days, turning eighteen on August ninth, the day we bombed Nagasaki. He would have looked great in an Air Force uniform. I'm pretty sure he wanted to be a flyer, though I don't really remember him talking much about it. Father had fought in the trenches in the First World War and didn't want Spencer doing anything but cracking codes in an office somewhere. But then it was all moot anyway, since there were ticker-tape parades celebrating victory by the time Spencer would have been able to enlist. It pleased me no end to have a scar that might have been produced by a German bayonet or Japanese saber.

Aunt Lavinia was the first person to whom I showed my scar, not counting Spencer. She came to the house to visit me, apologizing for not having made it to the hospital. She had not felt up to the hypocrisy of being pleasant to Aunt Grace, she said, and besides, hospitals were singularly depressing: the caustic smell of disinfectant and the harsh lighting assailed the senses. Moreover, she made a policy of avoiding those places where Mr. Phipps was not welcome. She brought me gifts, however, "to appease me," and they did: a kazoo, a brass compass in a Moroccan leather case, a book with photographs of doorways in Europe, and a pair of army surplus goggles. I hadn't a clue as to what guided her selection of gifts, or where she found the particular items she proffered, but I was invariably pleased, charmed by the odd random notes she struck. Like the jangled tones she made with her bracelets, they resonated with her peculiar whimsy.

When she left, I took off my bathrobe and stood before the mirror wearing only my boxers and the goggles, smoking Spencer's cigarettes, and practicing my French inhale, training the smoke to curl up into my nostrils. I couldn't get it to look seductive; one nostril pulled the smoke up in a smooth wisp, while on the other side the smoke wafted unattractively past my nostril into my eyes, causing my face to squint in a pinched, blinded way. I gave up and went back to bed with the book of photographs and a tumbler of orange juice. I hadn't mentioned Lillian and neither had Aunt Lavinia.

Beckwith rang the bell about two hours later, clearly hoping to cadge dinner. He sniffed around the living room, making small talk before he helped himself to a drink and put Mahler on the record player. Something was wrong with his eyes: a yellowish discharge had gathered in the corners and his eyelashes were coated with a dried crud. He took off his glasses to wipe his eyes, revealing a deep, red indentation on either side of his nose, where the eyeglass frames pinched the bridge.

"Jesus, Beckwith, is that contagious?" I asked, averting my eyes and willing him to put his glasses back on and restore the barrier that separated me from his infection.

"I don't think so," he said unconvincingly. "It's getting better, anyhow." He massaged the bridge of his nose with his thumb and forefinger, as if deep in thought, and then, to my relief, replaced his horn-rims.

I stayed across the room, preempting him on the couch, which I lay across, invoking all the privileges of my invalid status. He took a seat in the club chair, and fished in the cigarette box for one of Spencer's Old Golds.

"Your Aunt Grace has fired me," he said. "Because I was out of town for a brief spell and it took me a while to return her call." Behind the film of infection, his eyes glinted with indignation.

I almost felt sorry for him; commiserating about Aunt Grace's many flaws would have been easy for me, but I saw him pocket a couple of smokes, which annoyed me.

"It wasn't exactly a tenured position," I said instead.

Beckwith huffed a little and then responded, "Actually, it's just as well. I shouldn't be frittering my time away on the privileged when my calling is with the workers, the downtrodden, and the exploited."

"You sound like the Statue of Liberty, Beckwith. What's the matter? You losing your edge?"

"I'm under the weather," he sighed.

"Have you seen a doctor?" I asked, softening as the notion of my liberation from Beckwith's draconian tutelage began to sink in.

Beckwith lit his cigarette, holding it between his thumb and first finger, so that he looked like someone about to conduct an interrogation. "Nah," he said, "I'm not about to contribute an obscene amount of money to some weasely flunky of the American Medical Association just so he can put braces on his creepy kid, or build a ghastly swimming pool in his bomb shelter. Besides, the body is self-healing."

"Oh yeah? Behold my healed self," I said, pulling up my pajama top to expose my scar. Beckwith came over and peered at my abdomen, oblivious to the inch-long head of ash on his cigarette, poised to fall directly on my tender wound.

"You have no way of knowing if that surgery was even necessary," he said, returning to the armchair.

"Oh for god's sake," I muttered. Beckwith was warming up for a rant, I could tell. I changed the subject abruptly. "Spencer's just about done, you know, with his book."

Beckwith's eyebrows arched imperiously over his oozing eyes. "Really!" he exclaimed. "I just hope the publishing world will accept gracefully the kind of talent and taste to which the industry is clearly unaccustomed."

I wasn't sure if there was a slight embedded in Beckwith's response, so I went on the defensive: "They're really good stories. I read a few. Spencer's shown me a couple, and it's terrific stuff."

"That's my point precisely. Your brother has a greater gift than you could possibly appreciate, hence my concern for its reception in the tainted halls of commerce. I myself was rudely rebuffed when I submitted a very discerning manifesto to editors at several well-known houses."

This struck me as a ludicrous parallel, but I let it go. "I'm not worried on Spencer's behalf, and you needn't lose sleep over it either," I said.

"Sleep is the great leveler of men," Beckwith replied, getting up to fix another drink. Holding the scotch bottle in one hand and his glass in the other, Beckwith lumbered into the kitchen, where he started rummaging in the freezer for more ice.

"What do you have by way of comestibles? Anything to complement our cocktails?" he asked, even though he was the only one drinking.

"There may be some crackers in the cupboard, or cashews. We didn't make any cheese balls or deviled eggs, if that's what you mean, but if you're really hungry, there's always Lucky's Diner."

Beckwith shuddered. "I know the place. The coffee is gray swill, too thin to even carry grease, but of course, judging a diner on its coffee is like measuring a woman by her ankles—very few are going to pass muster. The key is this: are the muffins fresh and is the bacon crisp? Also consider what is complimentary: two refills and dinner mints are the least you can expect in exchange for the heartburn. When these standards are applied, I'm afraid Lucky's doesn't acquit itself as a choice establishment."

I snorted and rearranged myself on the couch, tucking another pillow under my head. "Well, I should warn you, I think tonight's menu features lasagna, and we're fresh out of dinner mints," I said. I could hear Beckwith panting over an ice tray that required a certain muscle to force up the frozen metal spring that cracked the cubes. There was a sudden clatter and I knew, without lifting my head to look, that Beckwith had lost control of the tray and the cubes were all over the kitchen floor.

"A little hot water usually does the trick," I offered, now that it was too late for advice.

The room began to fill with the blue shadows of twilight, but neither of us bothered to turn on any lights. Beckwith slumped in the club chair, musing on the pernicious effects of poverty—almost, it would seem, as imperiling to the spirit as the wealth Beckwith decried with a plangency that might have been mistaken for yearning.

The evening had fully fallen by the time Spencer returned and found Beckwith and me sitting in the warm gloom listening to the record skip, without the energy to cross the floor and lift the needle or replace the record.

"Whose wake am I interrupting?" he asked as he entered the living room and snapped on the standing lamp by the couch.

Spencer lit a cigarette and stared at us, his head cocked slightly to the side. Then he turned and crossed the room to change the record, replacing Mahler with Ella Fitzgerald. He leaned over the record player for a moment or two, letting the music infuse his body until it started to pour out of him through his fingers and toes, which began to tap out a private code of sultry pleasure. When he turned again to face us, his eyes were soft and his face had a drunken quality to it, as if he were recalling a shameless indiscretion. But before I could comment on it, he drew himself up again and continued his circuit of the room, turning on all the lamps, one after another, systematically dispelling the sweet sadness of the dark.

It was only after Beckwith left and I was showing Spencer the spoils of Aunt Lavinia's visit, spread out on display across my rumpled bed, that he mentioned Lillian.

"By the way," he said, as casually as possible, "I ran into your friend Miss Dawes at the library."

"What was she doing there?" I asked, a touch defensively.

"The usual, getting books . . . She sends her regards, and suggested we get together when you're feeling better."

"Is that all?"

"What did you expect, Bucko?" Spencer asked softly, turning the compass in his hand.

"How long did you talk with her?" I asked, ignoring his question in favor of my own.

"Not too long, an hour maybe?"

"In the library?" I demanded.

Spencer pulled the coverlet straight, as if he were preparing to tuck me in.

"No, not in the library. You know they take a rather dim view of conversation on the premises. We went to the Algonquin and had tea."

"Are you seeing her again?" I asked, trying not to sound fierce, but my attempt to dissemble was awkward. The question sounded choked and painfully obvious in intent.

"I hope so," Spencer said, rising to leave the room. "I'll leave the door ajar. If you need anything, just call me."

It took me a very long time to fall asleep. The shaft of light from the living room, where Spencer was reading, pierced the room like a sharp lance, and my body was casting off heat like an overrevved engine. No sooner would I shift position in bed than I would instantly absorb the cool of the sheets, replacing it with my own feverish warmth.

I finally fell asleep to the gentle tap of Spencer's typewriter, like large beads of rain dripping from an eave, filling my room with invisible words that I knew must be meant for Lillian, words that hung in the heavy air, full of awe and longing.

The next morning I woke early and left the house while Spencer was still sleeping, his bedclothes wrestled into a damp clump at his feet. From the phone booth on the corner of Sixth Avenue, I called Aunt Lavinia; Ling answered on the third ring and refused to wake my aunt until eight. It was only seven-fifteen and I had already had three cups of coffee at Lucky's Diner.

I fabricated an intricate lie involving an urgent message I had to deliver to Lillian and managed to persuade Ling to give me her address. Actually, it was unclear how much of my lie he understood, and how much of his complicity was merely an expedient means of getting me off the phone.

"She at work. She work all days. You wait. Now I get street for you." He put the receiver down, and I could hear Mr. Phipps wheezing asthmatically into it, which I imagined had been left dangling on its cord in the kitchen. Then I heard the soft padding of Ling's small barefoot tread on the parquet floor, followed by the brisk click of Mr. Phipps's toenails trotting behind him. I plugged another nickel into the slotted mouth of the phone box, waiting for Ling to return.

I made him repeat the address four times before I let him off the phone because his English was so fractured and his accent so opaque that I didn't trust the numbers I had scratched in fountain pen on the back of my hand. Nonetheless, I liked the idea of wearing her coordinates on my skin: the blue digits had the bold intimacy of a tattoo. Ling's patience was exhausted by the time he hung up on me in the middle of an unfocused message I was asking him to relay to Aunt Lavinia.

I retucked my shirt in my pants and smoothed down my hair and then, on a whim, I descended the worn steps to the Seventh Avenue subway for a shoeshine. I took a seat next to a gentleman in a pinstriped suit who was reading the paper while his wing tips were buffed, and waited my turn. At Renwick we had had to shine our shoes every Sunday, and one Christmas I had been given a small wooden kit equipped with all the necessary accoutrements, but I had left it behind, imagining that my future would not exact such attention to detail, and that I was polished in more important ways.

The shoeshine boy, who was old enough to be a grandfather, lifted my right foot onto the metal stirrup and whistled. "You needs mo' than a shine, mister," he said, too loudly for my comfort. "You done wore out the sole." I nodded miserably, explaining that I was about to replace the shoes anyway.

"Don't need a throw dem out. Shoe's good leather," he said, spitting into his rag. I glanced around at the passersby who were heading for the turnstiles, hoping no one was listening to his scolding. To circumvent any further discussion of my footwear, I began to study the address penned in black ink on my hand.

"Dat's shor some tattoo," the shoeshine boy chuckled, but I ignored him, wondering how much I should tip, and whether he would embarrass me by commenting on it.

As he bent over my shoe, I looked down from my elevated perch and studied his forehead. It was a beautiful glossy brown, smooth as the shell of a chestnut, and it looked as if it might be cool to the touch, like marble. He was whistling, and despite myself, I began to smile, infected by his cheer. When he was done, my shoes looked transformed; there was such a high sheen to the polish that they seemed to glint in the dim light of the subway corridor. I thanked him profusely and reached into my pocket to pull out the coins to pay him, but he shrugged me off and, turning to the next customer, said, "Save them nickels up to get yo shoes fixed good." That kind of largesse slays me: I felt so humbled by the simple kindness of his act I teetered on humiliation and my thanks were awkward and unconvincingly effusive.

Because my feet now were the focal point of my attire, I decided to take the Madison Avenue bus uptown rather than walk and risk scuffing my newly refurbished loafers. But I might as well have saved the fare, for when I arrived at the address I had so laboriously extracted from Ling, it was immediately apparent that the limestone town house was in the midst of an extensive renovation. I had no sooner entered than I was coated with a thin, powdery film of plaster dust rising in waves as a crew of Italian workmen completed the demolition of a foyer wall. Other workers carrying tools or canvas drop cloths and ladders moved in and out of the entrance, forcing me to dodge back and forth until I could get the attention of the foreman, who directed me to the ballroom, "Down the hall, you can't miss it."

Lillian had her back to me and was crouching in front of a section of wood paneling, her blue work smock spreading out behind her in loose folds on the floor, like a wide cape. Her hair was gathered up in a knot from which a long loop of ponytail hung down her back.

She must have heard me enter, for without changing her position she turned her head and, seeing me, she smiled. "Gabriel, what on earth are you doing here? Do you come bearing the truth like a shield and arrow?" she asked. I hesitated, confused and embarrassed out of speech.

"Never mind," she said, rising from her crouch and approaching me with her palette still poised on her left hand. "I was only teasing you about your name. It means 'bearer of truth,' you know." She wiped her brush off on her smock and tucked it into her topknot, where it protruded like an eccentric hair ornament, reminiscent of the chopsticks Oriental women wore in the old woodblock prints my father had in his study.

"Yeah, I know," I said shyly.

"Did you miss me?" she asked with a laugh.

"Yup, I did," I said, smiling now.

"Well, good," she said. "Come talk to me while I finish this panel. I can't stop yet; the paint is wet." She turned back to the wall and kneeled before a section, leaning in close to the wood.

"What are you doing to the wood?"

"Faux-bois," she said. "It's not wood. It's plaster. I'm restoring the trompe l'oeil, making it look like rosewood with a mahogany inlay."

"Is it hard?" I asked, marveling at how, even close up, the illusion held.

"No, it's not really hard. It's just tedious and time-consuming. I have to concentrate, which will give you a chance to do most of the talking."

I sat down cross-legged beside her. "Lillian, will you make me a promise?" I asked.

"Maybe," she said without looking at me. She was using a comblike tool now, creating the swirl of the wood grain. "But first you'd have to show me your scar," she said, sighing and putting down the small forked tool.

I pulled up my shirt, displaying my scar for her, and she wiped her hand on the bottom of her smock and then lightly traced its contour with her finger. Her touch was quick and gentle but it seemed to burn all my nerve endings at once. I shuddered involuntarily.

"Did I hurt you?" she asked, pulling her hand back, as if she too had been burned.

"No, no," I said, "I'm fine, really. It just sort of tickled."

She pulled the brush out of her hair and began to feather in the darker creases of color that swirled into tiny black knots in the wood grain. "So what's the promise you've come to collect?"

"You mustn't marry Clayton. Promise me you won't."

"That's easy: I promise I won't marry Clayton. I can't imagine why you thought I would. He hasn't even asked me, dear boy, and I don't intend to let him. As Friedrich Nietzsche said, 'Is not life a thousand times too short for us to bore ourselves?' But that can't really be what you've come about, so tell me the truth, Gabriel."

I couldn't. Even if I had been able to articulate the inchoate mixture of feelings that prompted my visit, I would never have had the nerve to voice them. For one thing, I was loath to invoke Spencer by name, as if the mere mention of him might summon to the room the dormant power of his charm. A nervous laugh was all I could muster. "Hand me that jar," Lillian said, squinting at some invisible blemish on the wall.

I handed her the jar, filled with three fingers of an oily, dark liquid that gave off a pungent odor. "How did you learn to do this?" I asked.

"In Paris, after the war. I had hoped to study painting, like every other fool on the planet. But the only way I could go to the Beaux-Arts was as a model—which was fine in the end. I would pose for the students, and listen to the comments the instructor made, and then, on my breaks, I went around and looked at the paintings and saw what the comments had been addressing. It was an odd way to learn, I suppose, secondhand and indirect as it was, but it taught me a lot more than just painting and sketching. I learned to filter and focus, and maybe most of all, I learned patience."

"And that's how you learned to paint like this?"

Lillian stretched and rolled her neck from side to side. She looked tired, though it was well before noon; the morning light lay across the parquet floor like a glowing scrim, burnishing in long strokes the scuffed floor, striating the wood as it lifted the golden hues from this plank and that.

"No. At the time, I was living above a *relieur* shop in the sixth arrondissement. In exchange for my lodging, I spent my afternoons in the workroom, apprenticing to the bookbinder. Monsieur Levaux specialized in old and rare books, and you can't imagine how good they smelled; it was like breathing in the pure aroma of the words as the years of dust and neglect floated up off the page." Lillian laughed and put her brush down. "I used to inhale those texts until I sneezed, thinking I was somehow absorbing the spirit of the letters before it dispersed in the sunlight."

She shook her head. "I had all sorts of notions back then. For a while, I thought I had found what I wanted to do forever. Monsieur Levaux made his own marbleized endpapers; we only ordered from Italy when a customer requested a particular paper we couldn't make. It was those marbleized papers that led me here, though with the usual detours along the way. Monsieur Levaux became ill. His daughter closed the shop and I went to Italy for the winter. I stayed with one of Monsieur Levaux's clients, a difficult old woman who had a villa outside Florence. You see, she wanted someone to make an inventory of her library, to sort through books, make minor repairs, and separate out the ones that needed rebinding, recommending which she should sell and which she should keep. She hired me only because she liked the endpapers I had made for her copy of *Lord Chesterfield's Letters to His Son*. She said the endpapers matched the prose. I don't know exactly what she meant, but I was pleased to go to Italy, and I needed the job. It took me two months to put her library in order, and during that time she had a father-and-son team restoring the trompe l'oeil marble in the dining room. It seemed like magic, what they could do with paint. The Gambonos could turn a plaster wall into crumbling stone or bamboo lattice or carved oak paneling or an overgrown garden in which birds would come to roost. It would take your breath away, Gabriel. In an afternoon, they could add the veneer of centuries to a new room. I had never seen anything quite like it before, the way perspective could be used to redesign reality. It was a kind of epiphany for me. I realized I could train my brush to recover all the things I'd lost."

Lillian stood up. "I'm going to take a break. Let's go out and find some coffee." She reached out her hand and pulled me to my feet.

Wwe sat side by side on a park bench on Fifth Avenue, drinking our coffees from heavy white mugs Lillian had persuaded a waitress at Horn & Hardart to let us take off the premises. "It makes a big difference, you'll see, drinking from a real cup. It's more intimate: it extends your personal space out into the world—like having a parlor that extends to the horizon," she said. She also taught me to close my eyes for the first bite of Belgian chocolate. "The only countries that really know how to make chocolate are, in this order, Belgium, Switzerland, and Holland."

We had stopped at a gourmet shop on our way to Fifth Avenue, and Lillian had chosen, after considerable deliberation, two chocolate truffles. Mine was filled with hazelnut puree and hers had a white-chocolate cream center. The two chocolates cost more than I would have spent for lunch, but it only made them taste more forbidden and sumptuous. (Although we would often share chocolate after this, it was usually just a Hershey Bar or maybe a Baby Ruth.)

After we had savored the last traces of foreign sugar, I was feeling so relaxed and sated that I posed a question that rose to my lips before I had a chance to shape it with tact.

"Why do you go by different names?" I asked. She flinched slightly, enough to spill her coffee.

"To what names do you refer?" she demanded stiffly, ignoring the stain on her white shirt—a man's cotton dress shirt too large for her slight frame, it billowed over the khaki pants she wore.

I could feel across the wooden bench a tension rise between us that made me regret my question, but there was no solution other than to blunder forward.

"Elisa Linwald and Diana Liswell," I said sheepishly.

Lillian sipped her coffee for a moment, staring out at the traffic that moved in syncopated surges down the avenue.

"I think," she said slowly, "people take new names in the hope that by the power of logogenesis, they will become new people, as if by living a lie you can embody it, making it true."

She turned and looked at me, watching my face closely. I was put in mind of a conversation I had had with Spencer the week before, again during one of the bathtub sessions. He had adjusted the faucet to reduce the hot water flowing into the tub down to a mere trickle that compensated for what was siphoned off by the high-water drain, achieving a delicate balance in temperature and level. Spencer was making an analogy to something which I no longer recall, saying, "It's like your essay on *The Great Gatsby*. You reduced Jay to a 'phony,' which is not just a tragic misreading of the book, but more important, of human nature."

I swallowed nervously. "Are you in trouble?" I asked.

"Aren't we all?" she countered, rolling her eyes.

"Does it have something to do with that Cuban fellow?" I persisted.

Lillian looked confused. "Cuban fellow?" she repeated in bewilderment, and then her face lit up with a smile that seemed to stretch up to the corners of her eyes: "That was you! Oh my god. Nando was furious." She burst out laughing, covering her mouth with her hand, as if her hilarity might spill out onto the bench. Like the sparks that shimmer around a sparkler, her laughter seemed to brighten the air surrounding us.

"Nando is Argentine; he only works in a Cuban restaurant, and that's just until his wife has her baby. Then they'll go back to performing in nightclubs, I imagine. We're not lovers, if that's what you mean. He was just teaching me some steps." She paused and looked down at her paint-spattered hands, and then sighed. "I've had a few fellows in my life—but only one really mattered. And he betrayed me. Or so I thought. By the time I found out otherwise it was too late."

Her mood had shifted and her shoulders slumped with the weight of her private sadness. Then, with an almost forced briskness, she said, "But that's enough questions for now. People aren't nuts you crack open all at once. The pleasure in getting to know someone is meant to be savored, like the chocolate. You can't just gulp it down, you have to let it melt slowly, so your palate registers every little quiver of nuance. Besides, trust has to be earned, and I need to go back to work. And next time, it's your turn to do the talking."

We returned the cups and I walked her back to work. At the door, she paused and put her hand on my cheek. "Thanks for the visit. It was fun." I worried about the word "fun" all the way

downtown, turning it over and over in my mind, trying to decipher its meaning as though it were an opaque foreign term capable of yielding multiple and contradictory meanings. I couldn't
decide if Lillian had intended me to understand the word as a
boundary, circumscribing the kind of interaction permissible
between us, or if it was meant to trivialize our time together, and
render it inconsequential, or if in fact it was only a reflection of
pleasure.

When I returned to the house, Spencer was kneeling on the
floor of the living room, pages of his galleys spread out around
him like a large white jigsaw puzzle he had almost completed. He
held his hand up to silence me as he arranged another pile of
pages in a stack to his far left. "I've spent all morning rearranging
the sequence of the stories and I think I have it now. I'll be with
you in just a second."

He switched another two piles and, after a moment's hesita-
tion, switched them back. "There," he said, "I think that's it." I
hopscotched my way around his piles to the couch. "Spencer," I
asked, failing utterly to acknowledge his endeavor, "what does it
mean when someone says they've had fun? Is that a kind of put-
down—you know, a polite way of saying nothing better?"

"Don't be demented," Spencer said, searching amid his piles
for his lighter.

I was silent for a moment while I bit the cuticle on my
thumb. Then I tried again. "Isn't 'fun' one of those words, like
'nice,' that people say when there's nothing else to say?"

"You mean damning with faint praise?" Spencer asked, still
absorbed by the search for his lighter.

"Yeah," I said, "something like that."

"I think it depends on the context," he answered, finding the gold lighter with our father's monogram under the last pile he lifted. "I wouldn't pick apart a word unless there was some supporting evidence that it was warranted. Tell me who said what and why and I'll try to help you extract the hidden meaning. You know, sometimes people just say they've had fun because they did. Sometimes speech is like that—pure denotation," Spencer said, lighting a cigarette, smiling his ironic smile, "though I applaud your interest in nuance. Does this mean you've locked horns with Hadley again?"

"No, I ran into a friend, someone from Renwick, no one you'd know . . ." I tried to sound vague. Spencer was still smiling. "Well, I guess it doesn't matter then, what exactly your buddy meant, because he probably didn't give much thought to his choice of words. I'd relax, and worry about whether *you* had fun."

"Of course I had fun," I said irritably.

"Then a good time was had by all," Spencer continued. "It sounds so jolly I'm sorry I couldn't attend. Maybe you'll bring him around for more *fun* here at your lodgings."

"Stuff it," I said, tossing a cushion at his head.

He went back to his piles, stacking them in their new order until he had filled the cardboard box in which the manuscript would be returned. "We're all so different," he continued, "I, for example, am usually in a good mood after I've had an enjoyable encounter with a crony. You, on the other hand, become tetchy, and fretful. It is comforting," he concluded, riding his joke a little too far, "to see that individuality endures in the face of mass conformity."

I forced out a loud belch as the only riposte I could summon;

I was equally unwilling to disclose with any candor the particulars of my morning or suffer Spencer's annoying attempts at humoring it out of me.

"If you'll excuse me, I think I'll study my chemistry text now," I said, rising from the couch.

"My company's that bad?" Spencer queried, feigning a hurt expression. "Or are you just trying to get up to the high caliber of students you'll be consorting with at St. Ignatius?"

At that I hurled myself at him and knocked him off balance. In two quick moves I had failed to anticipate, Spencer had pinned me on the ground. Holding down my arms, he kneeled over me and said, "Listen, Gabriel, I can't know what's bothering you if you won't tell me, but I'm not about to let you take it out on me. If living here doesn't agree with you, you're welcome to call Aunt Grace at any time. I'd be sorry to see you go. Living with a relative is about the most difficult thing I know, besides traveling with a friend, but I think we've done pretty well. As you must have noticed, I'm not really set up for a permanent houseguest here, but I'm glad to share my home, such as it is, with you. I just wish you would be a little more forthright about what's going on. I had hoped you'd use this time to let me get to know you, and up until that weekend at Clayton's, I think you were. But recently, you've been withdrawn and secretive. I feel as if I've suddenly become an enemy, though I can't for the life of me figure out what I've done to harm you. So why don't you calm down and just tell me what's been bothering you."

"You're hurting my shoulder," I said.

Spencer shifted his weight and released me. "I'm sorry, I didn't mean to hurt you."

We stood up and faced each other and Spencer offered his hand. "Shake?" he asked.

I put my hand in his and squeezed as hard as I could, but he did not let go. If he had asked me for anything else in the world, I would gladly have surrendered it. But I couldn't mention Lillian. Whatever claim on her I had could only be preserved in silence.

The days of summer stretched out in a languid array: long and humid and vast, time had become a seamless ocean on which I floated, drifting to each distant night on imperceptible currents I had no desire to alter. Spencer and I spent hours marooned in the living room, dazed and indolent, reading and listening to the hi-fi spin the siren songs of Ella Fitzgerald, Dinah Washington, and Judy Garland. I spent most of my indoor time clad in only my boxer shorts, while Spencer puttered around in faded cotton pajama bottoms.

We drank iced tea by the pitcher, and took naps. Spencer was waiting to hear from his editor and I was just waiting; as if on a journey with no particular destination, there was no anticipated event which would signal arrival. Our conversation was torpid, only occasionally rising from a sluggish commentary on local news stories when an item in *Life* magazine or the *Saturday Evening Post* struck Spencer as noteworthy. Then, like a spark on tinder, our talk would flare up into vigorous discussions that left us sweating and exhausted, as though the labor of thought and the exercise of expression were sprints in which we raced from our recumbent postures.

Sometimes, late in the evening when the heat lifted from the pavement, rising up past our window in wavering sheets of distortion, damp and musty like the effluvium of the sleeping streets, we would talk about things previously unmentioned: our father's temper, our mother's illness, the reason Uncle Ambrose left Harvard, subjects that ventured into swampy ground.

Spencer was my Virgil; a patient guide to the nether rings of reality, he not only knew where to look as we reviewed our shared history, but how to look. My tendency was to rubberneck: linger over the sensational moments, juicing them for gory details, but Spencer's approach was more disciplined, philosophical. He looked for illumination in the darkness.

Once, in the lull that followed those late-night intimacies, I asked him if he ever thought about Lady Ambrosia Kenthy. "No, not in years. It's funny, I guess. More like absinthe than ambrosia—by the time you notice the bitter taste, it's gone."

We sat in silence for what seemed like an uncomfortably long time and I was tempted to bring up Lillian Dawes, not just as an anodyne to the moment, but because I was swelling with the urge to reciprocate in kind for the honesty Spencer had introduced into our dialogues. "Spencer," I started, but he was stubbing out his cigarette, gathering himself from the chair.

"Stay a minute, I want to tell you something," I said.

Then the phone rang. At that hour, it was an ominous signal of impending bad news, or a wrong number. It was much too late for socializing. Spencer answered it quickly, and turned his back to me, as though to shield me from the conversation. "Yes," he said, "yes, I will." There was silence on his end for a minute or so while the caller spoke, and then Spencer replied, "Fine, I'll bring the money to Hauser's office in the morning. Tell him not to answer the door until you get there. Better yet, send someone else. It's better if you aren't seen going there." Then he hung up the phone and sighed.

"What was that about?" I asked, rising to my feet, thrilled as much by the hushed tone as by the mysterious content of Spencer's conversation.

"It doesn't concern you," Spencer replied almost curtly.

"What's the matter? Don't you trust me?" I demanded, genuinely wounded by my exclusion from the drama.

"Gabriel, sometimes it's better not to be involved."

"You're involved," I insisted. "I just want to know what you're involved in."

Spencer sighed. "Someone Beckwith and I know has been ratted on. A subpoena has been issued for him to appear before the House UnAmerican Activities Committee. He's going to try to dodge it—leave the country for a while. I'm contributing some money to the cause. There, are you happy?"

"Oh," I said, my excitement instantly deflating. My disappointment was palpable.

"You shouldn't help this guy. You're not even a Communist. Beckwith's only coming to you because you have some money."

"Well, exactly. Under other circumstances I might be a coward, but this time it's pretty easy for me to do the right thing. Anyhow, all you need to do is keep your lips closed. If Aunt Grace finds out about this, she'll have a conniption."

"I know. I'm not a retard, Spencer."

It's late," he yawned. "I'm beat. I haven't slept well for weeks. Tell me tomorrow whatever it was you were about to divulge." He snapped off the lights as he left the room, leaving me in the dark, full of words I had to swallow.

I went to see Lillian with a regularity I tried to disguise as random by shuffling the days on which I visited, as well as the hours. If I timed my call to coincide with one of her breaks, we would take our coffees to the park and either sit on the benches or wander down the paths, depending on Lillian's mood.

Once I arrived at the "site," as she referred to it, before she had returned from lunch. At the time, she was restoring a ceiling fresco, one of those sentimental pastel depictions of cherubs hovering heavily in puffy clouds, everything overblown and sickeningly sweet, like Viennese pastry.

While I was waiting for Lillian to return, I had climbed up the tall scaffolding to lie on my back beneath the ceiling, pretending to be Michelangelo. I had been drowsing there for about twenty minutes, listening to the workmen in another room buff the floors, when I heard her arrive with Vanessa Demmerly, whose high heels pounded across the wood floor with the insistence of a woodpecker, echoing sharply in the empty room. I peered over the edge of the scaffold to observe them. Vanessa straightened her right stocking while she talked.

Vanessa was complaining about Harold Zimmermann, about how hairy his knuckles were, and the earrings he had given her that were merely cultured pearls, and his breath, which she found profoundly problematic.

"People are so disappointing," Vanessa concluded.

"Yes, it's actually comforting. At least you can count on it," Lillian said.

"I'm afraid I'm going to have to dispense with Harold. It's not working out and besides, I have other fish to fry."

"Oh god, you're incorrigible. What's wrong with Harold now that wasn't wrong with him before?" Lillian asked as she put on her smock and began her preparations to resume work.

"Harold is a bore," Vanessa said bluntly, lighting a cigarette and exhaling a gush of smoke.

"All your boyfriends have been bores," Lillian said, waving some of the smoke away.

"Besides," Vanessa went on, "he has no manners."

"Ah! No manners," Lillian repeated. "Well, manners *are* important. I've been living off them for years now."

"Of course manners are important. How else do we know we're better than other people?" Vanessa snapped back, laughing as she sat down on a packing crate, crossing her long legs and letting the pump on her left foot dangle from the toe.

"Honestly, I don't know how you do it," Lillian said, drying a paintbrush in an old rag, "sleeping with men so old they have pubic hair growing out of their ears and the smell of cigar smoke baked into their skin. At least Harold's not old, and he's almost rich enough to dispense with manners altogether."

"Well, in certain ways he's ancient, darling. In certain important ways."

Vanessa put her hand on Lillian's arm to press her point, "Let me put it like this—"

But Lillian broke in, "Don't tell me. I can imagine: the

spirit is willing but the flesh is weak," to which Vanessa nodded vigorously.

Lillian turned to face Vanessa. "So, who's next?"

Vanessa made her familiar moue, puffing out her lips, and then she said petulantly, "You are not being nearly sympathetic enough. For god's sake," she went on, in a wounded tone, "I think he's having me followed. Can you imagine? After the way he flirted with Miss Subway at that opening we all went to?"

"What makes you think you're being followed?" Lillian asked, looking up from the paints she was mixing.

"I don't *think* it—I know it," Vanessa said with a wry smile, as if it were in some way pleasing to her vanity. "There's a very dingy little man loitering where he clearly doesn't belong because he's always ill-dressed and frowsy and he stares in a very rude manner. I don't think Harold spent much on him, which is typical. You must have noticed him watching us all through lunch, and then as we walked back here, he was across the street, keeping pace with us."

Lillian started gnawing on her thumbnail. "I think I know who you mean. I've seen him too."

Vanessa snorted. "You see, it's as I say—Harold is having me watched."

"Then why is he hanging around here?" Lillian asked.

Vanessa made a dismissive expression and flicked her ash on the floor. "It's probably to make sure I'm with you and not someone else."

"About two months ago," Lillian said, "when I was staying in the back room at Marcus's gallery, someone came by asking all sorts of questions. Marcus didn't say a word. He's a champ about things like that, he had his framer deliver a message to me telling me where to meet him. He chose a truly depressing dive on Canal Street—we were the only ones in that bar who weren't professional drunks. Marcus was especially conspicuous—you know how tweedy he is, with his walking stick and silk cravat. It's the only time I've ever seen him wear sunglasses—he was so delighted by the drama of it all. He chose a booth with a view of the door and said about five times that his walking stick was a lethal weapon. Can you imagine? He kept glancing about for likely marks to bash with the polished ebony knob of his cane. But the absolute loveliest thing about Marcus is that he never asked a single question. All he said was, 'Show me the body and I'll bury it,'" Lillian repeated, laughing.

Vanessa stubbed out her cigarette on the packing crate. "Was it the same guy? The one who's been hanging around now?"

Lillian looked off across the room, at the open windows through which came the shrill squawk of urgency as an ambulance passed, answered by the rising chorus of car horns sounding down the avenue, familiar as querulous voices repeating an insignificant point with dull persistence.

"I don't know," she said thoughtfully. "Marcus only really described the clothes he wore: an expensive gray suit and striped college tie. He said the man's cologne spoke of 'empowered reticence.'"

"What the hell does that mean?" Vanessa asked, rummaging in her handbag for her lipstick.

"That's pure Marcus, he puts things so perfectly he makes everyone else's speech seem paltry."

"*He's* paltry," Vanessa muttered sullenly. "And he serves cheap wine at his openings. As if we won't notice because of all the 'By Joves' and 'Right thens' and 'Cheerios' he uses. I've always thought he was a fraud. He probably bought that RAF medal off a destitute war widow or else he buggered some general."

Lillian turned her back to me as she spread out drop cloths over a new patch of floor. "You're just annoyed because he accused you of thinking in headlines, and being a parasite."

"No," Vanessa interrupted, dropping her lipstick into her handbag and snapping it shut, "I hated him well before he said that."

"Anyway, after a couple of gimlets in that dive, we decided it would be prudent to show my work under a different name. I came up with Elisa Linwald. Marcus loved it, he thought the foreign angle was extra tricky. And damned if the work isn't selling better now, even though it remains conspicuously representational and decidedly uncontemporary."

"So," Vanessa said, standing and adjusting her hat without benefit of a mirror, "you think this guy might be following you, not me. Well, why? What could he possibly want with you? Is there an abandoned husband somewhere I don't know about?"

"No, of course not," Lillian said impatiently. "Look, I really had better get back to work."

Vanessa bristled visibly. "Well, I'm on my way out. I'm actually extremely late for an appointment. And I have to pick up Gloria at her piano lesson across town. What a waste of good money!" Vanessa strode to the door and then paused and turned, waving lavishly from the doorway, holding her white kid gloves in one hand so that the leather made a gentle thwacking sound as she flapped them theatrically overhead, as though performing for an imaginary audience fascinated by her every gesture, whether it was pulling on a stocking or putting off a suitor.

I was pleased to observe that Lillian completely ignored the ludicrous farewell.

"You can come down now," Lillian said when she had finished assembling her palette.

I peered down at her, juggling my embarrassment with the relief of discovery.

"The scaffold sways with too much weight, so we can't both be up there. Come on down. I have to finish the putti by the end of the day."

"Are you angry with me?" I asked as I climbed down the rickety ladder.

"I would be if I thought you had been eavesdropping intentionally. But there was no way you could know Vanessa would accompany me. I didn't know it myself, so you're off the hook this time. I am assuming that you would have announced your presence had it been anyone but Vanessa," she replied with more generosity than I deserved.

It had never occurred to me to cough or call out, and even now, I didn't mention what I knew about Prather's investigator, not wanting to reveal even a remote complicity in what she could only find distasteful and unwelcome. She had not seemed unduly disturbed, after all, and besides, she was beginning to trust me with confidences, revealing more details of her past, opening up chapters of her life she had previously kept sealed.

And like those books she had tried to inhale in Paris, I couldn't help wanting to absorb all of her, refracted through her anecdotes and memories, until I had distilled the essence of Lillian, as if she could only be revealed through a comprehensive study of her past, as if her soul was somehow held captive by the wide span of days for which I couldn't account.

If I had had the good sense to consult Spencer, he would have no doubt reminded me that you can only know a person in the present moment. The past is as irrelevant as the future: speculative and warped, fictionalized by a thousand distorting forces, and filtered through the mendacious scrim of emotion. Moreover, by our very nature we are in flux, evolving imperceptibly into new beings that share only the superficial manifestations of our earlier incarnations.

Spencer's insomnia worsened, and as a way to beguile the late hours of his wakefulness, we started to frequent jazz joints. Sometimes Spencer would spring for the expensive clubs that booked famous name acts, but mostly we went to dives without a cover charge, joints where the beer was flat and the patrons had a bohemian air but the music was usually decent. As we were coming out of a cramped basement club called Buddy's Big Time, a smoky, windowless room off the Bowery that would have been decidedly depressing had not the saxophonist been gifted with a talent that could make you weep, we had to pick our way over the passed-out rummies who littered the sidewalk like ragged bundles of flesh.

It was a grim sight: heaped against doorways and trash bins, curling here and there in fetal position, swollen, scabbed hands tucked under greasy heads, as if in grotesque imitation of the charmed sleep of children. We turned a corner, looking for a cab, and saw, at the end of an alley, the slim silhouette of a woman, moving from bum to bum, bending over them with a flashlight as if searching among the bleary, unfortunate faces for something precious, something the rest of the world had overlooked but that was hidden in plain view.

"What the devil is that woman doing?" Spencer asked. "It's not safe for a female to be wandering down here alone at this time of night. Even a hooker knows better than to test her luck with this bunch." He turned down the alley in pursuit, despite my protests that I was tired and it was late and none of our business anyway.

"You stay here and keep an eye out for a taxi," he commanded as he strode away. A wino shifted in his sleep, and muttered thickly a word so sodden with anger and despair as to be unrecognizable, and I quickly followed Spencer down the alley.

I had almost caught up with Spencer when the woman stepped into the umbrella of light shed by a neon sign glowing the word "Rooms," and I saw that it was Lillian, and she was crying. She was wearing an ivory sheath of a dress, with thin straps crossing behind over her shoulder blades, and in the stark light everything about her was pale, like a misplaced apparition. She was clutching something to her breast, which at first I thought was an evening bag, one of those tiny purses women carry that don't hold more than keys and a lipstick, so that, as Spencer put it, you end up carrying everything else they need or want. But when I got closer, I saw it was moving: she held a mewling kitten like a child clasps a rag doll, with an absentminded, almost clumsy protectiveness.

Spencer was holding her by the shoulders, and his face was a confused mix of relief and anger. It reminded me of the expression I'd seen on the faces of parents who had found a missing child, briefly separated in a crowd. There is a moment in which it is not clear if they will hug or scold their charge. Spencer did neither. He simply tipped his forehead into hers.

Maybe it was precisely because Spencer already knew her in some way that rendered unnecessary the revelations I had sought with my dogged questioning, making them seem in retrospect gratuitous and greedy, that she came home with us as if it had been obvious all along, as if she had been waiting in that seedy alley, with a flashlight and a kitten, for him to come and take her home.

In the taxi, she talked nonstop, a kaleidoscope of jagged fragments shaken out of sequence, the jumbled narrative spilling together, the Park Avenue party she had left, where there had been a bowl of white peaches, the kind that fill the market stalls in southern France this time of year, bursting with a juice so sweet and thick it runs down the chin to fill the hollow at the base of the throat like perfume. It was the same scent, she said, as the one she had carried with her on her blouse (spilled from a tin of peaches), when she ran away to find a father she never found. It was for her father she was looking still, among the rubble and discarded lives, measured out bottle by bottle between soup kitchens and flophouses, because she traded in all she had when she left in anger, on a northbound train, and later hitching rides and working shifts in orchards and in diners for quick money, leaving behind her the two people she loved for the answers that no longer mattered. But she was not yet seventeen when she left and had never ridden an elevator or eaten lobster or even seen the sea, so what could she know about mistakes that never end but lead you into alleys on sleepless nights like this one?

Well into morning she talked, curled up on the couch, the kitten dozing in her lap, its head resting on her arm, while

Spencer and I sat with our backs to the window, as if to block the light and hold back the day, which I worried might somehow take Lillian from us, the finale to a fairy tale, which leaves the woodcutter alone in the woods again.

But she was still there, asleep, Spencer's jacket tucked under her chin, the kitten purring loudly by her head, when I awoke in the early afternoon, having been unable to fend off sleep, having relinquished to Spencer my duties as a guardian. When she finally awoke, it was afternoon, and the room was flooded with a deep golden light that slanted into the room from the west.

Lillian asked for a towel, and I showed her to the claw-foot tub and gave her a new bar of soap, and wished that I had been more fastidious about keeping the bathroom clean. Spencer had made a litter box for the kitten out of an old roasting pan that he had filled with sand from a nearby construction site. He had already been out twice, and had brought back, in addition to the sand, two newspapers, the *Times* and the *Morning Mirror*, a dozen eggs, a loaf of bread fresh from the Italian bakery, still warm and smelling vaguely of yeast, and a brown paper bag filled with plums. Then he fell asleep on top of his bed, still wearing last night's clothes; he hadn't even bothered to take his shoes off.

When Lillian emerged from the bathroom, she was wearing Spencer's bathrobe, her hair wrapped in the bath towel like a turban. The silk robe was much too big; when she sat down, the collar gaped and I could see the skin below her clavicle bone, it was pale and freckled and there was the suggestion of a blue vein glowing under the shadow of the silk. Beads of water clung to her eyelashes, darkening them in clumps.

"Do you suppose you could do me a huge favor?" she asked, picking up a peach and rubbing its fur against her cheek.

"Anything," I said a little too quickly.

"Would you get me some clothes? I can't wear an evening dress before dusk." I nodded in understanding, although personally I thought it would be okay, as long as the dress was flattering, which it was. I had gleaned however, from conversations I had overheard between Aunt Grace and Hadley, that there was a complex code prescribing women's attire. Those who violated the rules, who wore, for example, white shoes after Labor Day, or red shoes in the evening, or wore colors darker than navy before tea were regarded with the same superior contempt reserved for the aesthetically bankrupt types who put sleeves on the arms of their upholstered chairs, or, god forbid, plastic slipcovers.

I would not have suspected that Lillian subscribed to these strictures—for she had generated a certain amount of comment from the women clustered around Clayton's pool because she had eschewed the bathing cap most women wore that made their heads look pinched and tiny. Though I had not witnessed this particular sartorial transgression, I imagined her long hair fanning out behind her as she swam, like a mermaid, undulating with her every stroke the way a sea fan flutters on coral, red and thin as the strands of a cobweb.

Nonetheless, these were matters that were beyond my province, so I took her keys, and consigned to memory the address of her apartment, the fifth-floor rear in a warehouse building in the meat-packing district near the river. Having set out, I became increasingly apprehensive as I neared the address Lillian had given me.

I had never been to that part of the city before, and it seemed as if the brutality of the business conducted there had darkened the dirty maze of streets, and stamped the faces of the men grimly sweeping thick pools of blood from the sidewalks onto the battered cobblestone paving. It was, even in daylight, a dismal neighborhood—not at all the kind of place for the likes of Lillian.

I was almost jumpy as I climbed the stairs of her shabby building. The metal steps slanted precariously toward the exterior wall, as if the structure itself was slouching in despair of so much dinginess and squalor. On each landing, littered with crushed cigarette butts, I looked around nervously for dangerous types, knife-wielding thugs or sleazy hookers, but the building was empty; only a pigeon had penetrated the forbidding premises, having erred in through a broken window. It huddled in the corner of the third landing, looking diseased and unhappy, training a dim bead of an eye on me as it took my measure. On the fifth-floor landing, I noticed in the corner what at first glance might have been the discarded stub of a cigar but was, in fact, some form of fossilized turd left, presumably, by a stray animal.

I was therefore entirely unprepared for Lillian's quarters. As the unmarked metal door swung open, I had the giddy experience described in children's books and fairy tales, of crossing into another world, a place as secret as it was enchanted. Suddenly, I was in the country, in a cozy room with wide pine floors and beadboard wainscoting. A sash window opened its shutters to a wide field of overgrown grass, and a wisteria vine edged its lush blossoms into the frame of the window. I must have stood in shock for a full minute until, like eyes adjusting to a dark room, I came to realize what she had done. It was only paint, all of it, save for the bedstead and the suitcase under it, but it was so real I had to run my hands across the flat surfaces of the wall, watching the fire-place mantel recede into one dimension, or the shutters, or the mirror, or the arrowheads arrayed on a shelf, even the bureau and the braided rag rug flattened beneath my touch.

The window was the masterpiece, however. Its idyllic scene of rural life was painted on a heavy sheet of linen inserted into the actual window frame so that her "view" was illuminated by what little light made its way in from an alley. The very air in the room seemed freshened by the suggested hum of wind weaving through grass, dispersing the fragrant waft of wisteria. I half expected to see bees trying to extract nectar from the purple buds, perma-nently wet with morning's condensation: the deceptive tricks of light and pigment. It was only when you stood right up against the window that you could see, like a pentimento, the bleak real-ity intrude in shadowy outlines against the cloth.

It was a remarkable feat of alchemy, for the transformation was complete, making, where one would least expect it, a home as inviting as any I had ever known. Even the narrow closet had been given a trim of mahogany molding, creating a doorway that hinted at other rooms and the rambling sprawl of an old house. It was there that I found her clothing. She had no more than six hangers' worth of items, a few dresses and a winter coat hanging on a metal rod, and on the plywood shelf above the clothes was a stack of folded slacks and sweaters, a pile of books, a black beaded evening bag, and a few hats. Her whole wardrobe repre-sented less clothing than Hadley packed for a weekend visit to her homestead. The spareness of Lillian's possessions, or rather the ascetic life it suggested, stood in sharp contrast to the fullness of the decor she had assembled by brush stroke, and the richness of the life she seemed to be leading in other parts of the city.

Confronted with the scant entirety of her wardrobe, I became paralyzed and decided to pack all of it. It could comfortably fit in a small suitcase, and I didn't want to reveal my ignorance of what constituted appropriate day wear. Under the bed, behind the luggage, I found her paint set, and a packet of postcards, bound with an elastic band, which a quick inspection revealed contained only glossy images of famous sites and monuments scattered across the globe, all unsent; their virgin backs remained unsullied by words.

I packed it all, taking pains to fold each garment neatly, placing her three pairs of shoes carefully on top, with the soles facing away from the fabric on which they rested, handling the thin shifts and patterned cottons with the reverential care due the shroud of Turin. My hands felt clumsy and large as the delicate silk scarves shivered beneath my touch.

The bathroom, I inferred, was down the hall, but I did not have the nerve to try the remaining flank of metal doors that ominously lined the poorly lit hall. On my way back to Spencer's apartment, I stopped at a Rexall and bought Lillian the three toiletries that seemed necessary: a toothbrush, a hairbrush (the expensive kind, with a wooden handle and natural bristles, made in Britain), and a bright red lipstick by Elizabeth Arden called Flamenco Rose. I had barely enough money to cover my purchases, and felt, as I counted out my change at the cashier, humiliated by my poverty and annoyed by the spectral presence of the Whitcomb heir who stood between myself and the cash that might have lined my pocket.

Willa Daniels, the last surviving legatee of Mr. Frederick Whitcomb, had come to represent in my agitated imagination the embodiment of all that wasn't fair: she was the bitch of fortune, the capricious hag spinning the wheels of fate like a crooked croupier, keeping the game in play just when it seemed the giant roulette wheel was ticking down to rest on my winning number. I blamed her, irrationally but nonetheless fiercely, for all the ills and misfortunes that beset my simple life, as if she were responsible for my expulsion from Renwick, or my faulty memory when it came to irregular French verbs, my inability to waltz without lurching, or the troubling problem of my brother's natural charm when it came to keeping company with Lillian Dawes.

I returned to the apartment to find that Spencer and Lillian had named the kitten in my absence. They both seemed delighted with the moniker Perseus, a choice which made me glad the selection process had taken place without me, for I was going to suggest Blackie, which now seemed painfully uninspired and juvenile.

And so began the days of Lillian. That night, when we were alone in the kitchen and I was watching her slice chicken gizzards for the cat, I said, "You should have said something about your room. It took my breath away. It's extraordinarily beautiful."

She wrinkled her nose. "You think?"

"Yup, really amazing," I said. "A work of art."

"Oh, not art," she said, shaking her head. "Art is long and my attention span is short," which made Spencer snort in laughter, spilling his coffee on the counter. Any fool could see how happy he was. He stood beside Lillian, letting his arm hang a hair's breadth away from hers, close enough to feel the heat from her skin without actually touching it. The room was charged with a giddiness that sparked us into laughter over the silliest things; like static electricity, every idea our tongues touched carried a humorous current.

I waited nervously at the end of that first evening, long after the plates had been cleared and the last record played, until conversation finally was overtaken by fatigue, settling over us as gently as a shadow, submerging us in a contented quiet. All evening I had wondered how the sleeping arrangements would unfold. At last, we stood up and exchanged good nights, and then, without any discussion, Lillian and Spencer retired to his room as I pretended to busy myself with a final glass of water.

In my narrow bed, I strained to hear sounds that would betray the privacy of a closed door, but the house was silent, and reluctantly I drifted off. In the morning, Spencer was already dressed when I emerged from exile wearing only pajama bottoms.

"Put on your robe," Spencer said primly, but Lillian called out from the bathroom, over the sound of running water, "Not on my account, I hope. A young torso decorated by a new scar is nothing that needs be hidden."

I made a face at Spencer to communicate a silent "so there," and took my place at the table. A moment later, Lillian joined us, wearing a sleeveless sundress and, I was pleased to observe, the crimson lipstick I had chosen for her. I could see from the way she let her hand brush Spencer's as she reached for her napkin that there was between them, no matter how discreet or shy, an intimacy from which I was excluded.

I stared at Spencer, but he was impervious to my outrage.

"Have some jam," he offered, as if that was what was lacking from the completion of my beatitude, as if the pulp of seedless raspberries could somehow compensate me for the vast domain of happiness he had claimed for himself.

"No, *thank you*," I said, trying to insert into those words as much irony as they could hold, but Lillian reached for the jar, and putting her hand lightly on mine, said, "Are you sure? This is the best there is, made by blind virgins in Belgian convents," and I surrendered, melting into utter acquiescence. I could have struggled against Spencer's charm, but I could not resist the overwhelming urge to enjoy Lillian in whatever measure was offered, so I let myself smile, and a sense of relief filled all of us, I think, for the small kitchen seemed flooded with light.

Our days passed quickly as we settled into the loose cadences of summer, and the comfortable vernacular of domesticity. Lillian contributed to the household a range of delicacies we would ordinarily forgo: translucent slices of smoked salmon, pine nuts, blood oranges, loquats and chocolate-dipped strawberries, woven twig baskets of candied apricots, and smoky teas that conjured up the exotic twang of the Orient.

Lillian's finances were oblique, but it seemed that she bothered to earn only what was necessary to allow herself certain extravagances, deriving an unabashed hedonistic delight from indulging in carefully chosen luxuries while observing in other areas of her life an almost penitential rigor of frugality. It gave me a twinge of pleasure to see her bath oils crowd the shelf in the bathroom, or to smell, upon entering the apartment, the mere shadow of her scent, barely discernible but haunting nonetheless. I was unfamiliar with this variety of perfume, elusive in its subtlety, tantalizingly muted, as if it were in a perpetual state of evaporation and no amount of inhalation could increase the fullness of its pale complexion.

Hadley and Aunt Grace both wore Bellissimo, a tenacious perfume, ostentatiously feminine, its floral notes as dominant as a brass horn, but Lillian's made you want to lean closer, to follow the movement of her shoulder with your nose, to gather to your face a handful of her hair.

In the kitchen, assorted jars of her French mustards and Danish honey and Turkish olives lined the counter, and she put sachets of lavender between the folded towels, and sprigs of lemon grass between the sheets. We lived like kings, or sultans, perhaps, since the heat persisted, stubborn and insistent, glazing us by midafternoon in a salty sheen, pressing down like a heavy hand, curtailing even the most modest ambition.

When it became unbearable, we went to movie matinees, selecting our theater based on proximity and the quality of air-conditioning, without reference to the film on offer. It was enough simply to escape the heat, we didn't require emotional transport as well. Lillian was always placed between us, and though she made a point of always taking, on the street, both of our arms, I would occasionally notice in the dim gloom of the darkened theater she had slipped her hand into Spencer's.

Lillian continued to see, from time to time, Vanessa Demmerly, meeting her for luncheon at the Colony or drinks at the bar of the Ritz, places Vanessa liked because the waiters fawned sufficiently. For these outings, Lillian would dress with unusual care, sometimes going to the effort of changing the buttons on an old jacket, or dying in the sink a pair of cotton gloves to match a dress she "borrowed" from Bonwit's, returning it the next day, crisply wrapped in layers of tissue paper, the receipt tucked under the blue ribbons that tied the box like a present.

According to Lillian, Vanessa Demmerly had a great many attributes and accomplishments, including the ability to make almost any man look good on the dance floor, knowing more about auto repair than the average mechanic, and being fiercely loyal (she still sent care packages to Johnny Lasker, a high school beau who was doing time in Sing Sing), and it was the latter that impressed Lillian, and allowed her to overlook the more glaring limitations.

"She can be abrasive, I'll grant you, and her conversation is sometimes tedious, but she sticks by her friends, and nothing shocks her."

Once, when Aunt Lavinia had given us tickets to a Noel Coward play on Broadway, we had bumped into Harold Zimmermann during intermission and he had stood us to a round of champagne before he too asked Lillian why she put up with Vanessa. She had replied, "For the same reason you do. I think we are both amused and somewhat fascinated by her shameless self-indulgence. Not that selfishness is that unusual, but her degree of candor about it is. In a funny way, she's more straight than most people, and her wants are so childish they're harmless. And she once did me a very good turn. Let's leave it at that."

Zimmermann had sandwiched her hand between his own large puffy paws, the kind that are always warm and a little moist, saying, "But she just doesn't seem like the sort of person someone of your . . . someone like you would pal around with." Lillian had

232

deftly withdrawn her hand and said, "Hence her charm." After that, I didn't question her allegiance further.

By July, Lillian's restoration work at the mansion was completed, but she evinced no concern about replacing her employment. From time to time, she would take a painting up to Marcus Enwright's gallery, but for the most part, she lolled around, reading French novels or German poetry or lazily listening to records, eating cherries from a bowl on her lap.

When she was feeling restless, she would take me out on jaunts: we went to the Cloisters, the zoo, the roller coaster at Coney Island; we rode the ferry back and forth to Staten Island, ate hot dogs on Brighton Beach, and in Chinatown I was introduced to exquisitely delicate dim sum in a filthy hole-in-the-wall Lillian insisted on.

"The food will be good, I can tell," she had said with unshakable confidence. The proprietor, a mummified specimen with eyes as shiny and black and hard as the shell of a beetle, served us himself, grunting with satisfaction as we ate. Throughout our meal, he fingered with greasy hands the long, thin threads of his mustache until they were as round and pointy as the whiskers of a catfish.

In Harlem, she made me taste the only vegetable Aunt Grace had never served, and which Uncle Ambrose, with a shiver of distaste deliberately mispronounced, calling it "colored greens." "You have to spark it up with Tabasco, otherwise it just tastes like lawn," my docent instructed me.

Lillian liked to pretend, especially when we were wandering midtown together, that we were foreigners. She taught me a secret language of her own devising that involved placing *z*'s or *sh*'s between syllables, and sometimes we carried a Baedeker's guide to Rumania, or a badly worn map of a distant and obscure city, like Fez or Quito, bought in the secondhand bookshops she liked to frequent.

She could keep a poker face longer than I when asking unintelligible directions of passersby, and pointing earnestly at a relief map of the Carpathian Mountains, signaling her confusion with the international hand gestures of helpless befuddlement. Our favorite response, and it happened more than you might think, was when the victim of our prank would study the map and then, nodding vigorously with an air of absolute authority, gesticulate a set of directions as deeply fraudulent as the inquiry.

Once we went into Saks Fifth Avenue, where Lillian demonstrated a point she had been making about diminishing perspective, creating for me an infinity of receding reflections by adjusting the side panels of a standing mirror. "Visual echoes," she called them, and it was as if a hot wind had thrilled the hair on the back of my neck and arms.

From time to time, Aunt Lavinia would summon us. She seemed, each time we saw her, to have grown sharper, as if she were being slowly whittled into more severe angles and points, although her irreverent sense of humor remained as supple and pliant as ever. If we were called for lunch, we would join her at a restaurant of her choosing, but dinners were always given at her house, in the formal dining room facing Central Park. Apparently, she was so impossibly fastidious about decor most restaurants were unequal to the aesthetic standards she required for the proper digestion of her largest meal.

It was true, I suppose, that she had a gift when it came to interiors. Her careful calibrations of color, the contrasting textures and tones combined in her selection of sumptuous fabrics, juxtaposed with the various "pieces" of antique furniture she had collected throughout her years in Europe, created an environment of richness that was too elegant to be cloying, too eccentric to seem fussy, and which made, indeed, a splendid backdrop for the kind of conversation she liked to inspire at her table. She was much less demanding, however, of the food she served, which was dependably good but never aspired to greatness.

"This arriviste reverence of food bores the bejesus out of me," she once commented. "It's pretentious and beside the point. When you come to *my* table, it must be for the company. The food is merely a means of sustaining the pursuit of other, more rewarding appetites."

Her guests were an odd lot, culled from diverse areas of the arts and letters, with the conspicuous exception of academics, against whom she openly discriminated, dismissing their work as "the search for lost allusions." They were, she felt, by and large a petty breed, "self-satisfied pedants, jackals picking over the carcasses of others' inspiration."

After a few soirees, it was clear that the three drawing room currencies she most valued were, in this order, the originality of thought, the dexterity of humor, and the rarity of beauty; everyone else was just social ballast. I didn't like to think what dispensation she made for me, for though her fondness was pronounced,

I couldn't help feeling it bore an alarming kinship to her affection for Mr. Phipps.

She did not, for example, take me by the elbow to meet Fabrizio Dalforno, or Mrs. Lattimer, or the great Richard Tivett, as she did Lillian, making introductions that I could see, even from across the room, were lavish effusions, skillfully designed to flatter and intrigue the parties in question, who usually remained so tightly bound in animated exchange they missed the first announcement of dinner.

Nor did she seat me with particular reference to my interests, as she did Spencer, so that I often spent the evening trapped by the dullard lover or spouse of someone whose cleverness was being savored in another conversation, a few tantalizing words of which washed across the vast gulf of the rosewood table, carried over on a wave of laughter.

The most egregious of this type was a man named Ross Ellman, whose passport to the evening was an enthralling woman with fierce, wiry hair, a quick tongue, and a loud, surprisingly seductive laugh. But Ross, her escort (I can't bear to think she might have actually married such a man), was a lethal combination of strident contention coupled with a vacuity of knowledge even I found appalling. The result generated a kind of boredom so painful to endure I tried to recall the mental strategies Red Tillock used to tell us about after "lights out" at Renwick, recounting the methods his oldest brother had devised to survive imprisonment in a Japanese camp. My solution was to try to count the straggling hairs on the dome of Ross's head, which rose up stiff and matted, like the fibers on a coconut shell.

After that particular dinner, Aunt Lavinia waylaid me in the hall as I was returning from a hiatus in the guest bathroom, where I had hidden from Ross for as long as I dared occupy a room so much in demand after the final espresso had been served, and the liqueurs were being poured. She pressed into my palm a gorgeously ornate silver penknife, which opened with a tiny blade on one side and a miniature scissors on the other. "You deserve a reward," she said, "and I'm afraid this is all I've got on hand that would be of any interest to you. Not that you're in need of survival tools," she added, "you've already demonstrated your abilities under duress." It was as close to an apology as she could come without deriding a guest still under her roof, and thus under the protective code of hospitality that Aunt Lavinia honored.

After that, the woman with the wiry hair was struck from the roster of guests allowed to grace Aunt Lavinia's magnificent rooms. It was understood by those who remained in the ranks that the woman's wit and wild flights of occasional brilliance came at too high a price, or at least, at a price that was unfair to impose on others to pay.

On the whole, however, Aunt Lavinia's dinner parties were a treat for which I was grateful. It was there, after all, that I met the dashing Monsieur Paniceau, who had been decorated by de Gaulle for his efforts in the Resistance, but I was more taken with another chapter of his life, the tales he spun while consuming quantities of a syrupy-sweet violet liqueur. It was a sissy drink only the most confident of rogues would make his own.

After a couple of fingers of this powerfully perfumed elixir, he told me, through the miasma of floral vapor and Gitane smoke, of the years he was engaged in a variety of smuggling operations. He began his crimes with the sale of black-market cigarettes in

Italy, for which he was briefly incarcerated. He then graduated to the more challenging and lucrative problem of smuggling stolen paintings out of France and into Switzerland, which he did by rolling the canvases around the middle of a pair of skis, on which were piled other skis and poles, all of which were mounted with a cord of hemp on the roof of an old *deux chevaux*.

The car's dashboard was littered with lift tickets from some of the more demanding slopes in the Alps, and as a final touch, the radio was tuned to a weather station as the car approached the border. The success of his plan was predicated on hiding the contraband out in the open. The stack of skis was obvious and familiar, and occasioned no further investigation, although several times his trunk and suitcases were searched, more out of boredom than suspicion, he conjectured.

But after a few successful runs, he abandoned this line of work. It was too dependent on the weather, he said. If you had to hold the goods for even a couple of rainy days, it dramatically increased the danger: "People get panicky and crack. One little leak and *pssst*," he hissed, clamping his fingers dramatically on the end of a candle he had just lifted to his cigarette, snuffing out the flame and spattering pearls of wax on Aunt Lavinia's finest table linen.

He was retired now, making his living as a calligrapher. A woman swaddled in brass jewelry told me that he was highly regarded in his new field, and had turned down the opportunity to be the chief calligrapher for the White House. It was hard to know if this was true, for that same woman had also told me that the color orange should be struck from the spectrum, and that the difference between love for sale and love for free was that love for sale costs a lot less.

Much as I admired Monsieur Paniceau for both his pluck and ingenuity, I was disturbed to find him later with Lillian in the front vestibule. They were speaking French and there was something in the rapidity of their exchange, and the way they abruptly stopped speaking when I entered, that suggested they had known each other elsewhere, in other circumstances.

"You've met Monsieur Paniceau, of course," Lillian said quickly, adding with a laugh that sounded slightly forced, "It's such a shame that he must leave us, just when the evening is gathering momentum." Monsieur Paniceau took her hand and held it to his lips a moment too long, so that the gesture was infused with something more complicated than cordiality. Before asking us to make his good-byes to Madame Lavinia, and the others, whom he indicated with a loose flick of his wrist, he gave Lillian a lingering look, and I was certain then that they had once been lovers. Then he collected his hat and umbrella from the brass stand and stepped swiftly, almost stealthily, into the elevator which had just opened its door on Aunt Lavinia's foyer.

Ling remained professionally indifferent to my presence, though he always greeted Lillian and Spencer with a rapturous barrage of broken English, showering them with shards of meaning I made no attempt to decipher. Spencer, I noticed, was always served the choicest cut of the roast, while the browned end slices were saved for me. During cocktails, Ling would work his lacquer tray through the room so that, inevitably, it was almost empty of appetizers by the time he reached my corner of the couch. If Lillian's dessert plate was festooned with candied violets, mine would have an exiguous broken petal or two.

The preferential treatment he showed to Lillian and Spencer was too subtle to warrant complaint, but evident nonetheless in the myriad details of his household duties. He couldn't help it; neither could Aunt Lavinia. Whatever charms Lillian and Spencer exerted individually were multiplied exponentially by their union: they were irresistible as a couple. Even the most embittered cynics fell under the sway of their allure.

I think this was partly because they tried so hard to repress the outward signs of their enviable concord, and the energy of that restraint, which sometimes forced Spencer's hands into his pockets, or Lillian's eyes to focus on her shoes, filled the space they inhabited with an infectious tension that enlivened us all: it was like watching lightning in a bottle.

It amused me to observe, throughout these evenings, Aunt Lavinia tote her handbag with her from room to room, setting down the bulging and misshapen lizard receptacle at the foot of her chair as she took her place at the head of the table, as if the caterer, or perhaps even one of her guests, was suspected of having designs on its mysterious contents.

Once, when I was seated to her right (an honor I was almost never accorded), I mischievously tried to nudge the capacious black satchel to the dark recesses under the table, hidden by the long lengths of tablecloth and satin runners. I did not succeed: my toe could not budge the bag, which had the compact heft of a small valise, but I did manage to mistakenly step on the buzzer which rang in the kitchen and prompted Ling to arrive with the next course.

Later, when I was discussing this quirk with Spencer, Lillian interrupted to elucidate the situation. "It's so she can have her various pills on hand. It's a point of pride with her not to let on about her many medications. They're all decanted into tins for breath mints or boxes of licorice bits or gummy chews, so that when she reaches into her bag no one even notices. And it works — neither of you suspected anything more than that she had a sweet tooth, but the fact of the matter is, I think she's quite ill."

We rode the rest of the way home in silence, with only the atonal humming of the cabdriver as a doleful accompaniment to my sense of shame.

Then, in the last days of August, Hadley showed up unexpectedly, having concluded, wrongly, that Spencer couldn't be counted on to maintain our phone service. She had intended to announce to us her engagement, but she was distracted from her purpose by the discovery of our *ménage*. Lillian was not in evidence, but her presence in our midst was undeniable: her stockings, like shimmering wind socks, were drying in front of the window; a tiny nest of hairpins was piled on the low table in front of the couch; an earring sparkled on the rug, flashing a white prick of light from the worn blue weave of the kilim. And of course, there was her scent, unmistakably female and lovely.

Spencer and Hadley argued. The air was blurred with bitter words that hung there like a nasty odor, refusing to dissipate. A call was made to Aunt Grace and within a matter of hours I was removed, despite my loud and pathetic protests, from the scene of "debauched impropriety." Lillian had still not returned by the time I was torn from Spencer's apartment, with the frenzied haste of a body being dragged from a burning car, but I was pleased to see, as I was hustled out the door, that Spencer had written in tiny letters, next to the addenda of Gabriel on the nameplate, the word "emeritus."

He must have gone out to the front door while Aunt Grace and Hadley packed and I pleaded, an operatic sense of urgency motivating the three of us. Perhaps Spencer went to the door to get a breath of air untainted by the moral censure that polluted the apartment, or perhaps it was simply to escape the unpleasant commotion that had consumed the rest of us. He might even have stood on the steps waiting for Lillian, to divert her from an encounter with the Furies we called family. I didn't even notice he had stepped away.

It was only later, in the evening, that I spoke to him, having waited until Aunt Grace had gone to bed before creeping downstairs, barefoot, to use the telephone in the kitchen. His voice sounded miserable and pinched. Apparently he had had a nasty spat with Lillian. It was complicated, he said. I felt sorry for him immediately, almost as sorry as I felt for myself. He was not, I knew, any good at fighting, and as an amateur, more likely to wound inadvertently than one more practiced in the art.

"Somehow or other, Perseus got out. The doors were open intermittently while we were moving your things out to the car. No one was paying attention. *I* wasn't paying attention," he corrected himself.

"She's upset?" I asked, already knowing the answer.

"She's destroyed. We spent hours looking for him. She's out there still."

"It was an accident," I said.

"No," he answered sharply, "it's a goddamned *metaphor.*"

243

That's when I realized he'd been drinking. I didn't know what to say. I could feel him drifting away, as if the trusting sweetness at his core was receding, like a bright birthday balloon, released in an unguarded moment from the grasp of a small, astonished hand.

It *was* complicated—he was right. He explained how he had given Lillian the first copy of his book, wedged between the explanation of my absence, the ransacked state of the house, and the discovery of Percy's absence. "She wept as if I'd struck her," he said, continuing his disjointed narrative.

"I would have waited, *should have waited*, of course, for a better moment, but I wanted to soften the jagged edges of the afternoon, distract her so she wouldn't be hurt. I didn't want her to feel like a moral disease from which you had to be shielded, even if my family was acting that way. I didn't want her to feel slighted. I thought we could just forge past the ugliness other people impose. Hubris, I admit it. The satisfaction of the book's small weight in my hand took away some of the sting of ... I didn't remember about the dedication. It was months ago, before I even—"

I interrupted, "What about the dedication?"

I had naturally assumed, at the time Spencer returned the corrected galleys, that I would get the dedication. I was the obvious choice: Lillian was at that time relegated to the realm of my private obsession, and who else was there to contend with my claim? Certainly not Hadley or Aunt Grace, or Uncle Ambrose, who was now too old and vague to even fully understand the gesture. Beckwith had squandered his shot at it by borrowing money once too often to receive the dedication as well as a handout, and Aunt Lavinia, while a possibility, seemed a dark horse. I had taken it for granted, in a way, but also had composed in my head a very touching, heartfelt thank-you I looked forward to delivering at the appropriate moment.

"I dedicated it to Willa Whitcomb Daniels," Spencer said, muffling a hiccup. I was silent for an interval as the disappointment tingled through me, settling in my extremities with a numbing cold. I was unprepared for this. I had been poised to be a peacemaker, offering to renounce, in subsequent printings, that honor that he might bestow it on his beloved.

"It seemed the right thing to do at the time. After all, *some* kind of restitution needs to be made, and it was unclear, it is still unclear, if we could make pecuniary amends." Spencer slurred the word "pecuniary," but I didn't correct his pronunciation. I was having too much trouble breathing.

"Who knows where the damn woman is," he went on, "certainly not the man we hired to find her, that's for sure. Always an address behind, chasing leads that lead nowhere. Not one piece of hard evidence to identify her. It's as if the Daniels girl never existed, but that's not the point. *The point*," he said, his voice growing tremulous with emotion, "the point is that Lillian had no reason to carry on like a mourner in a Greek tragedy. I told her the dedication didn't mean anything—there was no reason to be jealous of some poor little hayseed who probably couldn't even read. The dedication, as I told Lillian *repeatedly*, was my freedom from an obligation. You see, I was planning to ask her . . . I thought that now, with *my portion* of the money . . ."

I had stopped listening. There had been a moment when this phone call had reminded me of another phone call: the slurred shape of words, the sound of ice cubes shifting in a glass, and somewhere out of reach, a girl without a past. I had made the sickening connection that now seemed so amazingly obvious I was stunned by my obtuseness. In retrospect, I should have told Spencer right then. It would have sobered him in a second, and it would have restored the natural advantage he always had in life.

"Spencer," I should have shouted, "*she is Willa Daniels!* Don't you get it? Lillian Dawes, Diana Liswell, Elisa Linwald—you said it yourself: they're all anagrams. Anagrams of Willa Daniels. That's why you can't find her. She moved in with you."

But I was flustered. There was a knot in my throat, choking back this information, as if all the lies that it uncovered were my own. I felt the searing embarrassment of exposure on her behalf, and in an awkward sputter, the most I could do was counsel him to find the cat. "I mean, so much depends on it, after all, to make things right." There was a low, strangled sound on the other end of the line, as if the burden of my advice had pressed the breath out of Spencer. Then, as he assimilated the weight of the task before him, he moaned, "You're right, of course, it's up to me . . ." He clicked off without even a good-bye, and I was left shivering in the kitchen, listening to the harsh emptiness of the dial tone.

I tried to call him back but the phone rang unanswered. He was out, scouring the night alleys for the happiness he had so suddenly lost, moving among the trash bins and the broken men with a stumbling despair they might have recognized as their own.

I would later learn from Aunt Lavinia that Spencer had been out when Lillian returned to the house. He was out while she sat huddled in his chair, waiting with their cat she'd found cowering in the hallway behind Mrs. Marshall's weekly delivery of laundry. Spencer was out while she fretted, wild with remorse, wanting to cover him with words that carried the thrill of kisses, impatient to erase the dark smudge of anger that had eclipsed their golden noon. He was still out when she fell asleep in the chair and when she awoke stiff and confused and hurt. He was out when she fed Perseus one final time, made the bed she had not slept in for a night, and packed her clothes in the leather luggage that bore her mother's monogram, the faded gold initials "V. W."

By the time I was able to reach him on the phone again, three days had passed and he was fully aware of the nature of his mistake. Lillian had left. The rooms were still full of her, her bottles and boxes, bath salts and chocolate drops, hairpins and lipstick, all deceptively present, but she was gone.

"Her paraphernalia resonates through the house," Spencer said, "like the last chords in a nocturne." That was the kind of response he gave when asked for details. He was grief-stricken and made little sense. Sometimes he would just say the word *"Sostenuto"* in a pained whisper, as if no further explanation were possible.

She had left his book open on the desk. The dedication had been crossed out and beneath it she had written the words, "You have confused charity with love. What makes you think Willa Daniels would take either from the likes of you?"

$\mathbf{M}$y contact with Spencer over the next few weeks was limited, not only because if he was home he rarely answered the
phone, but also because the telephone at Aunt Grace's house was
constantly in use. Hadley's impending nuptials preoccupied Aunt
Grace with a feverish monomania. That Hadley had "snagged"
the socially prominent and financially dominant Clayton Prather
was an achievement Aunt Grace fully intended to celebrate with
all the pomp of a coronation.

Discussions of and interviews with florists, organists and
photographers, caterers and dressmakers consumed Aunt Grace
and Hadley like a wasting disease. I tried to remain out of the
sphere of contagion, lying low, keeping to my room (formerly
occupied by Hadley and still flounced with enough lace and pom-
pons to have outfitted any number of bridesmaids). I did not, for
example, mention Monsieur Paniceau when the subject of callig-
raphers for the invitations came up. Nor did I comment on the
advice Aunt Grace imparted as she followed Hadley around the
house with swatches of tulle and organdy in her hand, saying

things like, "Just remember, all men are a hideous compromise, so don't be disappointed by the particulars."

Hadley was invariably home on weekends and divided the time not devoted to arguing about appetizers or bud vases between practicing her new signature on every available scrap of paper and weighing herself on the doctor's scale in the bathroom, monitoring the progress of her reducing diet on an hourly basis. My only opportunity for escape (concocted out of desperation) were the handful of unsupervised Saturdays Aunt Grace allowed me to take the commuter train to Grand Central for the purpose of "finishing up" with Beckwith.

It was on those few occasions that I saw Spencer and Aunt Lavinia, both of whom Aunt Grace now considered bad influences. But I was learning discretion, and kept my visits secret, and if Aunt Grace guessed what I was doing when I claimed to miss my train, she was much too preoccupied to pursue it.

The speed with which Hadley's union was arranged occasioned unkind speculation from Aunt Lavinia, who wondered if perhaps a more pressing timetable than that of true love was driving the event. It was true that Hadley had met Clayton Prather only three months before their engagement was announced in the *New York Times*. Personally, I think when Prather met Hadley at the Lettimore dinner party it was her relationship to Spencer that secured his interest. Hadley was just a pawn in Prather's systematic assimilation of Spencer's world; like the family portraits he had purchased, or the witticisms he appropriated, she was the ostensible coup in his usurped collection of Spenceriana.

But the joke was on Prather, for not only did it not rankle Spencer, he applauded the match. "They're perfect for each other.

I should have thought of it myself." Spencer did not attend the wedding, however. "I don't think I'll attend the nuptials. I'll contrive to be out of town. Besides, it will add enormously to Prather's pleasure to think that I am miffed by his taking my only cousin for his bride. I'll send them instead an obscenely expensive present and everyone will be happy."

It was from Aunt Lavinia that I gleaned my news of Lillian, as I persisted in calling her despite all recent revelations. Somehow it seemed disloyal to her to so readily discard the world she had invented for us, and which still had for me much more substance than anything conjured up by her *real* name.

Spencer had telephoned Aunt Lavinia when he finally returned home empty-handed, stinking of filth and failure.

"She's gone," was all he said.

"Yes, I know," Aunt Lavinia had answered. "She came to my apartment directly upon leaving yours. The poor thing. What a state she was in. I had Ling make her scrambled eggs."

Aunt Lavinia and Lillian had talked in her bedroom for hours, until Aunt Lavinia grew hoarse, and Lillian had cried into no fewer than four of Aunt Lavinia's monogrammed Egyptian cotton handkerchiefs. (Aunt Lavinia claimed anything less fine gave her a rash.)

Later, while the curtains luffed sluggishly, and the ruddy light of late afternoon lapped at the edges of the windowsill, Lillian had slept on the daybed in the library, covered by a paisley shawl Aunt Lavinia herself had tucked around her guest, after having first drawn her a tepid bath (hot water was no good for delicate complexions) and poured her a large glass of red wine, from the private stock of vintages she kept locked in a Spanish walnut cabinet.

During this time Aunt Lavinia "bestirred" herself. She put on her black alligator pumps, which pinched in the toe and were therefore reserved for occasions of state, or when she wanted to intimidate administrative personnel. She put on her gray pearls, her navy suit, and her gold bangle bracelets and "had an audience" with the director of the Bank of New York, where she kept her private account. There she withdrew a substantial sum of money, which she had drawn up as a letter of credit for Lillian. She also emptied her bank vault of an emerald bracelet, a pearl necklace, and a silver compact, all of which she pressed on Lillian when she awoke.

The money, she explained, was from her own account and had nothing to do with the estate of her brother, Gordon Gibbs. She had earned it, with her beloved Monsieur Panisse, through judicious investments in real estate and art. It was, therefore, entirely uncomplicated by family matters: it was money that was meant to be squandered, and Aunt Lavinia was running out of time. Lillian protested and Aunt Lavinia insisted.

"We Gibbses have always had a penchant for grand gestures and draconian measures. It represents a fundamental flaw in our nature—that certain emotions rarely find expression, but when they do, it is usually in the vocabulary of excess.

"You're twenty-six," Aunt Lavinia instructed her, "go and take the world to the brink of amazement. That's what I would do, if I were you. Life should have no limits but those of the imagination. You and I both know this is an extraordinary opportunity for you. Don't insult my intuition. About people I am rarely wrong: you are proud but you are not a fool. Now, ring the bell for Ling. It's time for Mr. Phipps to have a walk, and I need to rest. It is not easy handing over the torch of unrealized dreams. Oh, and wear something festive for dinner. I'm taking us out tonight. I think we should have something that requires a really good white wine. Champagne is such a cliché—it gives me a migraine just thinking about it."

"Did you mention me?" Spencer had asked, when Aunt Lavinia recounted to him these events.

"No. I thought it would be in bad taste to mention you before she did, and she didn't. I didn't want to meddle."

"As if handing her a small fortune wasn't meddling."

"My dear fellow, this is *my* money we're talking about now, and I will do with it exactly as I please. If you intend to become brutish, I'm afraid I'll have to ring off."

Aunt Lavinia could be exasperating. It was another Gibbs trait, but one that seemed to surface more dominantly in the female line. Among the male Gibbses, it was only a recessive gene, as far as I could tell.

Three days after my eighteenth birthday, and a week before I was to be deposited at St. Ignatius, Aunt Lavinia took me in a taxicab to the offices of Shackney and Hart, the law firm handling the estate of my father. We met with a senior partner, Mr. Voller, in an office with huge glass windows facing a gargoyle perched on the crown of an adjacent building. The simian features and leering grimace of the stone creature, now dripping residual rainwater from the downward slant of its mouth, reminded me strangely of Mr. Voller.

Many things about him were distasteful: his lips, for example, were thick and pendulous and perpetually wet, giving them a glossy, obscene shine. It was one of Mr. Voller's nervous habits to lick them, a tic I found mesmerizing and disturbing in equal measure. Because Mr. Voller's nose had been broken, he seemed to have nasal problems, but to me it looked as if the sheer weight of his lower lip, and the force of gravity, were pulling his mouth open. Even the truth, that Mr. Voller was a mouth-breather, disgusted me.

You could see Mr. Voller had been in the army—his office was decorated with souvenirs of that experience, and if he had never fully readjusted to civilian life, he had at least found in the law an arena in which a man with the social skills of a tank could maneuver effectively. I signed papers and forms; I pretended to listen to him bark out debilitating advice and admonishments about responsibility, protecting capital, and various rates of return.

When we left Mr. Voller's office, I was rich. The first hint of autumn was in the air and I was itchy with excitement. Every season has a different way of announcing itself, Lillian had told me, and standing impatiently at a crosswalk, I suddenly registered the delicate distinctions she had intimated were there, in the quality of light reflected from a bank of windows, or the shifting palette of sky breaking between the buildings, or even the texture of wind as it rubs around a corner, redefining the sensations of the city, as if its very pulse and pull had subtly shifted tempo. I felt a swooning flash of unadulterated joy run through my loins, as quick and ephemeral as the dizzy rush of blood when you tip your head back on the upward trajectory of a swing.

"Aunt Lavinia, let's go to the Plaza and have those finger sandwiches and tea cakes you like so much," I suggested. "It'll be my treat. I feel the need to splurge. I'm thinking maybe a dozen eclairs a piece, what do you say?"

Aunt Lavinia patted my arm and laughed. "You're such a child, my dear, but then, so am I. Lead the way—it has always been my policy to encourage harmless vice and undeserved indulgence."

We sat at a small round table positioned as far from the piano as was possible, and while I consumed two pots of Lapsang tea, a plate of cucumber sandwiches, and three eclairs, Aunt Lavina talked. She told me a long story, strange and poignant and familiar, the way any tale that touches you strikes some note that you already know, hidden in your heart, waiting to be sounded by a certain phrase or conjured image, and once given shape, takes its place in the indefinable locus of the soul. Spencer called this phenomenon *déjà lu*, and it explained, he said, how the kinship established by certain works of art was as powerful and compelling as any ties of blood.

It was Lillian's story, and I understood when it ended that she had been telling it to me over and over again, all those evasions and distortions just variations on the truth, which ran through every lie with the ineluctable rush of a river. She had been trying to tell it all along, in the only way she could, through the filter of necessary fictions, and I, who fetishized the world of facts, had missed it.

I had been raised to think that truth went in one direction only, like a sharp arrow, and that it could be identified as quickly as a color. It had made me anxious to think that things were ambiguous or shifting, or that experience, like light passing through a prism, could take on various hues when regarded from different angles. I suppose that kind of certainty, and the comfort it affords, is a characteristic of youth. The ability to keep life tidy (as if the virtues of childhood, making the bed and sorting socks, could be extended into the world at large) was part of the regimental order I associated with adulthood. It was Aunt Lavinia who taught me that afternoon that the acceptance of complexity and contradiction were in fact more useful tools with which to navigate the world.

Aunt Lavinia smoked a couple more of her particularly stinky brand of Egyptian cigarettes, and then I paid the check and we left.

For someone who almost unerringly knew the right thing to do in a situation, Spencer proved hopeless when it came to love. First, he had moped about for weeks, like a sick dog, hardly eating, keeping out of sight, dazed, listless, and disheveled when he did appear. Even Beckwith was concerned. It was pretty much our only subject for discussion in my last sessions with him.

"Why don't you just call her or send her flowers?" Beckwith had suggested. "Buy her something. All women are venal at heart, it's just a matter of degree." Spencer, prostrate on the couch, had only moaned, and removed the book covering his face.

"She's not like that. Besides, I don't know where she is."

"Your aunt must know."

"She claims she doesn't. Says she hasn't seen her since the day she gave away all her money."

"You see, I told you all women are venal," Beckwith said with dull satisfaction.

Spencer had propped himself up on an elbow and said,

"Beckwith, you are so full of crap I ought to beat it out of you but I don't want to sully my heirlooms. Just get out."

It was two weeks until he spoke to Beckwith again. I think at that point Spencer had given up hope of hearing from Lillian. It never occurred to him that she might be waiting to hear from him, that she had gone to the Sherry Netherland Hotel, as she had always said she would as soon as she could afford it, adding that if we were very good, we could come too. It was less obvious, she felt, than the Ritz as an enclave of privilege, and the name amused her: she inverted it to become the Nether Sherrylands, a kind of fairyland of patrician promise.

Spencer was probably too distraught or guilty to imagine that she might be checking hourly with the concierge for a message, waiting for him before allowing herself to order room service, which she had never had and which was at the top of the list of experiences she intended to cross off one by one.

She had talked about room service in a way that made me certain she would be disappointed by it when it finally arrived, but I didn't say anything, for at the time, it was her chief hankering. I know because she had shown me her list—places to go, mostly, or activities, such as riding an elephant, tasting truffles, snorkeling, seeing the aurora borealis, and traveling anywhere by airplane. I remember there were also items for acquisition as well: they included a music box that played Chopin, a cashmere coat, a monkey, either rhesus or capuchin, a cameo brooch, black satin evening gloves, and a grandfather clock that chimed.

I could have told him she was probably at the Sherry Netherland, memorizing the menu in her room, if Spencer had asked me, but he didn't. We were not talking much at the time.

His depression was like a dark sea I couldn't cross. To be totally candid, it frightened me, and I turned away.

Beckwith's second assay was more successful. "Look, let's face it. You're letting this eat you inside out. You're just going to have to find her. That's all there is to it. Find her and fix it up." Spencer roused himself from the couch and lit a cigarette.

"I can't leave the cat. Ever again." As proof, he picked up Perseus, who had grown obese in his care, and nuzzled him into a loud purr.

"I'll keep the cat," Beckwith offered. "I'm good with animals," and because Spencer must have looked at him as if doubting the veracity of his claim, he added gingerly, "Better than I am with people, if you must know. Anyway, you've got to at least get off the couch. Go on a trip. Do something."

When Beckwith left, Spencer, desperate to put himself to sleep, retired to bed with the final report he had received from the investigator who had dropped it off days before in exchange for a final check, which closed the case. In the morning, Spencer awoke inspired: he booked a ticket on the evening train to Washington, D.C., with a connection to the small town of Winsville. He left Perseus in Beckwith's care, with a two-page instruction manual detailing the cat's habits and preferences, both alimentary and tactile, and became, in his way, a man of action. The great indoorsman was at large.

It was at about this point that Aunt Lavinia had received the third in a series of phone calls from Lillian. It was true, Aunt Lavinia *didn't* know where Lillian was, as she made a point of not asking that kind of thing. She asked instead for an accounting of Lillian's expenditures.

"It doesn't sound like you're being bold enough. I've made you a woman of means, for Lord's sake. You're no longer a spectator in the world of privilege, you're a participant. Go forth and participate. Opulence is no place for the squeamish. It requires flair, a lack of qualms. Entitlement, in a word. It's in your blood, my dear. Your mother was a Whitcomb, don't forget. This is the chance to have the life your mother threw away." Lillian thanked her again, and said her good-byes. She would be traveling soon, she said, by airplane.

"Ask for a window seat, a deck of cards, and extra blankets," Aunt Lavinia advised.

Winsville, Spencer was told by its proud inhabitants, had grown and almost flourished, in the years that followed the war, but Spencer could still see what Willa Daniels had left when she was not quite seventeen. He paced the dusty lanes and drank Cokes on the porch of the general store. He talked to everyone who would stop, and found that more than a few folks grew expansive on the subject of the Daniels family, and Willa in particular.

One farmer showed Spencer the callused hand he claimed Willa had bitten when they were children, but mostly the recollections were fond and slightly exalted by the passage of time. An old woman, pitifully bent by arthritis, had walked Spencer up to the grave site on the old property. You could still see the charred outlines of a house, and there were fresh flowers on the graves of her brother and mother.

Miss Markham's failing eyes had misted as she told her version of events. "But you should probably see Addison Aimes.

Addison knew her best. Not just because he and his father were the only neighbors for better than a mile. Addison used to follow her like a puppy, like a big-pawed puppy. They were inseparable, those two. He lives up top that hill now, with his wife and babies, in the yellow house.

"They say things work out for the best, but I don't know about that. I'm so old and I still don't know if I believe it. Do you believe it, Mr. Gibbs?" she asked, and Spencer saw by the way her hand trembled as she fretted a wad of tissue that she was asking him in earnest for an answer.

"Addison was supposed to meet her at the train. It was all he could talk about after she left. They were running off together; it was all arranged. You see, she'd found out her father was still alive. And even though her mother only lied to protect her, Willa was young and headstrong, and already looking for a reason to leave. It would have been hard for her to go otherwise. Her mother and Addison were her whole world. But of course, he never made it to the train, what with all that happened that night up here at the Daniels's house. That fire was the worst one this county had seen for decades. But the terrible thing was that she didn't know what kept him from her. She was two miles off, waiting down by the tracks. Willa must have heard the bells, but there was no reason to suppose they meant anything to her.

"It was a full two years before she knew. And that was just by chance—because she bought some winter boots from an itinerant who had passed this way and maybe stopped to work. The boots were almost new and stuffed into the toes to fill them out was an old newspaper, *The Winsville Gazette*, full of the story of the fire, with a picture of her mother on the bottom. She wrote to me at once, told me it had nearly destroyed her, what she thought was Addison's betrayal, that he didn't come with or even after her. And she asked me to pass along a letter to Addison Aimes. She was right to suppose he'd moved.

"You see, he'd married. At first, it was because he had to—there was a baby on the way, but then he made his peace with luck, and I think he was happy. So I never gave him the letter. What do you think, Mr. Gibbs? Did I do right? You see, I always figured Willa was a citizen of the world, the kind of restless spirit that was too big for our little town. She had gifts that were meant for more than we could muster."

Spencer found himself crying. Miss Markham handed him her tissue, shaking out the worst wrinkles first, and watching with old, clouded eyes as he blew his nose. "Miss Markham," Spencer said, "I think forever comes too fast for all of us."

She nodded. "That's what I think too. But I didn't tell any of this to that other man who came through a while back, trying to poke up her story. I didn't like his face. It wasn't one to trust." She gave Spencer her arm and together they walked back down the road into Winsville.

In the morning, he came home. Before he had even unpacked, he called Aunt Lavinia.

"I've been such a fool," he said.

"I know," she answered.

"How did you know?" Spencer asked.

Lavinia sighed. "I knew her mother ever so slightly, way back when. We went to the same dancing school and Ambrose had a crush on her for a time. Undeclared, of course. Vienna Whitcomb had a quality you don't forget easily. And her daughter has some of it too. Same eyes, and elongated neck, certain gestures . . . the giddy way her laughter rises. I didn't put it together immediately, I'll admit, but by the time I did, I had come to respect her secret. I know a thing or two about wanting to put your past behind you, and I'm all for self-invention. I thought I'd leave it to her to reveal herself or not. I didn't foresee the two of you . . . well, that's one of the reasons I gave her my money. So that she could take us or leave us as she pleased, without that as a consideration."

Three weeks into my first term at St. Ignatius, Aunt Lavinia left for a weekend in the country with Mr. Phipps, to visit friends. The leaves were turning early that year and the hills were all aglow. In a quick note she sent to me to fill an otherwise empty mailbox, Aunt Lavinia excused her brevity, saying she and her hosts were "off to shop the roadside produce stands for ears of late corn and baskets of early apples." Mr. Phipps had been left to guard the hearth, she added in an exuberant postscript.

The property was fenced in and Mr. Phipps was not given to wandering, so I imagine Aunt Lavinia enjoyed her pastoral ramble without concern. It is not known what lured Mr. Phipps into the swimming pool. Probably he had chased something—a leaf or bird or butterfly, but having fallen or jumped into the pool, there was no one home to hear his frantic barking. The sides too steep for him to clamber out, and even if he had found the metal ladder on the far side of the pool, the distance between its rungs was too wide for his stubby legs; when he became too weary to swim, he drowned.

Aunt Lavinia unraveled. Her grief was epic and complete.

Mr. Phipps had been, she told Spencer, the only inducement she could name for prolonging her corporeal existence. "I have cancer," she told him. "That's why I came back to the States. You all may have flattered yourself it had to do with family but no, discovering I had relatives I could care about was an unexpected dividend. I only returned to see doctors. Well, I've seen them, and the fact is that I'm dying and there is not a damn thing they can do about it. I swore to myself I would not leave Mr. Phipps behind. No matter what, I'd just have to eke it out while he was still alive. But now he's gone and I can end this miserable charade. I really hate having to be brave—it's enough to have had to be clever. I'm no good at suffering. I just don't have the temperament."

She gave Spencer a detailed list of instructions, right down to the label of wine she wanted served at the bereavement. She had typed up her obituary, "modestly glowing," arranged with Frank Campbell's funeral home the service she wanted, "nothing overtly religious," and chosen the Waldorf for the site of her "departure," as she dubbed it. "I have always disliked the Waldorf. They give themselves airs, but it's really a manqué establishment. This is my little revenge."

Spencer tried to reason with her.

"Don't. I beg of you," Aunt Lavinia had implored. "Sentiment is a second-rate emotion—it's too easy, too cheap, like nostalgia. I won't permit it, not from you." She had tried to get a prescription for morphine from her doctors, but "those overpaid asses" were no help at all. She had had to concoct her own formula for death, "following in the footsteps of Socrates, but with a detour through the garden." Her brew consisted of Seconal and *muguet des bois,* the lovely, lethal lily of the valley, "just as toxic as hemlock, but more feminine. And make sure the floral bouquets at the memorial are full of *muguet*. My private joke: a matching accessory. They'll have to be flown in, of course. We're four months past bloom in this zone."

When he realized he could not stop her, Spencer had offered to be there with her at the Waldorf. "Absolutely not." She had been adamant. "That's the whole point of going to a hotel. It will be less troubling for strangers. Be sure to tip the maid generously, or whoever it is who discovers me. Poisons are always a messy business. I do appreciate the offer, but no. I came into the world alone and I will leave it alone. I would have made an exception for Mr. Phipps, of course. Animals don't feel guilt. They don't need to."

She planned the day of her demise to precede Hadley's wedding by less than a week. Aunt Lavinia liked the idea of stealing Hadley's thunder, as well as skipping out on the obligatory present. It made her cackle with delight: "Grace will have to wear black to her daughter's wedding. It's pure genius, don't you think?"

Both the funeral and the wedding coincided with my midterm examinations, and as a result, I had to miss both. It didn't matter though. I had no particular interest in participating in the celebration of Hadley, and Aunt Lavinia, well, she was easy to honor no matter where you were. I climbed to the top of the bell tower in the chapel and carved Aunt Lavinia's initials and her dates in the weathered wood. When I was through crying, I wiped my nose with the sleeve of my blazer and rang the chapel bell, hard, gathering the junior classmen from all over the campus like the pied piper. "A great soul is gone," I told the swelling crowd, "and she was family to me," I proclaimed theatrically. I think Lavinia would have liked that.

It was Wincett who gave Spencer his first lead, from someone in the Cairo office who had taken the report. She had come wearing her loneliness like a halo, lovely and untouchable as a mirage, thin as a papyrus reed, with the pallor of illness but a steady, sure stride, walking into the Viceroy Club as if she owned it, asking the astonished bar boy for a gin and tonic. "No ice," she added in Arabic before collapsing.

Between Wadi Halfa and Adindan, below the first cataract of the Nile and the winter resort of Aswan, on a strip of parched land with nothing but a few tired water buffalo, and the stray cur, ragged and yellow, it was an odd place for a woman, but she looked not even that—barely more than a girl with a small scuffed valise, and tennis shoes stained the color of iodine from the red dunes miles away, in the interior of the desert, to which there was no road.

That was how Major Azziz found her—lying on the blue tile floor, under the maudlin portrait of Lord Kitchener, with the three staff boys hovering nervously over her fallen body, fanning off the flies. She was carried to the third floor, to a small room with an arched window facing east. For five days, during which her fever didn't break, Abdou, the youngest of the staff boys, fed her white rice and boiled bananas rolled between the palms of his hands into tiny balls, the same size he fed his songbirds. Every three hours, Abdou or his brother Ahmed would wipe her forehead, her arms, the insides of her wrists, and the bottoms of her feet with rubbing alcohol Major Azziz brought from the dispensary at Wadi Halfa. In her sleep she muttered the fractured phrases of delirium and sighed, exhaling sorrow with her breath.

It was Abdou who thought she said the word, "Vienna," an artifact of meaning in the shards of syllables she threw from her burning body. But it didn't matter: she was still a cipher. In her luggage no passport was found, only a few books, a paint box, a change of clothes, and a tattered collection of maps.

Major Azziz sat on a wooden folding chair, straddling the doorway into the room on the third floor where the girl curled like a wounded animal in the center of a sagging army cot. He was tired and hot and the air in his lungs felt heavy and gritty. It seemed to him that he had been tired and hot for most of his adult life. But for the green necklace of the Nile and its banks, it was a lunar landscape, not fit for humans. Even animals, Major Azziz reflected, remembering the carcass of a mule he had passed on the road, could barely scratch out a life.

A small electric fan scalloped the edges of the mosquito net with its whining, ineffective breeze. He rubbed his eyebrows, a gesture of fatigue he had developed since his posting in the south. In the morning, a Fatima would arrive from the Aswan clinic to nurse the girl. Major Azziz had sent for her immediately, but travel was slow. It was a delicate situation and he was sensitive to the facts as they would be appreciated in Cairo: the girl was white and most likely a Brit. There could be, therefore, no suggestion of impropriety, nothing that might alarm the most prudish embassy matron, such as the idea of dark-skinned native boys rubbing alcohol on the feverish body of a white woman.

But that was only the cusp of the complexity. No one on either side of the border stops would want to assume responsibility for this girl, who had all the portents of bad luck: no money, no name, and no companion. Her illness was another complication; dengue fever most likely. The absence of a passport meant moving her would be tricky, though it was obviously desirable to get her out of the Sudan, preferably to Cairo, where the various embassies could concern themselves with her identity while the Anglo-American Hospital undertook to improve her health.

Recent events—the extension of martial law, Nasser's plans for the Aswan High Dam and the dispute with the Sudan over water rights, talk of an impending coup—meant that the best way to handle the situation was to make it someone else's problem. As soon as she could travel, he would hire a *falouka* to take her away. There was no room for a scandal now—there had been rumors that U.S. and British financial aid might be withdrawn from the Sudan as a means of pressuring a resolution. Relations between the countries were, in diplomatic parlance, "strained." The report that Wincett forwarded to Spencer had been marked *Confidential* and required clearance even for Wincett to gain access.

He would do what he could, Wincett assured Spencer, to find out where she had gone from Cairo. He had a friend at Interpol who could make inquiries with the various customs and passport control agencies, but it was a slow and delicate business: people were reluctant to put their jobs on the line. It took time to find the ones responsive to "baksheesh."

In December, with the first snows, the ads for Kane Cola began to blanket the city. Every billboard and newsstand, subway car and magazine repeated Lillian's quiet smile: there was no escape. She was everywhere, like the duplication of a thousand suns on the inner eye of one who has stared too long at the sky.

Spencer was furious. He confronted Clayton, who shrugged and smiled genially, saying, "I would have gotten a release if I had known where to find her. But the deadlines for print ads are very stiff, and it's all in the family now. I'll cut you in, don't worry." That's when Spencer broke his beautiful nose, giving his face, if not his temperament, the character it had previously lacked.

All this Spencer told me at the Oak Room over a farewell dinner. I was out of school on Christmas holidays, and we had arranged to meet before Spencer departed for India, where he believed, because of Wincett's intelligence, Lillian now was.

I had brought him two packages. One contained the pith helmet Aunt Lavinia had given me, and which I was turning over to Spencer for good luck and because he would need it more than I. The other package, smaller than a packet of cigarettes, contained a cameo brooch for Lillian, which I had purchased that afternoon at one of the snobbiest stores on Fifth Avenue. I had wanted to get her something from her list, and it was the least cumbersome of the items I could recall.

We sat for a very long time at the table, smoking and drinking long after an indifferent meal. It was a very heady evening as I remember it; Spencer was brimming with confidence and his excitement infused the occasion with a sense of euphoric expectation I still associate with the Christmas Eves when one is too small to know disappointment, too naive to question the reality of Santa. Everything was arranged. Spencer had disposed of his apartment, stored his furniture, packed his trunk, and since Beckwith had refused to return Perseus, visited them one final time in their overheated underworld. Spencer was going to head for Tiruchchirappalli, in the Tamil Nadu province of southern India. He drew a map for me on a soggy cocktail napkin. Spencer remembered Lillian talking about the temples there, and the sacred elephants. It had stuck in his memory, he said, because she was convinced that the temples were shaped like little Eiffel Towers. It was a place, she said, that had long been on her private list of wonders to be seen.

If she was not there, he would continue down to the very tip, to Kanniyakumari. It was a name neither of us had forgotten, for we had accused her of having made it up. When she found it for us in Spencer's atlas, she could barely contain her glee, capering around the room, repeating the name in victory.

As the waiters discreetly piled up the chairs on vacant tables and began to sweep the floor, we gathered ourselves up and prepared to confront the cold. Outside, a line of carriage horses shivered under heavy blankets, snorting steam into the biting air, like white puffs of smoke that made me drunkenly think of domesticated dragons. On the corner, under a streetlight, we embraced—in a manly sort of way—and said good-bye.

"Don't forget to swim in the waters of Kanniyakumari," I shouted to Spencer from across the street. "Lillian said it was supposed to be good luck, because the three oceans meet there, and wash away your sins!"

Spencer had hailed a Checker cab, and just before he folded himself into the backseat he called back, "No, the riptides are too strong—you can only dip a toe." He smiled and waved as the taxi pulled away, shouting from the window, "But don't worry, I'll do at least that!"

Personally, I believe he did. After the first fourteen months had passed without a word, Aunt Grace stopped asking me if I had heard from Spencer. She had grown old all of a sudden. What with Hadley's long and bitter divorce, and Clayton's financial ruin—Kane Cola had never caught on and then his holdings in Cuba were lost in the revolution—Aunt Grace withered like the last leaf that clings to a bare branch.

I think maybe it pained her to think, as I did, of Spencer and Lillian together, riding elephants and feeding truffles to their pet monkey, enjoying so much happiness that the rest of the world was forgotten.

Acknowledgments

I remain deeply grateful for the support, suggestions, and unfailing confidence of Bill Gaythwaite, Bill Clegg, and Marjorie Braman. I am also thankful to The Bogliasco Foundation for my residency there, and to Eden Collinsworth, Annabel Davis-Goff, Kathy Anderson, and Katie Nelson for their encouragement when it was so badly needed.